Book Cover by Angie Cottingham

2nd edition 2023

THE WEAVER CHRONICLES

BOOK ONE

ANGIE COTTINGHAM

This is book one in a paranormal, why choose, meaning that the main female character will have more than two mates and will not have to choose between them. While not extremely triggering, this book contains some graphic sexual situations and language that may be unsuitable for readers under the age of 18. There is also one scene that could be depicted as rape but had to be included for the storyline to make sense. - Reader discretion advised.

CONTENTS

PROLOGUE

I n the beginning, there was darkness, in which
reigned demons and other dark creatures,
Creatures of magic and elemental powers. Creatures forged from the fires of Hell itself. The
creator saw fit to balance this darkness with light.
For every dark creature, there would be its counter.
There were Demons and Angels, Unseelie and Seelie Fae, etc. Humans were forged and given free will
to choose their paths and natures. A world was
created for them that was just as balanced with all
the elements.

As angels were the first light creatures created,
they became jealous of all the creator had given to
humans. They attempted to overturn the creator
and take over Heaven. Some fell to earth to wreak
havoc on humans. One such angel was Lucifer,
the first angel. He led a coup in Heaven, but the
creator slipped into another realm and locked it
from anyone who could enter.

Lucifer then went to earth to rule over the humans. Humans, however, weren't keen to be led and fought back. If he couldn't rule over them, he would find a way to destroy them. A woman stepped forward to help him. Lilith was the most beautiful creature he had ever laid eyes on. Smooth, creamy skin with long blonde hair and eyes as green as the fresh, dewy grass. Lucifer was immediately enamored with her. Lilith became pregnant, and Lucifer had tamed down a little, no longer feeling the need to destroy that which the creator made. There was a child born of their love. He was a skilled supernatural. And at the age of majority, he could shift into a massive lizard–like beast with the ability to breathe fire. And thus, dragons were born.

One day, while Lilith was gathering herbs, she came upon a man who could control beasts. His name was Adam. Despite all her love of Lucifer, Lilith felt drawn to Adam and began an affair. She became pregnant again. When this child was born, it was with the ability to shift forms into that of a wolf. And thus, shifters were born.

Lucifer was livid and heartbroken at the truth that this new child was not his. In his wrath, he wanted to ruin Adam. He discovered Adam himself had another mate and a child, Abel. Her name was Eve. She, too, was beautiful and the opposite of Lilith. Her long ebony hair and bright blue eyes would shame the most beautiful sapphires. Lucifer seduced Eve to steal her away from Adam. The child created in this union, Cain, would be forced to walk the earth through eternity cursed to drink the blood of others to survive after killing his brother Abel.

All children created by Lilith and Lucifer had darkness in their hearts. The balance was broken, and Eve felt horrible for what she had done, begging the creator for forgiveness. Seeing how humble she was, the creator bestowed one more child upon Eve. A special child. This child would be known as a weaver.

She held the power to create or destroy. She had both light and darkness. She could walk all the realms bringing balance or destruction. She could walk and weave dreams and nightmares. Eve named this blessed child Neveah. As Neveah grew into her powers, so had the darkness. Lilith and Lucifer wreaked havoc on all the realms.

Years went by with more and more creatures being created—witches on the dark side and elementals on the light. Shifters took on the form of all the different animals, predators, and prey.

Neveah, tired of the fight for balance, decided it was time to put an end to Lilith and Lucifer. Lucifer was cast into and locked away in Hell. She then created purgatory where spirits walked, watching and guarding the entrance to ensure he couldn't escape.

Realms were created for those creatures that preferred to leave Earth. Fae was given the kingdom of Elfame. The dragons, the most dangerous of the new creatures, were given a realm called "The Sacred Realm." Demons were relegated to Hell or The Nightmare Lands. The angels then helped Neveah create a task force to police the rest of the supernatural on Earth and the portals for the realms themselves.

Human minds were wiped of all knowledge of the supernatural, and a law was instituted that the magical creatures were to keep their true selves hidden. A council was formed to maintain the rules and the task force. This council consisted of the strongest of each supernatural species, who were then in charge of maintaining their species. The same line would always hold that seat on the council unless a line ended, at which point a vote would be taken to elect a new member.

A deal was made with Lucifer that any evil human soul would be sent to him in The Nightmare Lands upon death. Any Light soul was sent to Heaven. Lilith was banished to the void to live out her existence alone. The void was locked to anyone and anything, so any of her creations couldn't escape. Her cage was only strong for 2,000 years.

After that, it would begin to weaken, and she'd be able to find a way to break free.

The prophecy says that the Creator and Neveah made a key that would show itself when the time came, and this was the only way to relock Lilith and her minions back into her cage. Neveah's line held the key. When the time came, one would step forward with the same power to weave the very fabric of existence. When this time came, the fight for the world itself would commence.

Centuries went by, evil and darkness trying to creep into the world again. The council's longest-running line of the supernatural saw fit to create an academy where they could train new taskforce members. The Academy was named The Supernatural Academy of Excellence and was concealed with magic on Earth. To humans, the Academy was known as Winthrope Academy of Excellence, named after its creator and council head, Marcus Winthrope. No one knew the future, but the council and the academy were determined to be prepared for anything.

1

REEGAN

"What's wrong, mommy? Why are you and daddy crying?" The little girl asks. Her mother nods, "It's going to be alright, baby. Everything will be ok.

"Esme, they're going to come. It's time, my love.", her daddy says, looking at her mommy lovingly. "You felt that spike in power the same as I did. The task force will come and bring Hell with it."

"I know, Max. I know!" Esme screams. "Dammit. She's still too young for her powers to be this strong." Daddy gives her a look and a nod, "Call Marcus. He's the only one that can protect her." Esme snatches up her phone and dials. There's another voice on the other end, but the little girl can't hear it since it's muffled. He's coming to take her away. She begins to cry. A loud crash takes place downstairs. It sounds like the door was blown off its hinges. "Esme, hide her, now!" Max hisses.

Esme looks down at the little girl, "Ok, baby. Do you want to play hide and seek?" she asks with a watery smile. "The little girl beams a huge smile to her mommy excitedly, nodding her head. "Go quietly to your special hiding place, and don't come out until a man named Marcus finds you, ok. You can trust only Marcus, do you understand?" With a nod, the little girl gets up and runs.

Under her bed and against the wall is a tiny crawl space that only she can fit in. She gets in and replaces the grate over it. She places her hand over her mouth to keep from making any noise. All she can hear is grunts and a sharp noise like a slap. "Where is she?" someone yells. "Go to Hell, you bastard!" she hears Esme scream back. Her mommy never curses. Is she ok? There's a bang she hasn't heard before, loud footsteps echo around the house, and then all falls silent. She wants to check on her mommy but is afraid she'll be in trouble.

So much time passes. She can't be sure if it's been a few minutes or hours. Laying on her stomach inside her hiding spot, she can't see anything though she can hear muffled voices. One of them is strangely familiar. Her bed is moved. She tries to crawl further into the space in the wall where she hides, but there's no more room. The grate is removed, and a hand grabs her. With a yelp, she is pulled from her hiding space. She screams, kicks, and scratches, but the hands are relentless and refuse to release her.

"It's ok.", that familiar voice insists. "I've got you, sweetheart. It's all going to be ok." She looks up into the face of a man she vaguely recognizes. He has solid features, but those eyes. They look like her mommy's eyes.

"Who are you?" she squeaks. He searches her face for a minute before answering,

"I'm Marcus." His eyes are soft. He looks like he wants to say something else but doesn't.

"I'm Reegan, and I'm 5. Mommy said I could trust you?" she says like it's a question.

Marcus snickers with a smile and says, "Yes, *Little Bit*, you can. I'm going to take you somewhere safe."

"Where's mommy? Where's daddy? I heard a big bang. They hit mommy. She made me hide. I could've fought.", Reegan states with a look of pride on her face. Marcus doesn't respond. He picks her up and carries her down to a large black car. He sits inside, covers her with his jacket, and drives away.

I wake with a start. I'm sweating. It's still dark outside. These dreams have been coming more and more regularly the closer my birthday gets. I never see the little girl's face, but I know she's me. I can feel it. Are these memories resurfacing? I don't remember my parents. The only details I know are that my mother's eyes are the same steel gray as Marcus'. My father's smile was a little lopsided and childish. I didn't know until I was eleven that Marcus was my grandfather. He wasn't around much as I was growing up. I know he holds a council seat and founded the academy that trains the task force. I dream of being on the task force, but Marcus says that isn't possible for me. I am the heir to his seat. I'm an elemental. I can control the elements: water, earth, wind, fire, and spirit. According to Marcus, I am rare. Only a few possess all the elemental powers, and I am blessed to be one. There's something else about me that even I don't know. Marcus won't tell me anything.

No matter how often I ask, he says, "You are other. You are more." I don't know if he even knows what else there is.

Since I was twelve, I have dreamed, not like the dreams or recollections I've been having recently but lucid dreaming. I can walk into other people's dreams, shape them, and create them. I only did that once. I don't remember the details of that night, but I also have that recollection dream. Everything

always looks like it's underwater. I hope it stays
that way because it always feels like I will lose a
part of myself if I remember the details. A few
months after my twelfth birthday, I dreamt of a
boy with striking ice-blue eyes and dark hair. I
knew he was older than me, but not by much. His
name was Ash. I don't know if he was real or one
of my dream creations. I told him my name was
Winnie. That's not the complete truth. Winnie is
my middle name, a way to shorten Winthrope so
I'd always carry my family's legacy with me. We're
always within my dreamscape. I know because
it is modeled after my favorite place in the Fae
realm, Elfame. None of that matters because Ash
shouldn't remember the dreams when he wakes
up. No one else ever has.

Since my parents died, I have lived half my life in
the human world and the other half in Elfame with
the royal family. I am some long distant relation
to the Fae. History says that the Fae birthed the
Elementals, which use natural elements. Well, the
light Fae did. The Dark Fae birthed witches and
warlocks, blood magic. I live with the King and
Queen of Elfame, Dain, and Alita, along with their
daughter Maddie and their sons Aldair and Kalan.

Maddie has been my best friend since I first lived
with them at five. The boys have always been like
brothers, but Kalan and I have grown to be more
than that over the past year. We haven't passed

tender kisses and handholding, but I wouldn't mind if he took it further. The King and Queen don't seem to mind our budding relationship. Now that I think about it, our relationship started getting more romantic around the same time the dreams started coming more often, and the feeling of change within me began to take place.

I don't know how long I lay here pondering everything, but the sun is starting to rise, which means it's time for me to do the same. I make my way over to the window to watch the sunrise over the mountain of Elfame. It's my favorite place in all the realms. It's a massive thing covered in trees, and at the tip, you can see the steam rising from the crevice in the center. On one side, there's a beautiful rainbow-colored waterfall that lands into a clear blue pool beneath. Maddie and I used to skip lessons to swim in the cool water. It always felt like the safest place in the realm and beyond. Like it was fortified in magic that no other person could touch. In the other direction, far to the east, I can see the hint of the ocean and the pink sand beaches we used to explore as children. Closer to the palace are the gardens. It's so lush and filled with all sorts of fruit trees. If I were imagining the human's Garden of Eden, this is what I'd see.

After taking in my fill of the view, I head to the shower to prepare for the day. Today, we go back to Earth for the summer there. Summer on Earth, and Winter in Elfame. That's been my life for the past almost 17 years. I always look forward to this time. There will be no responsibilities or lessons—just fun to be had pretending to be human for a little while. After showering and changing into skinny black jeans and a black tank that molds my curves, I head to the dining room. When I enter, the queen is already sitting, making the arrangements.

"Your Majesty." I greet her with a dip of my head.

"Don't be cheeky, dear.", she responds with a mischievous smile on her beautiful face. Alita is a classic beauty that carries herself with such grace. She has long blonde hair that reaches just above her waist and crystal green eyes.

"Ok, Alita. So, what's our plan for this trip? Will we be staying at the house in Pismo again?" I ask conversationally. Sometimes, we change our plans but mostly stay at the family estate.

"Not this year. I'm glad it's just the two of us right now. We need to talk." Alita has a severe look on her face that has me somewhat shrinking in my seat. I'm curious about what she needs to say that she doesn't want the others here while she says it.

"This year, our trip will coincide with your grandfather's schedule. We are going to Tennessee and staying at the Winthrope family estate. I received a letter from Marcus' assistant Rebecca that we were requested, and that's what we will be doing. I wanted to talk to you before the others to prepare you. I know you haven't seen Marcus in some time, and I didn't know how you would feel about it." She gives me a kind smile.

Before I can respond, chatter reaches us from the hallway. Maddie and the boys enter. Maddie has a massive smile from some joke Aldair has told, but Kalan's eyes are locked on me. He is so handsome with his dark hair and grass-green eyes. He has high cheekbones and skin that's sun-kissed. His lips are full and soft. He comes around the table and gives me a timid kiss. I just want to grab him and deepen it, but I won't since everyone is in the room.

"Good morning, beautiful.", Kalan whispers to me.

I smile at him as Margo and Marie, the kitchen staff, bring in breakfast. It's quite a spread of pancakes, eggs, sausage, bacon, and fresh fruit. I fill my plate and dig into the fluffy eggs, moaning at the buttery flavor. Kalan stares at my mouth with a heated look. Yeah, it won't be long before we explode. That thought sends a delicious shiver down my spine as a blush rises to my cheeks. Kalan notices that as well, and a smirk takes over his face. He has to know where my thoughts have taken me.

A throat clears from the doorway, pulling me from our staring match. There, with a smile on his face, stands Dain. "Well, family, are we ready for our vacation?" he asks, pointedly looking at me.

Everyone begins excitedly talking about what we'll be getting into, but all I manage to do is nod my head at Dain. This whole thing feels like an omen of sorts. I haven't seen Grandfather in six years. I don't know if I want to see him. He leaves me here for years without making an appearance, and when he does, he refuses to answer any questions about my otherness. "Good, then eat and go get ready. We leave in 3 hours.", Dain states with all the air of the king he is. He's so very punctual. A giggle leaves my lips, but I quickly finish my food. Once I'm done, I excuse myself and head toward my room.

REEGAN

I'm all packed and ready to go when a knock sounds on the door. "Come in.", I call. The door opens, and in walks Kalan. He looks at me as I pat the bed for him to come and sit. He walks with such a swagger that it causes my breath to catch in my chest. I know he's going to kiss me. As he leans down, I weave my fingers through his hair and give a tiny tug. He tries to make the kiss tentative, but I want, no, I need more. I nip his bottom lip, and a growl rises from his chest. I open my mouth, and his tongue invades, fighting a battle with mine. He presses me down into the bed, and I all but melt at his touch. I grind my center against his hardness, trying to get a desperately needed release.

"Baby, stop.", he says, pulling away. He must see the hurt in my eyes because he quickly reassures me, "I want you so badly. You drive me crazy, but we can't do this now. I only came up here to see if you were ready. Everyone is waiting. And you, love, will make us late if you keep touching me like that."

I huff out a breath, "Fine, but this is far from fin
ished.", I say smarmily. He just chuckles and helps
me readjust myself. I smooth down my long purple
hair and try to regain my equilibrium. Once I feel
somewhat back to normal, I take Kalan's hand and
head down to meet everyone in the portal room.

I always hate traveling through portals. They
feel wholly unnatural to me. I'm not sure why. I
never look forward to the portals, but I am looking forward to the destination. I'm still reluctant
to see my grandfather. We always travel to the
West Coast on our trips to the human realm, but
for once, we visit a completely different place, Tennessee. I have never seen my grandfather's estate,
so regardless of my nervousness about seeing him,
I am looking forward to a new adventure.

"Now that we're all here," Alita begins, "we're
looking forward to this, and you all need to be on
your best behavior. This is the town in which the
Council resides. We are guests, so please, for the
love of the Creator, don't do anything to embarrass us." This is said as she looks at Aldair, which
makes sense. He has always been the prankster of
the group. " Now, go. Rodriq will be waiting on the
other side.", Alita says.

We make our way through the portal, me and
Kalan going through it hand in hand. Maddie
comes through next with Aldair, and then Dain
and Alita join us last. As Alita said, Rodriq is wait-

ing for us in a huge black SUV. He must have left yesterday to make accommodations. That would explain not having lessons. He's looking down at his phone, but as if he felt the portal magic ripple, he looks up.

He smiles when he spots us until his eyes land on Maddie in her crop top and cut-off shorts. "Princess, where's the rest of your outfit? Did the portal swallow it?" he huffs. I see the firelight in her eyes as she looks him up and down. Her favorite pastime is giving him shit, especially since it's his job to tutor and protect us. Oh, and did I mention that they are in love, but each refuses to acknowledge those feelings?

"I don't know, Rodriq. Perhaps the stable boy removed them for me." she snarks. There's a fire in Rodriq's eyes, and it's not the flirtatious one I saw. Now it is wholly anger taking over his handsome face.

Before he can do or say something he regrets, I tell him, "Come now, Rodriq, she's only dressing the way human girls do. You know we have to fit in." He physically shakes himself to get rid of the angry look, which is highly adorable. If they weren't clueless, they'd make a fantastic couple. As it is, I am trying to find a way to force them together.

Maddie and Aldair are lucky. They get to choose whom they love and marry. As the heir apparent, Kalan will be required to marry someone of class.

Someone that has highbred Fae blood. We haven't talked about that aspect of our relationship yet. While I want to, he seems to be ignoring the truth. We aren't destined to spend our lives together. This is just a passing thing. So why does that thought make my heart squeeze painfully in my chest?

We all pile into the SUV, cramming me in the back between Aldair and Kalan. Kalan's hand automatically reaches for mine as we settle. It's mid-morning when we get to the estate. "Kids, go enjoy your day and explore the city. Dinner tonight at nine.", Dain calls as we all head to our designated rooms.

I head over to my bags sitting on the foot of the bed, and pull out a sapphire blue peasant top that matches my eyes. I check myself in the mirror and deem myself worthy of exploring the town. When Alita told me where we would be going this morning, I researched and discovered there are so many different things to do, such as drive go-karts and play mini-golf. I knew this vacation would be enjoyable. There are even an amusement park and an aquarium I am dying to check out. I know that won't happen today. We will have to check out the town, the shopping and of course the food. I can't wait!

3

TRENT

We're walking along the strip we know so well. Growing up in the area has been amazing. If only we didn't have to go to the academy. Classes start in two weeks, meaning we don't have much time to get to know the tourists that frequent the area. Asher and I returned to town early to enjoy the city and the beautiful females that cling to this place at the beginning of the season– the beginning of summer marks the beginning of the term for us. Well, I'm going to enjoy the females while I can. I'm an easygoing guy, maybe what you'd call a lady's man. I love women too much to get myself tied down in a relationship. Because of this, I've garnered quite a reputation among the female population.

I look over at my best friend. He used to be like the rest of us. No worries about spending one night with a woman and then letting her go. That was before Calista. He and Calista have been together for the past two years. I don't know what he sees in her. She's a conniving bitch. None of us like her, and we're all waiting with bated breath for the day to come when he finally wakes up and dumps her dumb ass.

That's another reason we came back early. She won't be back until classes resume, so this is a vacation from the drama. Of course, that was my idea. I figured he needed a break after dealing with her for the past... however many days. I love this place this time of year since there are hotties everywhere, and they won't be staying long. It's the perfect environment for a few tremendous one-night stands before my life is zapped away and replaced by another year at the academy.

Even in my mind, I sound like a pig, but most people don't know about our lives; they don't know that all we have is time spent training to take our parent's spots on a council we want nothing to do with. Plus, I know I'm a good-looking guy and care about the pleasure I give to the women I fuck. I always make sure they come before I do. See, how nice of me, right? I also make certain that we don't see each other again afterward. If that makes me an asshole, lock me up and throw away the key.

We're just passing by one of the many food stalls when I hear a tinkling laugh that shoots electricity straight up my spine. I turn my head at the same time she does. She has a radiant smile and the most unique eyes I've ever seen. They're a gorgeous sapphire blue. I've never seen eyes that color before. Her hair is purple and runs in waves down her back. Dyed or natural, I'm not sure. One thing is certain. She is not human, but I can't get a read on her. I can see the glow of her eyes that gives her away as supernatural, but her aura is locked down tight, making it impossible to tell her race. And with just that little bit of information, I'm intrigued.

I peruse her. Starting at her feet, I take her in. She's tall and willowy with curves in all the right places. She's wearing a pair of Chucks, skinny black jeans that look like they were painted on, and a blue top that matches her eyes and shows off the swell of what I can tell are perfect breasts. *Yes, asshole pig here, remember.* She's smiling and laughing with another female, a Fae. The Fae is petite with fiery red hair and green eyes. She's dressed in a crop top and shorts with a pair of sandals on her feet. She's cute, but she has nothing on the beauty beside her. Beauty would be the perfect name for her. If I couldn't read auras, I'd swear the little one was a leprechaun, with her fiery red hair and slight stature.

"I think I'm in love," I say to myself. I know Asher isn't paying any attention to my musings. I'm sure he's stuck on his phone answering texts from Calista, insert shiver here, or his dad Senior Hayworth. Yes, that's his name. Pretentious right?

I'm surprised Asher didn't come out with the name Junior, except his mom is the sweetest dragon you'll ever meet and gave him his name. I still don't know how she stomachs that asshole she calls a husband. Unfortunately, Ash is just like his mom and can't see the disaster of a mating he's headed for.

"You are at least three times a week, man.", Ash answers. I guess he wasn't caught up on his phone. I looked over, and nope, I wasn't wrong. He's texting. I see it's Calista, so I take his phone and turn it off.

"What the hell, dude?" He asks. Someone has to save him from himself, and since I'm here, I guess the task is delegated to me.

"Man, stop. We came back early to escape her drama, not to continue dealing with it." I give him a look trying to convey that I mean business. "If you take it out again, I will throw it in one of the deep fryers in that food truck," I tell him while pointing at a truck that boasts famous funnel cakes.

"She's my girlfriend dickhead.", Ash fumes. She may be, but that doesn't mean I have to hear about it right now.

"Shit, you don't even like that bitch. You feel you have to do what Daddy says instead of living your life for you.", I admonish with an eyebrow raised, daring him to contradict me.

"Whatever, man. You know it's complicated.", he answers. "I don't have much choice in any of this shit, and she's hot as hell."

"Nah, man, it's not that complicated. And hot doesn't detract from the craziness, bro.", I say with an eye roll. He knows I'm right; he just refuses to admit he's got no problem being stuck under Senior's thumb.

"If you say so. So, who's the new love of your life?" he says as he throws his arm over my shoulder. I point toward where she's standing by the food truck. They haven't moved more than a few steps so he can see her. Right now, she's turned away, but even he can see how banging her body is. "Let's go get some street tacos.", Asher laughs, pulling me toward where the girls stand. I must admit that even though he claims to be taken, he is an excellent wingman.

The line moves quickly when we reach it, and as the girls make their orders and prepare to pay, I speak, "I've got these ladies. We'll also take six short rib tacos with slaw, please." Asher doesn't like slaw, but oh well. He'll have to get over it since I spoke first.

The girls turn, and those beautiful eyes shine at me. They take my breath away, "Um... Thanks, that's not necessary.", the hottie with sapphire eyes says with a small smile. I can see the slightest blush color her cheeks, making her look even more magnificent.

The redhead elbows her, "It's not necessary, but it's appreciated. Thank you.", she says. I can see her darting her eyes back and forth between sapphire and me.

I can't take my eyes off this purple-headed beauty in front of me. I feel a weird pull to her that I've never felt before. As if drawn to a magnet, I find myself leaning close to her, grabbing her hand in mine. It's so warm, and her skin is so soft. I kiss her hand, "It's my pleasure to feed beautiful women. I'm Trenton, and you are?" I plead. I need to hear her voice again. I need to know the name of the woman that has me, a certifiable male slut, enamored.

She opens her lips to speak but is interrupted by a sharp inhale from my best friend, "Winnie?" he asks. He looks like he has just seen a ghost and doesn't know what to do with it. His jaw is almost hitting the ground, and his eyes hold not just surprise but what looks like... hurt.

"I'm so sorry; I think you have the wrong person. I'm Reegan." she stutters, panic and recognition flaring in her eyes. She's scared. Is she afraid of Asher? Why? And where do they know each other from?

I can tell she knows Asher but doesn't want that fact known. She looks fearful for some reason. I find myself desperately wanting to take that fear away. "So, what brings you to Gatlinburg?" I ask them, hoping to change the subject.

The redhead doesn't miss a beat, "We're actually on vacation. I'm Maddie, by the way. It's nice to meet you." she holds out her hand, and I take it for a quick shake. I glance back at Reegan and see relief flash in those beautiful eyes. Crisis averted, but I'm even more intrigued by this magnificent creature.

"Trenton, but you can call me Trent, and this guy here is Asher." I nod toward my friend, who looks at Reegan like she's an enigma. I kind of feel the same way.

Asher finally breaks whatever spell he was under and looks at both girls, "Would you ladies like to sit with us to eat?" he asks with hope in his eyes. He looks at Maddie instead of Reegan. I think he knows she'd be quick to say no.

"Sure. That sounds great!" Maddie answers excitedly. Her excitement is infectious, and I find myself smiling as we walk over and grab an empty table.

We converse with small talk for a while, and then Reegan looks over Ash's shoulder, her whole face lighting up. Damn, I'd give anything to have that look directed at me. I turn around to see none other than the Seelie prince striding toward us with another man. I assume it's his brother. I've never met the princes, but our training has made it imperative that we know everything about the ruling families.

"Hey, baby. Who are your new.... friends?" the dark-haired prince asks. Gods, she has a boyfriend, and he's a possessive son of a bitch if the look in his eyes is any indication. Dammit. Of course, she'd be dating a mother fucking prince.

"Hey, Kalan. This is Trent and Asher. They were nice enough to buy us lunch. Wasn't that sweet of them?" Reegan smiles, tilting her head up to look at him. He kisses her lips, and I have to physically keep myself from growling at him. Maddie looks at me right then and giggles a little. I rub my chest above my heart as it tugs, causing Maddie to look at me with a frown.

"Yeah, nice. Are you ready to go? We should head back to the house. I'm sure mom and dad are waiting, and I want some alone time with you." he says, kissing her hair.

"Oh. Okay. Trent and Asher, it was nice meeting you. Thank you for lunch.", Reegan says as she takes Kalan's hand and rises from her seat. She grabs her trash and walks away but looks over her shoulder, shooting a look at Asher, and then gives me a wave and a smile.

At the same time, the douche looks over his shoulder, sending me a scathing look. Damn, if looks could kill! I'd kick his ass if it weren't for me not wanting to see this beautiful creature sad. As she walks away, I realize I don't know her last name. I'll probably never see her again.

After they walk away, I ask Ash, "What the hell was that, bro? Did you really know her? From where? I have so many questions." I stammer.

"I just thought she looked familiar. That's all.", he says, but I can see in his eyes that he's lying. We never lie to each other. So what's so important about this girl to him that he feels the need to keep it to himself? Is he afraid I'll tell Calista? Because that will never happen. Bros before hos and all that nonsense.

"Yeah, I call bullshit, but I won't push right now. That doesn't mean you won't be filling me in later." He just laughs. We get up, all thoughts of finding a woman to spend the evening with gone. I found one. I just hope I see her again.

4

ASHER

I am not mistaken about knowing that beautiful creature. Except her name isn't Reegan. It's Winnie. At least that's what she told me in a dream when I was fifteen. I know it sounds weird. How could I meet someone in a dream? I saw the recognition in her eyes and the sheer panic at the fact that I recognized her. Why is she hiding who she is? Is she in trouble? She seemed scared of me, but I don't understand why. I never did anything in those dreams but be her friend.

I never doubted she was an actual person when she first appeared in a dream. I remember them so vividly. I fell in love with her in those dreams, though I was always afraid to say the words aloud, fearing the dreams wouldn't be real. Then after two years of nearly meeting nightly in the dreamscape, as she called it, she disappeared.

I felt like a piece of me had been torn out then. Like a vital part of my being was missing. I tried to forget her. I tried to move on without looking back, but truthfully. I have dreamt almost every night of sapphire eyes and a radiant smile that was always just for me. I became thankful I never spoke the words my heart ached for me to speak. Eight years have passed, but the feelings remain. I'm not sure what to do. I'm with Calista now, and two years isn't anything to balk at when it comes to supernaturals. I'm sure she's making plans for the future. I know my father is.

"*Mine!*" my dragon bellows in my head. "*Yes, she is,*" I answer.

When I saw that smile on her lips today as she looked upon her boyfriend, I felt a pang of jealousy but quickly squashed it down. I have no claim on her anymore. I don't know that I ever did. But in those dreams, it felt like she was mine. I don't know what kind of supernatural she is. I couldn't read her power even if I wanted to. They outlawed that many years ago when witches would spell a super to find weaknesses to take advantage of. Trent could read her aura if he wanted to. He'd be able to determine what species she is, but very few know he has that ability, so he keeps it on a tight leash so that the wrong people don't find out. I don't doubt he's already read her, but would he give me that information?

I always wondered what it would be like to meet her in real life, outside the dreams. She's so much more beautiful than I ever imagined. She's still the girl I saw in my dreams all those years ago, but now she's more. She's grown into a woman. Her hair is longer, but still that perfect shade of amethyst, and her eyes are crystalline sapphire I loved getting lost in.

Her body is another story altogether. That is the most significant change. Her breasts are full and round. Her curves are more prominent, but you can also see how athletic she is. She's the perfect mix of hard and soft. And when she walked away, giving me the perfect view of her tight ass in those jeans, I had to bite the inside of my cheek to keep from groaning.

Just thinking of her has me hard as steel in my jeans. I grab my cock to relieve some of the pressure building there. Now is not the time for it when Trent and I have plans in the gym. She has a boyfriend, and I have a girlfriend, but I can't keep myself from imagining she and I together again like we used to be. And if my dragon agrees, maybe it's possible.

My phone pings as I lie on my bed in the house the guys and I share. I look down and see a text from Jaymeson:

Jaymes: Are you guys home already?

Me: I got back in yesterday. Checked out the town scene today. When are you guys coming back?

Jaymes: I'll be there tomorrow. Not sure about Bentley.

Me: Ok. Tell Bentley to text us and let us know. We have to make plans for the newbs this year.

I get up off my bed, and my phone pings again. I see Calista's name. I don't want to deal with her, so I turn it off. She's another issue I seriously need to figure out. Trent was right. I don't like her, though I used to. Over the last two years, something has changed between us. When we're together, I feel like I'm in love with her. When we're apart, I feel like I'm waking up from a coma. I can remember every detail of what's happened while I'm with her, though other things feel like they happened to someone else. The more we're togther, the more time I seem to lose. When we're separated, I find myself not wanting to be back in her presence. The one thing she has going for her is that she's a good lover. She's seriously a freak between the sheets, and I love that. She was never much of a challenge, but she doesn't shy away from my more violent proclivities, and I enjoy exploring her kinks. To most people, she's the perfect specimen. Tall with long blonde hair and hazel eyes. But those who really know her know she's a sadistic bitch. Maybe that's why my dad seems so keen on our relationship.

The real reason is one I don't want to dwell on. I know he likes Calista because she's the most powerful spell caster of our time. As the dragon council leader and descendant of Lucifer himself– all dragons are descendants of the devil– dad thinks he should be the head of it all. Calista's dad, a witch, tends to agree with him, so they've made some deal with each other. I don't know what that deal is, but I know I am a pawn in this game, and until I graduate, I don't have much choice. I wonder if Calista does. Does she truly want to be with me, or is she using me the same way my father is?

Done with thoughts of my dad, Calista, and the Council, I make my way to the gym. I spend a reasonable amount of time here every night with Trent. My dragon needs it. It helps me to relax and blow off steam in a safe way. I turn the treadmill up to the highest level, and I run. I ran for about an hour, just getting lost in the motion. When I'm done there, I walk over to the mats with the punching bag hanging from the ceiling. I give it a go for a while until I wear myself out. I can't let my dragon out to roam on the first night of the summer season in Pigeon Forge. That would be suicide since the council has rules against it and even my father wouldn't be able to save me if I somehow outed the supernatural world.

Trent is in the corner of the room working on his Elemental powers. He holds all of them except Spirit, making him the strongest and rarest of all Elementals, including his mom, who has the council position. She's also half dragon. His dad is part of the current task force and will teach fighting tactics this year. He's a strong elemental in his own right, and we're pretty sure he has skills none of us have seen. Bentley's uncle also teaches at the academy. The only council member that doesn't do much is my dad. He's a pompous prick that feels as if he's too good to take on the task of teaching future generations.

I make my way back upstairs and head for the shower. My body is tired, but my head still wants to run with thoughts of Reegan. I'm hard as fuck, with the views of that luscious body I got a glimpse of today running through my mind. I strip down and climb under the water. I slick up my body and take my cock in my hand. I hiss at the feeling. I grip it hard and jerk up and down, circling the head with every pass. It doesn't take long before I feel the tingle in the bottom of my spine and my balls tightening up. With a grunt, I come on the shower wall. I watch as the water washes the evidence down the drain. I quickly finish my shower and dry off. I throw on a pair of sweats that sit low on my hips and drop onto my pillows. I'm out in a matter of minutes. That night like so many before, I dream of sapphire eyes.

5

REEGAN

What does it mean that after all these years, the one person I never thought I'd see finds me in the middle of a crowd at a food stall? Not just that he found me but that he remembered me. How is that possible? He shouldn't be able to remember anything from the dreamscape. No one else ever does.

I remember the shock of electricity that ran up my arm when Trent touched me and the skip of my heart at his voice. He is one of the most beautiful men I've ever seen. Dark brown hair with blonde highlights from spending much time in the sun. His amber eyes were filled with mischief. He doesn't take much seriously, I'd say. I didn't get the chance to explore him further since Ash interrupted my perusal.

When I heard the old name come from the other man, I panicked. As soon as I saw him, I knew he was my Ash, but I didn't know how to tell him. I freaked out at that moment. I was so thankful to

Trent for taking the conversation back. I know he saw the look on my face, but I was relieved when he didn't ask questions. I'll just have to be more careful when I'm in town. It's a big town with many tourists, so I doubt I'll see him again. That thought helps me relax.

I know dream walking isn't a typical trait of supes. I've heard tales of witches and spells that allow dream walking, or memory walking, as they call it. But, as far as I know, none have the power to create dreams. To change dreams. Ash is beyond what I ever imagined he would grow up to be. His black hair and baby blue eyes were just as I remembered them, but he grew into a wonderfully beautiful man. I noticed hints of tattoos peeking below his sleeves, and I would have given anything to trace and see them all.

Since parting the little sitting area with Maddie and Kalan, I have felt this pressure in my chest, like someone is lightly sitting on it. Every once in a while, I feel a tug. What is that? I don't quite know, but it feels as if those two men are essential to something. Ash was always important to me, but when the dreams ended, I chalked it up to my imagination, creating someone to ease my loneliness. I can admit that I was lusting after both Ash and Trent, but it felt more like they were connected to me somehow.

Right on the tail of this feeling is one of guilt. I'm with Kalan and genuinely love him, so I shouldn't lust after anyone else. But I already know there's no future with us, so I'll bide my time, love him the best way I can, and then worry about anything else when our time together ends. He can claim that he won't leave me when it comes time for him to ascend the throne, and if I asked, I'm sure that is the exact reassurance he'd try to give me, but his people will always come first. I understand that even if it does hurt my heart to think of losing him. These feelings war within me as I toss and turn in my bed, unable to find enough peace to sleep. I'm afraid of what my dreams will bring me.

A soft knock on my door has me turning over. As if I conjured him, a sexy-looking Kalan walks in. His green eyes lock onto me. He's wearing low-slung silk pajama bottoms that show off that delicious v below his abs. I want to lick every one of them. His dirty blonde hair is tousled like he's run his hands through it a dozen times. He seems a little nervous, though I'm not sure why.

Kalan is ten years my senior, and from what I've heard *and seen* over the years, he is pretty well experienced, so it makes no sense that he's scared to enter my room. Does he think I'd turn him away? We haven't talked about the future, and I love him, though I've never said the words. He's never made me any promises, and I've never expected him to.

I know he loves me. It's in the way he looks at me, holds me, and kisses me. He makes me feel cherished.

I push the covers back and throw my legs over the side of the bed. Kalan's eyes drop to my legs, and I remember I'm only in a tank and panties. As his eyes travel up my body, I feel the heat rising in my core. "By the creator, you are beautiful," I hear him say reverently. A blush creeps up my neck and cheeks as I make my way over to him. I stop just shy of our bodies connecting though I can feel his heat through my tank. I can feel his breath on my face.

I lean on my tiptoes and press my lips softly to his. As soon as our lips meet, it's as if a dam broke, and we're both drowning. He immediately takes over, the kiss turning demanding. One of his hands curls into the hair on the back of my head while the other makes its way down to just above my ass. All thoughts are gone. The only thing that exists at this moment is his mouth on mine. I can't think of anything other than his touch. I gasp. He takes the opportunity to insert his tongue into my mouth. This kiss is so different from the others we've shared. I can't help but wonder what it would be like to have that mouth between my thighs. This is what our light kisses and petting have been leading to. This is the culmination of two years of holding myself back. Of him holding himself back from me.

He breaks the kiss giving me time to catch my breath. His eyes have darkened from that sea green to almost emerald. I go to pull away, to walk toward the bed. Kalan has other ideas, however. He grabs my thighs and lifts me in his arms, forcing me to wrap my legs around his waist. I feel how hard he is as my center sits on top of his groin. I can't help but grind my center down on him. A growl leaves his mouth, but he doesn't say anything as he takes me over and throws me down on the bed. A small giggle leaves my lips as he follows down after me finding my mouth again. He nestles between my legs, and I moan. His hands are everywhere, and I'd rather it be his lips. He rises on his knees and grabs the hem of my tiny tank.

"Let me see you, baby.", he says huskily.

I raise a little and help him pull the tank over my head. He leans back, perusing me like a present he just unwrapped. My nipples pebble under his gaze, and he leans forward, taking one into his mouth. His tongue laves at the pebbled nipple, and I feel his teeth graze against it. He bites down on the underside of my breast, eliciting another moan from my mouth. I'm at a loss for words with the feelings overwhelming me. Kalan's hand makes its way down my body to my covered pussy.

He cups me, and a hiss leaves his mouth. "You're so hot and already so wet for me. I can feel your wetness through the fabric. Tell me what you want, Reegan."

My name is like a prayer on his lips. All of a sudden, I become shy. How do I tell this gorgeous man that I want him to taste me? I just shake my head. "Tell me, love. Do you want me to eat you? Fill you so full you'll be feeling me inside you for days?" he asks.

"Yes" is the only word I can form. I look into Kalan's eyes. The heat I see there takes my breath away.

"Your wish is my command, Princess." he chuckles as he kisses his way down my body. When he reaches my belly button, he pulls on the ring I have there, eliciting another moan from me.

Once he's flat on his stomach, he begins kissing my thighs. I can feel his hot breath on my center. I feel him kiss my pussy. He blows that breath across my panty-clad center, making me shiver. He swipes his tongue across my lips with a groan. Then he slowly begins to slide my panties down my legs. His mouth returns to my core with another lick, making me arch off the bed with a guttural moan.

Using his hands, he spreads me wider, spearing his tongue inside. "Reegan, you taste amazing. So sweet. You're going to become my favorite dessert. ", he says, then continues to eat me as if I'm his last meal.

His tongue spears my heat over and over. Then his lips find my clit. I can feel a tightening in my stomach. I'm so close. When his teeth graze me and bite down lightly, I orgasm, screaming his name. Kalan continues his ministrations with his mouth. As he swirls his tongue on my clit, he inserts one finger into my pussy and begins moving it in and out, curling as he finds that bundle of nerves inside. I'm riding that precipice again, Kalan taking me higher and higher. He then adds a second finger scissoring them until I crash over the edge.

My legs are shaking, and I feel boneless. Kalan crawls back up my body, stopping at my breasts. He takes one nipple in his mouth and sucks. He releases it with a pop before moving back up to my mouth. I can taste myself on his lips and tongue. It has me groaning and rearing to go again. I reach between us, placing my hand beneath his waist-band, finding his hard length. I can feel how big he is. My breath catches in my throat.

"Now it's my turn to see you.", I say breathlessly. "Please, Kalan," I beg.

Kalan gets up and slides his pants off. My mouth drops open, and I can feel my eyes bulge out. He's not just big. He's huge. No way that will fit in my pussy. He's long, not overly so, but he's super thick. I'm scared he's going to rip me open. He must see the fear in my eyes because he leans down, kissing me softly.

"It's ok, baby. I'll be gentle and go slow.", he reassures. He kisses me again as he climbs back between my thighs.

We kiss some more, and I feel my body return to life. Kalan reaches between us, rubbing his palm on my clit. I can feel my release leaking down my thighs. Kalan removes his hand, glistening with my cream, and rubs it up and down his length. I lick my lips. I wonder how he tastes.

"I'll fuck that mouth soon enough, beautiful, but I want to feel you come apart on my cock tonight." Damn. He can talk *dirty*. I'm panting, and he hasn't even attempted to enter me yet. "Are you ready? You know I'd never rush you."

"I've been ready," I answer.

Kalan positions himself, rubbing the head of his cock against my clit. He lowers himself, his cock slowly entering. Inch by agonizing inch enters my body. It feels foreign but not in a bad way. Once he hits a particular spot, he pauses. Then before I can speak, he surges forward. I cry out. The pain is sharp but not agonizingly so.

"You're so fucking tight," Kalan hisses.

He gives me a minute to adjust to having him inside me, and then he slowly starts to move. As he picks up the pace, I begin to feel that sensation again of rising. I'm moaning and writhing. I'm a mess. When I feel like I'm going to crash over again, Kalan changes positions.

He rises to his knees and holds my legs over his shoulders. From this position, I can feel him *everywhere*. He speeds up his pace hitting the spot so deep inside me that I never knew existed before this moment. I come screaming his name. A few more pumps of his hips, and he follows me with a groan.

He releases my legs and then collapses next to me. After his breathing regulates, he gets up and heads to the bathroom. He returns with a warm washcloth. He cleans me up gently and then throws the cloth in the hamper. He returns to the bed, pulls me into him, and covers us with a light sheet. I snuggle into his chest with my head over his heart. The rhythm of his heart has my eyes drooping closed.

Right before I fall asleep, I feel Kalan kiss my hair and hear him whisper, "I love you, Reegan."

Kalan

I lay here watching Reegan sleep. Things are changing. I can feel it. I love this woman to a depth I never thought I'd feel for anyone. She's burrowed so deep in me that my soul feels connected to her. *"Mate,"* my mind screams at me. We've all heard the legends of fated mates, but usually, it's reserved for the shifter race. It's not to say the other races don't have them, but it's extremely rare. That's the only explanation for how my soul felt as if part of it now belonged to this gorgeous creature lying in my arms. Is it possible that we're fated? I've always felt a pull toward Reegan, even when we were young, but I didn't know what it meant. I was too busy sowing my wild oats to care about anything outside of the line of women I was fucking and trying to skirt my princely responsibilities.

A burning sensation on my side has me arching off the bed, causing me to yell out. Once I regain my ability to breathe, I lower the sheet to see what caused the sensation. What I find leaves me reeling. There, by my right hip, is a mark. It looks like an infinity symbol with a feather. What the hell does this mean? I reach down to feel it and hiss through my teeth. The mark is tender, like the tattoo on my left shoulder felt when I first got it a few years ago.

I'm preparing to wake Reegan when she arches off the bed and gasps. Her eyes are closed. She's still asleep, but I see a mark on her upper right rib. It's a pair of wings surrounding the sun—the mark of the Seelie Fae, my people's mark. "*My mark,*" my mind screams. Ironic, considering fae haven't had wings for centuries. Well, there's all the proof I need that we're fated. Isn't that what happens? We share a mark to prove our mating. I trace my fingers over my mark on her flawless skin. It's

beautiful. She remains sleeping even while I touch
her, even after what had to be the same sensation I
felt only moments ago.

I slightly shake her, "Beautiful, wake up, baby."
She doesn't stir, so I try again. She mumbles some-
thing incoherent and moves to roll away from me.
She comes to with a hiss.

"What the hell Kalan!" she says, thinking I
caused her discomfort. She looks down at the spot
and sees the murk. A large gasp leaves her, and
then, all of a sudden, she breaks down in tears.

6

REEGAN

"Beautiful, what's wrong? Please don't cry.", I hear Kalan say as I hide my head in his chest. I can't help crying. I know what the mark means. He's my mate. My fated mate at that. I know a little about mates because Rodriq claimed there was a time when they weren't so rare. He made sure I knew everything there was to know about our history. He claimed it was because he believed that one day if we weren't careful, history would repeat itself.

"They're happy tears, Kalan.", I tell him hoping he doesn't hear the worry in my voice.

I don't know what this means for us. He's supposed to be King, but the laws of Elfame forbid any other race to sit on a throne. I'm not Fae. So even though I am elated to have a mate, nothing changes. What's that mean for us? Even as true mates, we aren't above fae law. I've heard stories about mates forming a bond and then walking away from it. Everyone has a choice, right? But those that do ignore the bond slowly go insane. Women and men have been known to take their own lives or the lives of whatever partner they end up with. Once the bond is sealed, it can't be undone except through death. Kalan places his finger under my chin and lifts it. I lower my eyes.

"Agra, talk to me, please," he says, pulling me into his lap.

Beloved. "We're fated, Kalan, and that makes me so happy, but what of the future? You're to be the King one day, and the laws forbid you to marry a non-fae."

He frowns as if this just came to his attention. "Fuck the laws, beautiful. They don't mention fated mates. There's no way Dad and Mom would ever deny me the happiness of having my fated by my side."

"But what if they do Kalan? Your parents are nothing if not respectful of laws and traditions. You can fuck whom you like, so long as you marry a fae. Your people will think me lesser and not worthy to stand with you.", I tell him, my heart tearing in two.

"Our people, Reegan. They've been your people for most of your life and you. You know how rare fated mates are for our kind. They won't be able to deny the bond." he tries to placate me, but I still think it's a shot in the dark. "And if they don't want us together, then they don't want me as the king. I'll abdicate the throne, let Aldair rule. I don't care. I won't give you up. I loved you before this bond, and I will love you for all the days of my life."

I snuggle into his embrace, content, for the time being, just being held in his arms. Then it hits me that I haven't seen my mark on him. Did the bond not completely take?

"Kalan! My mark? I didn't see my mark on you!"

"Oh," he laughs. I guess I forgot. Here." he says, pulling down the sheet. There on his hip, I can see the symbol, but I don't know what it is. It's not like any marks I've ever seen in the histories.

"What's it mean? I've never seen a mark like this. Shouldn't it be the elemental mark? I ask, confused. I know I have other abilities, but the elemental powers are the only ones to show themselves and stay consistent over the years.

"I don't know, beautiful, but we'll figure it out together.", he reassures me.

I snuggle back into his embrace and sigh. So many questions are pulling at me, but I have no answers yet. The queen may have some answers, but I plan to seek out Marcus. If anyone knows what this mark is, it will be him. He's my grandfather, and it's time he stops hiding from me.

I must have fallen asleep because I woke drowsy to a fantastic feeling between my legs. I look down and see Kalan's green eyes looking back at me.

"Breakfast isn't for another couple of hours, beautiful, so I thought I'd go for my dessert now.", he chuckles.

He dips back down and closes his mouth around my clit. I buck up into his mouth, threading my fingers through his blonde hair. I moan as he laps at me. I crest that wave again while his tongue fucks me right through it. The next thing I know, I'm flipped onto my stomach with my ass in the air. He enters me slowly, moaning as he penetrates me inch by inch. When he's fully seated, he pauses. Then he begins to move. Speeding up his strokes until all I can do is pant and groan as he hits so deep inside me that I'll be walking funny for the next few days.

"You feel so good.", he groans.

"Kalan!" I scream as I orgasm again.

With a few more groans, Kalan follows with his caveman-like scream. He collapses along my back, peppering kisses on my shoulders. He rolls off of me, pulling me with him.

"In case you didn't hear me last night, I love you, Reegan. That mark just cements what I've felt for so long. Even without that mark, I would choose you, and to hell with anyone that went against it. I'd give up my throne for you. It will be years before it is time for me to rule, and I'm sure Aldair will happily lead in my stead.", he says.

I can't help the smile that graces my lips. I turn to look at him, and I can see the sincerity in his eyes. "I love you too, my prince.", I answer, giving him a small kiss.

"We should probably get cleaned up. While I'd love nothing more than to stay in this bed all day with you, I know those questions running rampant in your mind need answers. So get that sexy ass up, and let me help you wash your hair." He smiles lasciviously.

I do as he says, getting up and heading into the shower. I turn on the water to its hottest setting. Stepping into the water, a breath leaves me. The water feels so good running over my muscles. Kalan steps in behind me, pulling me back into his chest. He squeezes shampoo into his hand and massages it into my scalp and hair. It feels so good; I love that he's being so attentive to me.

Kalan ignores my moans and moves to rinse my hair. He then uses the conditioner, taking more time to massage it in. After that's done, he soaps up my body rubbing it into my skin slowly, torturously. He must see the fire banking in my eyes because he leans down and bites down on my lower lip. I groan, pushing my naked body into his. He wraps his arms around me and kisses me hard. Too soon, he pulls away, laughing at the sound of protest that leaves my mouth.

"Now, now, beautiful. We don't have time for any more play right now, but I promise we will continue this.", he states. I just huff with a pout. He laughs again as he grabs the shampoo for himself. He quickly washes and turns off the water.

We step out of the shower onto the heated floors. He grabs a towel for himself and then one for me. He helps to dry me then he dries himself as I dress in my bra and panties. After he is done, I make my way to the closet. I pull out a pair of deep brown leggings, a green crop top, and my black sneakers. After breakfast and answers, I'll spend most of the morning in the gym, *training*, so this is my go-to for the day.

More like being tortured by Rodriq. I swear that man hates me. He seems to go out of his way to make my life hell. We spend two hours every day doing physical training—another three with me practicing my elemental powers. You'd think they'd come easy to me, but they don't. Rodriq says it's because I hold all of them, making it harder to gain control. I can tell, though, that he's getting frustrated with me. I'm just as frustrated with my slow development.

Kalan's voice takes me from my musing. "Are you ready for breakfast, beautiful?" he asks. He leans down and places a kiss on my neck.

"Yep," I say, popping the p and giving him a big smile. He grabs my hand, dragging me in for a kiss.

When he lets up, he's also smiling. He pulls me out of the room and toward the smell of bacon.

7

REEGAN

E veryone is already sitting around the table when we enter the dining room. Aldair gives me a conspiratorial wink. I'm sure he knows what went down with Kalan and me last night, considering his bedroom is adjacent to mine.

"Oh, my Creator! When did you get a tattoo, and why didn't you tell me?" Maddie screams, making me jump. "I would have come with you."

Every pair of eyes lands on me, and I can feel my face heating. I had forgotten about the mark when I chose this top. "Um.... Yeah, so last night... Kalan and I...", I stutter.

Kalan grabs my hand. I can feel him sending a calm feeling through our bond. *Our bond!* "We all need to talk.", he states.

He leads me to a chair, pulling it out for me to sit. He then sits next to me and grabs my hand again. "So, last night, Reegan and I took our relationship to the next level. Imagine my surprise when suddenly I felt a burning sensation and discovered a mark right above my hip. The next thing I know, Reegan is bowing off the bed, and a mark appears on her ribs. She slept through it, and I had to wake her so she could see. Her mark is the Seelie crest." He lifts my arm so everyone can see, puffing his chest with pride. "Mine is something else entirely.", he continues. He stands and lowers his pants so the mark on his hip is visible.

A sharp gasp escapes Alita's lips as she whispers, "Weaver.", surprise and excitement coloring her face.

Dain gives her a sharp look. One everyone seems oblivious to except for Rodriq and me. "I guess you guys know something we don't.", I state, glaring at Dain. He has the decency to look guilty, but he doesn't respond. Rodriq says, "You need to speak to your grandfather."

With that, he gets up and leaves the room. I eye Alita, hoping she'll give me some glimpse as to waht they're keeping from me. She looks like she wants to say something but Dain's hand on her shoulder keeps her saying from it. "I'll call Marcus.", Dain says, exiting as well.

"Alita, please tell us what's going on.", I plead. I can tell it's tearing her up inside to not be able to say anything, so I give a nod instead of pushing.

"I wish I could, sweetheart, but I can't. Marcus has the answers, but I want you to know that this is a blessing. Fated mates are nearly unheard of for the Fae and the fact that you two are fated means everything. You, sweet girl, are special. That's all I can say. I love you both so much, and I am so happy for you two," she says as she gracefully gets up, hugs me tightly, and leaves.

I released the breath I didn't realize I was holding as I looked down at my plate. Kalan has filled it with food that suddenly doesn't seem appetizing. I force myself to eat to give myself something to do. The adults leaving makes me feel as if I have a plague they needed to escape.

Maddie comes around the table, taking the seat on my other side. "Hey, I'm sorry. But the mark is a good thing, right?" she asks. "Now we'll truly be sisters."

"Of course it is. It's a great thing!" I snap back. I flinch, realizing I'm taking my frustrations out on my best friend. "I'm sorry, I just don't know what to think right now. I love that I'm fated to be with Kalan, but I can't help feeling like there's so much more to it. And no one will give me answers. Maddie, I've never seen anything like the mark Kalan got from me. It's not been in any texts we've studied for years. What does that mean? Am I that different? Am I broken or something?"

Maddie doesn't answer because she doesn't know. She wraps her arms around me and holds me close to her while I cry out all my frustration.

A while later, after I've eaten what I could, everyone else quiet, I stand to head to the gym. While Rodriq loves to torture me, I have found that physical exercise helps clear my head. "I'm gonna head to the gym.", I say. "Better yet, I'm gonna go for a run."

Kalan reaches out to me. "Come on. I'll go with you," he tells me, reaching for my hand.

I slowly shake my head. I need some time. I say as much, "I wanna be alone for a bit. I need to get my thoughts together before I have to see my grandfather.", I say.

"There's nothing wrong with you, Reegan. You are perfect. You are mine.", he answers vehemently.

I raise my hand and cup his cheek. Giving him a small smile, I say, "And you, sweet prince are mine. I love you. I'll be back soon, ok."

Kalan nods and kisses me sweetly before pulling away. I turn on my heel and head toward the entrance of the estate. I fling open the door and take off running. I don't know where I'm going, but I love the wind whipping through my hair as I run faster and faster. I need this. I need to just feel the elements around me, to ground me. I spot a path cut into the woods and head in that direction.

Asher

I don't know why I'm out here running.
I never run outside. Why would I with the
state-of-the-art gym I had installed in the house?
Something felt off this morning, and my dragon
was urging me to run. I ran the six miles from the
house up to the Winthrope estate and veered off
onto a path through the woods. It's been a long time
since I've been up here.

When we were kids, we loved to get a look at the
mysterious Winthrope Mansion. It always seemed
empty. A shell that hid so many secrets. We never
had the guts to get too close. As I ran past, I
noticed cars in the drive. Did Marcus finally have
company? We all know he's somewhat reclusive,
only coming around to do his duties on the council
and to welcome the new students when the school
year starts. Otherwise, he's off galivanting to do
whatever a man of his status does.

But today, the property felt different. There was
a buzz of activity that was hard to ignore. Who
could be visiting? Marcus didn't talk about his
past, but the rumor mill had always been busy
with conspiracies about the man. He had lost his
daughter almost twenty years ago, along with her

husband. He withdrew after that, only doing the bare minimum, leaving most of his council tasks to his assistants Rebecca and Rodriq. Rodriq is another mystery. No one knows much about him other than he is only in town for a few months and teaches offensive magics and history for one term out of the year.

I'm so caught up in my thoughts that I don't even realize I've reached the lake until my dragon huffs at me. I look out toward the dock, and that's when I notice purple hair. As if she can sense me, Reegan's sapphire eyes look up and meet my gaze. My breath catches in my throat. She is stunning with the lake as a backdrop as she swings in the old swing we hung in the tree when we were kids. I search her eyes, looking for anything there. All I see is his resignation.

There's no sense of panic or even recognition today. It saddens me, and my dragon begins to beat inside my head. He wants to be with her; he needs to know she sees us, sees him. *"Me too, buddy. Me too"*. I make my way over to her. As I go around to her back, she straightens. I flinch. Is she scared of me? She surprises me by relaxing as soon as that thought comes to my mind. I take the ropes of the swing and pull them back. I then let go as she swings forward. When she comes back, I push the swing again. I feel electricity race up my arms with every brush of my hand to her skin. We stay like this for a while, neither speaking.

Eventually, she puts her feet down, stopping the swing. She gets up and walks over to the dock. She sits down and pulls off her shoes, placing her feet in the cool water.

"It's beautiful here.", she states quietly. "Why are you here, Asher?" she asks hesitantly.

"So you're not denying that you know me any—more?" I retort. She doesn't answer, so I continue asking," Who are you, Winnie or Reegan? How are you here?"

"I can't tell you any of that.", she answers after a minute. She looks away from me then, and I can't have that. I need to see in those sapphire eyes. I clasp her chin and turn her back to me, seeing the tears building in her eyes.

"Then at least tell me this, was any of it real? I thought you loved me, or were just dreams? Tell me, *Reegan,* was any of it real?"

Again, she doesn't answer, which, for me, is enough. I get ready to open my mouth again but pause—my phone chirps with a call. As I look at the screen, I huff. Reegan sees it. "Girlfriend?" she asks. This time I don't answer. "Hmmm, well, you should probably get back to her. I need to get back myself.", she snarks.

I look up into her eyes and see, is that jealousy? "Huh. Yeah, maybe I should. I've wasted enough time out here today.", I snap back. I get up and start running back toward home.

I hear her call out, "You're a hypocrite, Ash!!!" All I can see as I run is the hurt in those sapphire eyes, which guts me.

8

REEGAN

My chest is tight, and I find myself crying again. Why do I feel so bereft? I feel so much jealousy, and I genuinely hate myself at this moment. I have Kalan, and he should be enough. He has to be enough. Asher isn't mine anymore. He never really was. He was only a dream. He has a girlfriend; I bet she's beautiful and not broken like me. I bet she knows exactly who and what she is. I have no clue who I am anymore. I'm at a total loss. I look down at the notifications on my phone. Damn, I've been out here for a while. The sun is setting. I open my text messages to find several from Kalan:

Kalan: Baby, are you ok? I thought you'd be back by now. I'm starting to worry. (That was over an hour ago).

Kalan: Beautiful, please let me know you're ok.

Kalan: Reegan, please answer me.

Kalan: Reegan Winthrope, I'm coming after you if I don't hear from you in the next 5 minutes. (The most recent was sent 10 minutes ago).

Me: I'm ok, Kalan. I promise. I just... got caught up. I'm headed back now.

I see the dots telling me he is typing something.

Kalan: Thank the Creator! Come home, beautiful. Your grandfather will be here for dinner.

I get up, dust off my leggings, put my phone in my pocket and take off at a brisk pace back to the house, not knowing what to expect when I get there. I walk into the house, and the first thing I hear is heavy footsteps rounding the corner. Kalan runs to me, pulling me in for a hug. He squeezes me like he hasn't just seen me this morning. I melt into him, his comfort helping to ease my raging thoughts. Guilt begins to eat at me over my encounter with Asher. I'm back to feeling like I was doing something wrong.

My muscles tighten. Kalan pulls away, looking down at me. "What's going on, Reegan? Are you hurt? Did something happen while you were gone?" he bombards me with questions.

"Nothing is wrong. I'm fine.", I answer. I see in his eyes that he doesn't believe me. Damn this bond. Damn my itchy eyes. I know they must be red-rimmed.

"You don't want to tell me, that's fine. I'll get it from you eventually.", he states as he turns on his heel and stalks away. Shit. I'm a mess of confusion, and I'm irritated as fuck. What now?

I make my way upstairs to shower off the funk from running. Once I'm dressed and feeling a little more myself, I head out to look for Kalan. I owe him an apology and need to find a way to let him know I'm okay without giving away the secret I've kept about myself for most of my life.

I find Kalan in the game room, beer in hand, as he plays a game of pool with Aldair. "I call dibs on the winner.", I say lightly.

Kalan turns at the sound of my voice. His eyes widen and heat. I knew this outfit would be perfect for tonight. I'm wearing a black midi skirt that reaches mid-thigh with purple lace inlays on the sides showing off my upper thighs. I paired it with a purple wrap shirt with peasant-style sleeves. I am wearing knee-high riding boots with silver buckles. I make my way over to Kalan. While the shoes add height, I still have to stand on my toes to kiss him.

"Hey, baby.", I whisper, giving him a sultry smile.

"Feeling better?" he asks. I can tell he's still somewhat upset by the events earlier, so I try to reassure him.

"I'm getting there. I am ok. None of what I'm feeling right now has anything to do with how much I love you. Please believe me. I'll tell you everything when I can." I promise.

He must see the sincerity in my eyes because he physically relaxes returning to his game. Of course,

Aldair wins. Kalan was way too distracted to even try. I play Aldair and lose. It didn't help that Kalan couldn't keep his hands to himself the entire time.

Aldair just laughed at us. Giving me a wink and an "I'm out. Don't ruin the furniture", he leaves the room.

I squeal in surprise as Kalan lifts me by my thighs and sits me on the pool table, stepping between my legs. "You look good enough to eat. Did you wear this outfit for my benefit?", He asks hungrily.

"I wore it for Aldair.", I tease. A growl leaves his lips, but he holds a look of humor on his face. "Yes, my prince, I wore this for you. Do you like it?" I ask.

"I'd like you better out of it, but I'll take care of that later.", he states with his head held high.

I lift my chin, "Promises, promises." I tease, jumping down from the table. I throw him a saucy wink as I head out the door toward the dining room. I am determined to enjoy dinner with my family, and I will get answers if I have to tie Marcus down to get them.

Kalan

I can read Reegan's emotions as if they're my own now that we're bonded. Something is going on.

Every time she looks at me, she feels a sense of guilt.
On the tail end of that, shame. When she came in
earlier she smelt different. There was a somewhat
familiar scent attached to her skin that made my
hackles rise. I didn't mean to snap at her but I'm
feeling confused and bereft. I don't know what to
say to reassure her that everything will be ok, so
I will bide my time, show her how much I adore
her and hope she'll tell me when she's ready. What
other choice do I have? I follow her to the dining
room. We take our seats and wait for the others to
join us. I place my hand on her hand where it sits on
top of the table, giving it a reassuring squeeze. She
smiles at me, and I get lost in the look of love in her
eyes. I lean down, pressing a kiss to her forehead.
She giggles a little.

"Awe! Look at you two, so in love.", Maddie teases
as she enters.

I glare at my sister, hoping she won't push
the teasing too far and embarrass the gorgeous
woman sitting by my side. Maddie sits across from
me while Aldair enters, taking the chair opposite
Reegan. We chat idly as we await the entrance of
our parents. I think back to this morning. I saw
the surprise in my parent's eyes at the news that
Reegan and I were fated. That look turned into
elation in my mother, but I saw the face of dis-
appointment in my dad. Was it because she's not
royal? She is more regal than half of the women in

Elfame. I can't help but feel the look had more to do with me than Reegan. Technically, I can't rule without a queen, and the law says she must be fae. But it never mentions fated mates, so maybe there's a loophole. I meant what I told Reegan. I will abdicate the throne before I ever let her go. We are fated; even without that, I would give everything, including my life, to this precious woman. She owns me, heart and soul, and has for some time.

We age differently, so while I am ten years her senior, my looks make me seem more her age. I haven't lived a celibate life; some would call me promiscuous. When she turned 16, the legal age for marriage in Elfame, something changed within me, and I began to see her as a woman and not the small child she was when Marcus dropped her on our doorstep. Since then, I have been with women, I am no saint, but I have held out a hope that she would be mine. It was always as if she called to me in a way. Like siren song stuck in my head. A couple of years ago, I noticed her looking at me. When I'd catch her, she'd turn her head, a beautiful blush covering her cheeks. I started flirting with her. It was innocent enough, but I felt myself falling more and more for her as time went by.

It took a year for me to get up the courage to try to court her. I didn't want to just fuck her. I wanted to fuck her badly, but I also wanted a relationship for the first time in my life. I knew then she would mine. We began dating, and now, here we are. I was a patient man with her, letting the chemistry between us build and build until I knew it would explode. And explode it did. I can't get enough of this woman.

She is responsive to my touch, leaning into me when I'm close, arching and moaning beautifully when I have my head between her legs. And Creator, being inside her is Heaven! I could drown in her. I'd gladly die a thousand deaths to sink into her every night for the rest of my life. And now, I'm hard as fuck. I shift in my chair to discreetly readjust my cock. It won't do for Dad and Mom to walk in and realize their son is sporting a massive erection at the dinner table. If I keep this up, it will be a very long night.

Finally, my parents enter, along with Rodriq and Marcus in tow. Reegan stands and steps over to her grandfather, hugging him. "Hey, Little Bit.", I hear him say. "I've missed you, sweetheart."

"Hi, grandpa.", she responds. "It's good to see you too." She smiles at him, but it doesn't quite reach her eyes.

Before she can say anything else, mom interjects. "Reegan, dear, sit. Let's eat, and then we can talk." Reegan looks livid but nods and sits back down.

Dinner is served. If I didn't know any better, I'd assume this talk would be difficult based on what's served for dinner alone. Everything in this spread of food is one of Reegan's favorites. Grilled lamb, roasted red potatoes, asparagus with a cream sauce, salad, and even dessert, key lime pie. She senses the same thing I do. Her eyes meet mine, but she doesn't say anything as she loads her plate with some of everything and digs in. I can't help the small huff of a laugh that escapes me with how vigorously she's eating. She wants this dinner over with so that she can get the answers she seeks. I can't blame her much. I can feel her emotions, and honestly, they're breaking my heart as each minute passes. I'll admit to being curious as well. The mark I carry is a mystery. Reegan is a mystery, and I can't wait to unravel them all.

"How was your run, Little Bit?" Marcus asks. I don't know if he's asking because he honestly wants to know or if it's an attempt to stall the coming conversation.

"It was terrific. I found the lake, so I spent some time there just thinking and feeling the elements around me.", she answers, but I see a shadow fall over her eyes.

So, something did happen while she was gone. What could have happened, I wonder, and why wouldn't she just tell me? I will get to the bottom of that. But first, Marcus owes us some answers.

"That's wonderful. I was going to take you around the estate tomorrow and show you around." he continues their conversation. I know

now he's stalling. I can feel it. Reegan must sense it as well because she huffs.

Once everyone eats, Rodriq speaks, "Well, shall we move this conversation to the parlor over drinks?" He gives Marcus a pointed look, to which he answers with an incline of his head. We all get up from the table. I place my hand on the small of Reegan's back and lead her out of the room.

9

REEGAN

I'm nervous as I enter the parlor. I'm unsure what to expect from grandfather, but I am hoping for answers. I don't know what to do with myself, so I stand awkwardly by the door. Grandfather sees me and waves me over.

"Ok, Little Bit, why don't we start with you asking questions, and you tell me what you know or think you do, and we'll go from there., he states.

"That's just it, *Grandpa*. I don't know anything. I have many questions, though, like, "What am I? With the mark, I know I'm not at all what I've believed my whole life. Do the marks indeed mean that Kalan and I are fated? Why am I different?" The questions come rapid–fire from my brain, and I can't contain them all, so they come out in a rush.

Grandpa chuckles but then gets a serious look of concentration on his face like he's thinking of how to answer. "Let's start with the mating marks. Yes, those marks mean that you and Kalan are fated. While it is scarce in the Fae world, it is not impossible. The other questions will have to wait for just a bit. I need to explain something first, and I need to ensure you are ready for these answers. They will change everything."

I straighten my spine, lift my chin and tell him, "I'm sure. Tell me everything."

"Ok then, I assume you implicitly trust everyone in this room?" he asks. I look around the room before giving a nod of my head.

Grundfather stares at me, trying to decipher if I am telling the truth. When he's convinced, he begins again, "It is imperative that what we are about to discuss does not leave this room. It goes no further than here unless deemed necessary." he eyeballs each person, and at their assent, he continues, "You have all heard the story of our creation and Lilith. What isn't in any text is that they knew she would escape when her prison was created in the void. You also aren't aware that she was imprisoned not by the creator but by a weaver." I am about to interrupt him when he looks at me and says," Please, Little Bit, let me finish, and then you may ask your questions if they aren't answered in my explanation."

I nod again. He takes a breath and goes back to his story. "Where was I? Oh yes, the weaver. The creator saw fit during the time of great darkness to forge a being that could hold both light and dark powers. She alone held every power from creation to destruction, elemental magic to blood magic, and everything in between. She could walk all the realms and lock them if she saw fit. She was the catalyst for Lilith's demise. Neveah, the original weaver, was a stunning woman with pure white hair and sapphire eyes. No other supernatural carried or has carried that eye color. Once Lilith was locked away, Neveah mated a male, Samael Winthrope. He was the first Winthrope to hold a council seat. Neveah lived out her life with Samael–and several other mates that came along in that time– having a family, until one day, she just disappeared along with Samael. Their line, though, remains strong. Reegan, you are the last of that line."

"So, I'm a weaver. Was mom also a weaver?" I ask, trying not to cry at my mention of the woman that birthed me. I steel myself. I refuse to let the tears fall.

"No, she was not. She was elemental like me. There hasn't been another weaver since Neveah. Not until you. When you were born, we took one look at your eyes, and we knew.", he responds. "A prophecy mentions that the weaver holds the key to keeping Lilith locked away. Her prison has been weakening. Her minions are beginning to trickle through. Once the locks are weakened enough, she will escape, and then there will be war among the supernatural. You are the only one that can stop her."

I physically stop breathing at hearing these words. How the hell and I supposed to stop the mother of all supernatural creatures? I ask as much.

"I don't know more about the prophecy than that, but I know your powers are growing, and the answers will come to you as they do. I believe in you. Some want Lilith to rule, so you must be on your guard. These people would try to use you for their gain. Your powers are special, Little Bit. What you will be able to do with them could either save or doom us all." he looks so severe as he speaks.

"But what will I be able to do?" I am confused. How does he not know?

"That is another mystery. Not all of Neveah's powers were ever truly known. What we know is that you can hold them all, and more, outside of shifting, that is. Where dark creatures are prone to evil and light creatures, good, you dear, are a perfect combination of both. You are neither light nor dark, which allows you to tip the scales one way or the other. You are balanced in human form. I don't wish to scare you. That is not my intention. But you need to be aware that you will likely have to do things that will seem beyond your caring heart, but do not fear. You are good. You will do what needs to be done."

With that, the conversation is over. Or so I
thought. My mind is running rampant with
thoughts that I can't fathom. Why me?

"Now, onto brighter topics." Grandfather's mood
switches like that of a light bulb. I am dumbfounded
that he could drop all these truths on me and then
just let it all go with a smile. It's frustrating, but I
can tell that there will be no more answers from
him tonight. "The true reason for your visit.", he
continues. "You, sweetheart, are here to attend the
academy."

Now I am baffled. It was my understanding that
I would never attend the academy. That it was beneath my station.

Grandfather must see the confusion on my face
because he chuckles before he continues, "I could
not let you get your hopes up for an academy spot
because you will never be a part of the task force,
but as you are my heir apparent, you are required
to attend for two years. In that time, you will learn
more about our world and how to protect it and
yourself. You will then spend time every evening
here with myself and Rodriq, learning more about
what powers you possess. You will attend the academy as an elemental. No one else can know about
your otherness. There are evil beings on the council. Those that believe that Lilith should be released
to lead. You are the key in more ways than one." He
pauses to take a breath.

I sit with bated breath, waiting for him to continue. When he does, I'm floored. I didn't think this conversation could get any weirder, but I can't help the shiver of excitement that shoots through me at the idea that my dream will finally come true. I am going to attend the academy!

My thoughts are interrupted again by Dain, "Maddie will attend the academy with you. She is the heir to Alita's council position, so she will train to take over." At this revelation, Maddie squeals, causing all of us to laugh.

He turns to Kalan, "Kalan, I know what you're thinking. I know you want to be here with Reegan, but you must return to Elfame for a time." When Kalan goes to argue, the King stops him with his hand raised. "I am not purposefully keeping you from your mate. You will be able to visit with Reegan, but you cannot just give up your responsibilities to the kingdom. I will not allow you to abdicate your throne, My throne." Dain admonishes. "Don't look at me like that, Kalan. You are my son, and much like me, you would give up everything for the woman who holds your heart. I have many years left, son, and you will have many years to prepare yourself to take my place. And when the time comes, Elfame will be lucky to have Reegan Winthrope as its queen."

I am speechless. No words will exit my mouth. I must look like a fish out of the water as my mouth opens and then closes again, over and over. Kalan just gives me a huge smile and a wink.

"Unfortunately, we will be leaving tomorrow for our return. The girls will have only a week to prepare for the academy and learn the area. They need no distractions." Alita says. At this, both our smiles drop. He's leaving tomorrow. One week until we enter the academy.

Suddenly, I feel less and less ready. That night, Kalan makes love to me into the following day. He promises to be back as soon as possible and to call or text daily. With a kiss, he is gone.

The following week passes in a flurry of training and lessons on what will be expected of us once classes start. The closer the time comes, the more nervous I become and excited. I take my mind off everything as I watch Maddie give Rodriq hell. Their flirting continues to grow with every passing day. I'm waiting for one of them to finally unblind themselves so they can see what I'm sure everyone else does. They are the perfect couple. And now, after finding my very own fated, as rare as it is, I could see Maddie and Rodriq being fated as well. Wouldn't that be something? When I can't distract myself from the goings-on of these two, I spend time at the lake. It's quickly becoming my favorite place. I sit in the swing for hours, or with my toes in the water, just thinking over every bit of information I was given in the conversation last week. I'm slowly making peace with what I am. It just feels right. More and more nights, I dream of my past. I am slowly starting to remember things. I still can't see my mother's face, but I can see her steel-grey eyes. I still see my father's smile.

The night of their deaths plays on a loop inside my head. It still feels foggy, however. I also recall a time after moving to Elfame when I was scared and poofed out of existence in one room and found myself in another. I found I liked that new part of myself, so I would do it to have fun trying to scare Alita. It took her a while to figure out how I was showing up behind her out of the blue, but once she did, she called Marcus. After his visit, I could no longer pull off that feat.

The night before classes start, Maddie and I decide to explore the town again. We have dinner at one of the many dinner theaters and enjoy our time together. I know things will change tomorrow, so tonight, I hold tightly to my best friend and pray to anyone who listens that it will always be this way.

10

REEGAN

The morning comes too soon. As I get up and prepare for the day, nervous energy surrounds me. I choose pair of skinny jeans with strategic rips in the knees and thigh area and a white cold shoulder top that ties around my waist. I put my hair up in a high sleek ponytail. My makeup is on point. I used brown and green to make my blue eyes pop. I look good if I do say so myself.

As I exit, I see Maddie had similar ideas and dressed to impress in black pants and a pink top that goes well with her red hair. She kept her hair down, with the curls cascading down her back, hitting just above her ass. I whistle at her and get a snarky wink in return. It makes me chuckle as we make our way to the kitchens for e breakfast. After eating, we are ushered into a black town car and escorted to the academy grounds. I didn't realize how close the estate was to the academy, but it makes sense, given that my grandfather owns the school.

The academy is gorgeous. It is the perfect mix of gothic and modern. The grey stone of the walls is light, while the topiaries give it that old-world feel. I take in all the beauty as we're led up the stone steps into the main building. Off to the sides are other structures surrounding the pristine grounds. I can't make them all out. This campus is massive!

Rodriq leads us to the administration office and leaves us in the hands of Rebecca. At least that's what the plaque on her desk says. She is a beautiful woman. She looks to be no more than her late thirties but looking into her eyes; I know she must be much older.

"Ahh, you must be Reegan.", she says. Before I can offer her my hand, she has rounded the desk and has me locked in a hug. "It is so good to finally meet you.", she says as she pulls away to look at me. "I'm Rebecca, Marcus' um... assistant."

As she says this, a blush graces her cheeks. Its cute and while I want to ask if she and my grandpa are seeing each other, I don't want to be rude. "Anyway, here are your packets. There's a map in there as well as your schedules. I have a couple of students coming to show you around."

Before she can finish what she's saying, the door opens. Shit. It's Asher, and what was his name, Trent? They both look at me with surprise, and Trent takes on a sly grin while Ash looks like I'm shit on the bottom of his shoe.

"Gentlemen, this is Reegan Winthrope and Maddison, princess of Elfame.", Rebecca introduces.

At this, Asher's head whips up with a look of surprise. He now knows who I am. Then a look of confusion takes over his face. "We've met.", he says.

I drop my eyes to the floor. Trent takes over the conversation telling us how good it is to have us here, while Rebecca looks between Asher and me like we're a puzzle she must figure out. Well, good luck with that.

"Come on. We have just enough time to show you some of the campuses before classes start for the day", Trent says gently, looking at me. With a nod, he turns, and we follow.

We spend the next twenty minutes walking the grounds and getting to know the buildings. Trent seems easygoing and quite the lady's man. All the girls that pass give him glances and smiles while trying their best to get his attention. He smiles back but makes no move to go toward any of them. Asher seems determined to ignore me as he converses with Maddie asking questions about Elfame. I can't help looking their way when Ash laughs. As he tells her about his time at the academy, a beaming smile graces his face. It makes me sad that he seems so at ease with her and that the two of us will never be comfortable together again. More so because of the secret I can't share with him.

"Hey, beauty. Wanna talk about it?" Trent asks, pulling my attention to him. He's very observant. I'll have to remember that about him in the future.

"No. Not really.", I respond. He gives me a know-ing smile but lets it drop.

"Ok, what's your first class?" he asks instead. I pull out my schedule and hand it to him. "Nice, you have Elemental Studies with me. The professor is cool. It's this way", he finishes pointing to the right.

Maddie has class across campus, so Ash offers to escort her. We hug and then go our separate ways with a promise to meet up for lunch. We enter the room, and I freeze. Standing at the front of the room is none other than Rodriq.

"Ms. Winthrope, take a seat.", he says. I laugh at the stuffiness in his voice but do as he says.

"Do you two know each other?" Trent asks. He raises an eyebrow. Creator, that looks sexy as hell.

"Only since I was five," I respond.

He gives me an appraising look but doesn't say anything else. Rodriq begins his lecture with what will be expected in this class. Two days a week, we will have skills and aptitudes in the arena to go over everything we learned throughout the week. After going over the syllabus, he launches into the first lesson on the history of elementals.

My next class is Supernatural Politics. I'm in this one alone. Trent said that was because all the other heirs had grown engrossed in this life. I suppose that makes sense. I notice that my daily schedule changes, not the classes themselves, but their time slots. This should be oh so much fun (insert sarcasm here).

Trent drops me off with the guarantee to pick me up at the door after class for lunch. Trent is also in this class but claims he has another task to do. I sit beside a petite girl with coal-black hair and black eyes. She looks at me and then looks at the door.

"You're new.", she says. I just look at her and nod. "And already you have the attention of the Elite.", she states with a huff.

"The Elite?" I question. I know she's speaking of Trent, but I have no idea what the elite is.

"Mm-hmm, the strongest of our kind. Heirs to council seats. The Elite." she says this as if I should already know. "Trent Strong is the elemental E lite.", she says, nodding toward the door. "Then there's Jaymeson Matthews. He's a shifter. Bentley Morley is half Angel, half-demon, and of course, the King, Asher Hayworth, is a dragon. Last but certainly not least, at least in her eyes, is Calista Woods, a witch/vampire hybrid." She speaks of Calista with an eye roll. Before I get a chance to ask questions, the professor walks in and jumps right into the lesson. I didn't even have time to get this girl's name.

When class ends, I'm about to ask her name when I hear Trent behind me. He grabs my bag and starts to lead me out. With a glance over his shoulder, he says," Sarina, looking good today."

He gives her a wink. She flips him the bird. He laughs and keeps walking. I look back to Sarina, and she smiles at me. Maybe, I should try to make friends with her. As we walk down the hall, people start whispering. I can't make out what they're saying, but occasionally, Trent flinches. I'm sure he can hear them, and he isn't liking what's being said. He keeps walking with his hand lightly on my lower back. We're quiet as we walk across campus. I'm stuck in my thoughts, and Trent seems content to let me be. The more I'm with him, the more comfortable I feel. His hand hasn't left me, and I find I don't mind.

"So, Lunch isn't for another hour. Is there anything you want to see or questions you want to ask?" he questions, stopping and sitting on a bench.

There are a dozen, but I settle for asking the one burning brighter in my mind. "Tell me about the Elite," I order. I'm super curious about them. More wondering why Sarina only mentioned one female member.

"That's easy. It's the name the students gave to the heirs to council seats. Well, to the more powerful of us anyway. We run the school and keep everyone in line. And, Ms. Winthrope, you are an heir. Time will tell if you are an Elite.", he says with a smile. "Now, I have a question for you.", he says pointedly. "What's the deal with you and Asher?"

"That's a tough question to answer. He thinks I'm someone he once knew, but even if I were, I'm not that person anymore." It's the only answer I can give him, even though it was a non-answer.

"I see. You're as secretive as he is. That's ok. I'll let you keep your secrets.... for now.", he laughs.

We sit for a while with Trent telling me stories of his childhood and me regaling him with tales of mine. The time passes effortlessly here with him. I could probably sit with him forever and be ok with that. At that thought, I think of Kalan, and then I get an overwhelming sense of melancholy. I miss him dearly and can't wait until he comes for a visit, but here, with Trent, I feel this is precisely where I'm supposed to be.

"Lunchtime, Beauty, let's go eat.", Trent says, reaching out his hand. I place mine in his, and he helps me to my feet. I expect him to let go, but he surprises me by smiling and leading on, hand in hand, to the dining room.

11

TRENT

Creator, she is gorgeous. That's all I can think about as I take her in. That, and she's an enigma. I was shocked to find her standing in the admin office this morning. That shock turned into happiness at the thought of her being here, near me, every day.

I know she holds secrets—lots of them. I want to know them all. Alas, that isn't in the cards for me...yet. Reegan seems super comfortable with me though. Already, I feel this need to touch her. To be close to her. She doesn't seem to mind the small touches, which makes my heart leap. I don't know what's gotten into me. I never give a shit about holding hands with a girl, but for some reason, *I want* to hold Reegan's. I want to get closer to her. I can't help being curious about her and Asher. I've known him for most of my life, and I don't ever remember him reacting this way to any girl. Not even Calista, that slimy witch. Creator, do I despise that woman and the person Asher becomes when they're together.

Their relationship started as just a quick fuck at a party. He didn't even know her name, but as soon as his father discovered who she was, he forced Asher into a relationship with the vapid girl in hopes of gaining an alliance with her father and securing more power. Pfft, like the man needs a more oversized head than he already has. I'm almost certain that Calista seduced Ash on purpose. She is just as power-hungry as Ash's dad. I know she started the rumors of them fucking, and I'm sure she told Senior Hayworth herself. She's a conniving one. I'll give her that. But I saw the way Asher looked at Reegan. I saw the hurt in his eyes when she said she didn't recognize him. He feels something for her and has for a long time. Neither of them will talk about it, but I am determined to get answers and *always* get what I want.

"So, Beauty, what do you think of our humble academy?" I ask, turning my gaze to Reegan.

"Humble?" she asks with a laugh. "It's not at all humble. What it is, is beautiful.", she says with a smile. "The view is amazing!" she exclaims.

"Yes, it is.", I answer, never taking my eyes off her.

She must know that comment was about her because she looks away, trying to hide the blush staining her cheeks. She doesn't even realize just how beautiful she is. If she were mine, no, when she is mine, I will make sure she knows every day.

"Hey baby.", a voice says behind me as arms wrap around my shoulders from behind. "I had so much fun last night. Want a repeat?" I turn to find none other than one of Calista's cronies standing there. What was her name again? Amber? Ashley? I know it starts with an A. "Adeline, remember?" she says, pointing to herself.

"Name doesn't ring a bell.", I find myself saying. She huffs and begins to walk away. "In all serious-ness, should I remember you?"

"We were only making out last night and I did that thing with my tongue."

"Oh right. Yeah it wasn't that memorable. Maybe next time." I say, old habits dying hard.

She sputters a little but gives me a brilliant smile as she walks away.

"You're a pig, Trenton Strong.", Reegan says with a huff. "You shouldn't treat women that way." Reegan gripes.

"If she has the balls to come up to me after last night, then she can handle a little truth. And it had to be a bad time because I would have remembered a girl with an ass like that." I wink. Reegan looks at me and then bursts out laughing. I love the sound. This may be the first time I have been able to indeed be myself around a girl. It's refreshing. The fact that she's laughing at my pigishness speaks for the kind of woman she is; One I definitely want to get to know.

"In all seriousness, Beauty, I am not a saint, but before I take a woman to my bed, I make sure she knows I have nothing to offer her except for a good fuck. I don't make promises, and I don't do relationships." This brings a frown to her face. Dammit. That should have never come out of my mouth. *I don't do relationships. What was I thinking?* Here I am wanting to get to know this girl and I tell her that all I can offer is a night in my bed. My head is a jumbled mess. Before I can say anything else, Reegan's stomach growls. "Come on, Beauty, let's get you something to eat."

I take her hand and pull her down the path toward food. We make our way further across campus toward the dining hall. I see the fae princess waiting for us as we approach the door. Well, she's waiting for Reegan. She rushes over, pulling Reegan in for a hug.

"I missed you today!" she says. "This place is amazing, Reegan!', she says as she bounces on her toes.

Seeing her excitement brings a smile to my beauty's face. Seeing that smile causes a tug in my chest. My hand finds its way there as I absentmindedly rub at the spot. Maddie turns my way with a smile as well. I pull my hand away but not before Maddie sees. A small gasp leaves her lips, but she says nothing as she looks between Reegan and me.

"Shall we eat?" I say, pulling them both along into the hall.

Reegan's mouth drops as we enter. Along the walls, there are foods from every realm available. Staff members are meandering about serving the students. There are tables spread out over the hall with students chattering about. In the corner, I see the guys already seated waiting for me, my plate already filled with all my favorites.

"You girls get whatever you like and meet at that table over there." I point to the corner. Reegan looks like she wants to protest, but I just put my finger over her lips. "No arguing, Beauty. I want you with me today." I finish. With that, I walk away.

I head over to our table and take my seat. I haven't even gotten to say hello before the questions start. "Is that the Winthrope heir?", Jaymeson asks. I give him a look that says, "*Are we asking stupid questions?*"

"Is she single? Creator, she's hot! You know what, don't answer that. I'll find out myself."

We didn't tell Jaymeson and Bentley about the girls we met in town right after we returned. They have no information about Reegan. Not that any of us knows a lot. We know Marcus claims her to be his granddaughter and that she's an elemental like him, but that's all we know. Except for Asher, since he's keeping his secrets to himself, the rest of us are at a loss. I notice the dining hall has gotten quieter.

I look around and realize they're all staring to-ward Reegan. And then I see why. There, kneeling on the ground is a waiter surrounded by the food he dropped. Then I notice a demon student laughing. He must have knocked the food out of his hands de-liberately. It happens pretty often. Reegan is on the ground helping him to clean it up while the other students look at her as if she's lost the plot. I can't help but smile at what she's doing. As I said, she's an enigma. I turn back to the guys and notice that they, too, are looking her way, giving smiles. Even Bentley has a slight tilt to his lips. Bentley never smiles. He doesn't say much, either. Not since his parents were killed seventeen years ago.

No one knows what happened to them. Their bodies were found in the woods outside their home, mutilated beyond recognition. Magic had to be used to identify them. The only reason Bentley didn't join them in death was that he was with us. Being too young to take his council seat, his uncle now sits in his stead until he finishes academy next year.

I see Reegan from the corner of my eye. She gets up from the ground and begins her trek across the dining hall. Following her is the waiter she helped. He's carrying her tray as she argues that she could do it herself. Of course, he doesn't listen. He con-tinues placing her plates in the empty spot next to

me. He then bows a little to Reegan, thanks her
again, and disappears into the kitchen. I pat the
seat beside me for her to sit down. She does, and
Maddie sits beside Asher across from her.

"Gentleman, this is Reegan, and this is Maddie.",
I introduce them. Then going around the table, I
present the guys. "You know Asher and me. This
is Jaymeson and Bentley." Jaymeson shakes hands
with both girls while Bentley inclines his head and
grunts.

Reegan looks at me, and I give my head a barely
perceptible shake. She frowns slightly, but then the
look is gone as Jaymeson draws her and Maddie
into a conversation. I place my arm on the back
of Reegan's chair and lean back. Asher gives me
a scathing look. I lift an eyebrow at him, and he
drops his gaze. He doesn't like me being so close to
her, but I don't care. I can't help it, and he hasn't
laid claim to her. And if it pisses him off, that's
just a bonus. I love to get him riled up. I don't
remove my hand from the back of her chair, but I
sit forward to eat my food while listening to con-
versations around me.

"So, Caleb is throwing a party Saturday. Are we
going?" Jaymeson asks, looking to Asher.

Before he can respond, I do, "Hell yeah. Beauty
and Maddie can come along.", I say, directing my
attention to the former. She blushes at my comment.

Maddie answers, "That sounds like fun. It'll be good to get to know more people, and I can always go for a good party."

"Well, then that's settled—party at Caleb's. We'll get there about nine if that works for everyone.", I tell them.

"Perfect.", Asher starts. "I'll let Marissa know. Maybe you can finally put that conquest to *bed.*", he finishes with a smug smile.

I feel Reegan stiffen beside me and pull away from the hand I still have on the back of her chair. As her ponytail slides through my fingertips, I look at Asher and mouth, "This is war."

He laughs and nods like he can't be bothered. "You know, I'm not much of a partier.", Reegan says with a small voice. "Maybe I'll sit this one out."

Asher now looks like he swallowed something sour. I can't help to feel a little vindicated by the look. "Come on, Beauty. It will be your first party. We'll all be there, so it should be fun. You don't even have to drink. I promise it will be fun." I lean in to whisper, "I want to get to know you."

She doesn't blush this time; she reluctantly agrees to go. She turns down my offer to pick them up and says she needs an address and will find her way there.

12

REEGAN

It shouldn't bother me that Trent is promiscuous or that he made it known he doesn't do relationships. He was bluntly honest which is refreshing to say the least, especially with all the bombshells that have been dropped on me lately. That doesn't stop the heaviness in my chest after hearing those things. It doesn't control how empty I feel without his touch, his fingers running through my hair. It doesn't make sense. I'm mated to a fantastic man, and that should be enough. He should be enough. He is enough, but that doesn't stop my heart from beating out of my chest when Trent touches me. It doesn't stop the blush on my cheeks when I think of him doing with me what he seems to do with many other girls.

I don't think he realized he was even doing it as we sat there eating and talking. But I felt the touch deep into my soul. It's the same feeling I have when Kalan touches me, and I am beginning to wonder if it means the same thing. That just leaves me con-

fused. I don't know if Trent feels it as well. It also
somewhat scares me. I don't want to do anything
to hurt Kalan, and I don't want to live without him,
but I feel as if I can't live without Trent in my life
either. It's much too soon for these thoughts.

I notice the smug look on Asher's face, which
makes me frown. Did he say those things on purpose to hurt me? To hurt Trent? The boy I knew
wouldn't be so crass. He wouldn't have said or done
something that deliberately hurt others. But just as
I am no longer the girl he knew, he is no longer that
same beautiful boy that joined me in my dreams.
He's still beautiful, but now there's a hardness to
him that seems impenetrable. I don't know if I
want the task of trying to break through the rock
that is now his heart. I don't know anything about
him anymore, and as he looks back at me, I can see
in his eyes that he has no intention of letting me
know him as he is now.

That makes my heart hurt in a way that has me
wanting to cry out. I bite the inside of my jaw to
keep those feelings from surfacing and turn away
from him toward Maddie. She knows something
is up. She stares at me with questions in her eyes.
I can't answer them now, but I know the time will
come soon that I will have to sit down for a conversation where I will have to give answers. I am
dreading it. Maddie has been my best friend for

almost our entire lives. I'm afraid she will hate me for keeping so many secrets from her.

I don't know what to make of the other men in the group. Jaymeson seems sweet and brainy. He's sexy in a studious way. He's built with lots of muscle. He has ash blonde hair, longer on top and shaved on the sides. His shirt draws tight across the muscles in his chest, and I can see the outlines of his abs through the fabric. He's a shifter of some kind. Based on the earthy scent I get, I'm thinking wolf or big cat. I can't help taking him in. When I reach his eyes, he just gives me a wink. I hear the grunt from Bentley across from us.

Now, this man is a mystery to me. I know he's been hurt, but I'm unsure how or why. He seems oddly familiar in a way, but he looks at me like I don't belong here. Maybe I don't, but I won't let his attitude bother me. He is another beautiful man. He has muscles for days. I swear his arms are the size of small tree trunks. His chestnut brown hair is longer, unkempt. His eyes are the color of a perfect summer sky. They stand out against his deep tan skin. He has high cheekbones; If I didn't know he was a supernatural creature, I'd almost swear he was what the humans call native American. What did Salina say, Bentley is half-demon, half-angel? That makes sense. He's as handsome as sin with an air of superiority that I have heard

only the angels carry. I'm curious about him more
than any of the others.—the mystery.

He has no tattoos that I can see, only a tiny
piercing through his eyebrow. He seems cleaner
cut than the others in his button-down black shirt
with the sleeves rolled up. I bite my lip and see heat
bank in his blue eyes as I look at him. Ok, so maybe
he's not as cold as he seems. I look away, blushing. Creator, all these guys have me blushing like
a virgin. I mean, I know I'm not that experienced.
Nowhere near as they are I'd bet, but the blushing
needs to stop. I'm a big girl.—a woman. I'm not
some teenage girl that's never been looked at with
lust.

"Move. You're in our seats", a snarky voice says.
I see a gorgeous blonde standing by the table with
that girl from the courtyard earlier. "Seriously, you
can sit with the plebs, or maybe you'd rather join
the servants in the kitchens.", she says haughtily.

"Do you always have to be a bitch? Can't you see
we're eating?" Trent answers back with a sneer.

She pays him no mind and just goes right over
and plops herself down in Asher's lap. Ahh... This
must be Calista. She drapes herself across him like
a coat. He looks down at her, and she raises her
head. He leans in and kisses her. All the while,
he looks toward me. Adeline drapes herself across
Trent's shoulders.

"It's ok, Trent. Suddenly I've lost my appetite.",
I say, placing my hand on his arm. I ignore the
electricity that shoots up my arm at the contact. I
rise from my seat. Trent grabs my hand.

"Want me to walk you to your next class, Beauty?" he asks. His eyes are somewhat pleading, but
right now, I need to get away from this scene, from
them.

"No. Thanks anyway. You should hang out here
with your girls.", I answer.

I can't help the hurt I feel. I don't know what's
gotten into me. I don't understand why I care
what either Trent or Asher does. They're virtual
strangers. I turn on my heel and walk away, leaving Maddie alone in the midst of them. Right now,
I don't care. As I exit, I hear laughter and know
it must be Calista and her cronies. I don't turn
around to see. I just hurry out toward the green-
house where my next class is being held.

I'm between classes in the bathroom an hour
later. I hear the door open but continue with my
business. I listen to girls talking, and then I hear
her voice. "Did you see her? She's not even pretty.
Don't worry about it. Trent would never be serious
about her. She's a new addition, a novelty, and once
he fucks her, it'll be done. He'll be all yours.", Calista
says.

"You didn't see the way he looked at her. He likes
her, Cal.", the other girl says.

"Adeline, she's a poser. I don't know where she came from, but Daddy promised that there was no way Marcus had a granddaughter. How could he? His family was killed years ago. And.... she's weak. I read her powers, and they're almost non-existent. There's no way she could hold a council seat. Daddy and Mr. Hayworth will make sure of that.", Calista says. She's a real piece of work.

"You read her powers? Calista, you need to be careful. You know what the council thinks about that.", Adeline admonishes.

"Please, they can't touch me. Besides, who's going to tell them? The imposter? As I said, there is no way she's a Winthrope. I mean, they died like twenty years ago.", she says like she knows everything.

I've had enough. I open the stall and walk to the sink. Adeline's eyes are wide, and Calista looks like she's not entirely sure what to say. Is that fear in her eyes? "My parents were killed seventeen years ago when I was five. If you want to spread rumors or talk about someone, you should get the facts rig ht.", I say as I dry my hands. "Oh, and Adeline, is it? I won't be fucking Trenton. He was nice enough to show me around today, but I have a boyfriend back in Elfame. Perhaps you've heard of him, Prince Kalan?" Calista's eyes are wide with surprise, and she chokes on her words. I lift my head, square my shoulders, and leave the bathroom in silence.

Classes for the rest of the day run smoothly. Some people stare. Others whisper. I ignore them. I'm not here to make friends, 4e am I? I need to grasp my powers to take my spot in the Supernatural community. I need to find all the answers to the questions still left unanswered. By the end of the day, I am ecstatic to go home. I need a long shower, a run, and a strong drink- not necessarily in that order. I need so many things, but the only thing I end up with is loneliness and a deep ache in my chest.

13

REEGAN

I spend hours in the gym trying and failing to get my thoughts and feelings under control. I'm pounding the punching bag when Maddie enters, looking elated about something. That is until she sees me sweaty and blood dripping from the cracked skin of my knuckles. I won't stop until she comes up and grabs my shoulder. "Hey, what's going on? I knew I should have come home with you.", she says with concern shining in her green eyes that remind me of her brother's.

"How was your study session?" I ask, trying to change the subject. I don't want to talk about myself. I don't want to talk about my feelings. I just want to be left alone to wallow in my misery. "Tell me all about it." I try to smile at her. I don't know if it's convincing, but I can see the excitement in her eyes. She's dying to tell me about her afternoon.

"Oh my, Reegan. I met a boy in my Fae History class, and he is so dreamy. He asked me to meet and study since he's never been to Elfame. I had such a good time with him. He asked me to be his date for the party Saturday. Can you believe it?" she asks.

"Of course, I can believe it. You're amazing, Maddie. Any guy would be lucky to date you. And I think you should go to the party with him. I'm just going to stay home and train. Rodriq will be here, as well as Grandpa, so maybe we can work out some of my other abilities." I tell her.

I'm hoping she's too excited at being asked out to see through my facade. She would stay with me that night if I asked, but I didn't want to ruin this experience for her.

"Ok, no more stalling. Please tell me what's going on between you, Trent, and Asher. We grew up together, so I know he's never been to Elfame, yet you seem to know him. How is that possible?" she asks. I can see the confusion on her face. I don't know how to tell her this. I know I can trust her, however. She may be the only person I can truly trust with everything. So I take a breath and then start.

"When I was twelve, I realized that I could dream. That's not the right way to say this. Of course, I could dream. What I mean is I could lucidly dream. I discovered this skill because you were having a nightmare. I could hear you crying out in your sleep from across the hall. I came in and tried to get you to calm down. When I touched you, I could see what you were dreaming, and I could control it and make it stop. I didn't know what to think.

I walked back to my room once you were calm and went back to sleep myself. The next morning you didn't say anything, so I started to think that maybe I, myself, had been dreaming because you didn't seem to remember any of the nightmare or me being there with you.", I explain.

She looks at me like she doesn't know what to say, then asks, "What does that have to do with Asher? I'm confused. Can you explain more to me, Reegan? Without all the information, I can't help. I want to help.

"I'm getting there. A few months after I entered your dream, a boy showed up in mine. He was a little older than me. We became friends, and he would visit my dreams every night. I don't know how I pulled a stranger into my dreams, but I knew they were mine because they always took place by the mountain cave or the waterfall in Elfame. He told me his name was Asher, and I told him my name was Winnie since that's what my dad always called me. We would talk about the academy and becoming a part of the task force. We talked about building a life together, Maddie. We had it all mapped out.

Anyway, the dreams kept happening every night for two years. When I turned fourteen, they stopped. Like you, I figured he wouldn't remember the dreams when he woke up. I don't know enough about dreams to answer how he would remember when he joined me in the dreamscape. I didn't even know if he was real or a figment of my imagination. I never forgot Asher, but I pushed those memories deep into the back of my mind. That's why I was so surprised when we met them in town. I knew who he was, but I freaked out."

Maddie looks at me with a smile and wipes the tears from beneath my eyes that I didn't even realize were there. "Reegan, sweetie. Thank you for trusting me with this. So, if I understand right, you thought when you were younger that you and Asher would end up together, but when the dreams stopped, you thought maybe you imagined him." I nod.

"Then he shows up out of nowhere, and those long-buried feelings have surfaced, and you don't know what to do with them." I nod again, still crying. "And now there's the complication of Kalan and Trent." I give her a look like she's crazy.

"Reegan, I'm not blind, and I like to think I'm smarter than your average bear. I see the way Trent is drawn to you. I see the way you were leaning into his touch. Did you ever think that maybe you are meant to have more than one mate?"

I'm shocked. Seriously, I can't even fathom having more than one mate. It's just not possible. "But Kalan. He's my mate, Maddie. I love him. I think a part of me always has.", I tell her. "I won't risk losing him over some misplaced lust in a man that is a self-claimed slut and uses women as conquests. I also will not risk what I have with Kalan for a childhood crush who is now with a bitch. He and Calista deserve each other from what I can see."

"Stop, Ree. Listen to me. Who says you have to lose Kalan? I spent most of my evening learning about mate bonds. After seeing how Trent was with you today, I needed to see what could be happening. From what I read, it is normal for the strong female supernatural to have more than one mate. The stronger the female, the more mates she could have. And since we don't know anything about what powers you hold as a Weaver, can we assume that you may need more than one mate to help you balance the powers? Marcus said something about you being the perfect balance of dark and light, but he didn't say the powers themselves would be balanced. And if Kalan loves you the way I believe he does, he will be ok, no matter how many mates may come into your life. I feel that Trent and Asher won't be the last." This she says with a smile and a wink.

We sit in silence for a few minutes, and then I think about something exciting happening to my bestie. We completely glossed over it. "Maddie, you had a study session with a boy today?"

At this, she blushes. She looks so happy. I want that for her, but a face appears in my mind at the end of that thought. *Rodriq.* This situation could be interesting. It could also blow up in her face if she's not careful.

"Yes, I did. His name is Kenneth, and he reminds me of those surfer guys we used to ogle when we'd vacation in Pismo. He's dreamy and so sweet. He carried my bag for me and refused to let the driver bring me home. Instead, he gave me a ride. He opened the door for me and everything!" she exclaims.

"Will you please go to the party Saturday. I already told him I wouldn't go without you and wouldn't make you feel like a fifth wheel either. He understands and would love it if you'd ride with us and hang with him and his friends. You must go. As heir to a council seat, you must mingle and get to know the people you represent." She goes on and on about the plans for Saturday.

I tell her about the incident in the bathroom with Calista and Adeline. She makes a plan of action that she says will guarantee Trent is mine and that Asher will be wondering what the hell he's doing with the witch. We laugh and joke, and it's the lightest I've felt since the bomb was dropped on me about what I am. I eat a late dinner, sitting at the kitchen counter after cleaning my hands and showering. After eating, I head to my room to finish some required reading. I haven't heard from Kalan, but I know he's busy. I turn on Netflix and start to watch a movie.

Lying in my bed, the loneliness, hurt, and guilt comes back tenfold. I miss Kalan. I'm broken over Asher's betrayal, even if he owes me nothing. I feel shame at wanting another man, even if it is fated. I question everything. Why me? It was nice to joke about Trent and Asher being mine, but I have to face facts. It wouldn't be right to Kalan so I need to keep my distance as much as possible.

The next thing I know, it's Tuesday morning. I skip breakfast and head out on a morning jog around the lake. I don't stay long, knowing I need to get to class. I wear a pair of jeans and a plain black tee. In Elemental skills, I take a seat in the front of the classroom and don't even glance back at Trent. I manage to dodge him and Asher all day. I pass Jaymeson in the hall and smile at him but keep walking. I don't see Bentley at all. I grab lunch but take it outside to the courtyard to eat alone. The waiter from Monday helps me carry it and ensures the mess is cleaned up when I'm done. The rest of the week is much the same. The only difference is that Jaymeson tries to speak to me in the hallway as we pass each other. I always say a quick hello but go on my way.

By Friday, Maddie was tired of my hiding, so she forced me to have lunch with Kenneth and his friends. Kenneth seems nice, and he treats Maddie like a queen. I don't remember his friends' names, which makes me feel like a bitch, and I promise

to get to know them better at the party tomorrow. Once the week is over, I'm so exhausted that
I want to crash into my bed. Of course, that won't
be happening. I have a note from my grandfather
telling me to spend time working on my elemental
powers. I do as he says, locking myself in the arena
outside. I spend several hours there, and when I'm
done, I go to my room and fall asleep before my head
hits the pillow.

14

REEGAN

Saturday comes much too quickly, and before I know it, I'm standing in front of the floor-length mirror in my room, admiring the black and purple bandage dress Maddie chose for me to wear. It is beautiful but a little uncomfortable. If I move the wrong way, I'll be flashing everyone my underwear. I match it with knee-high-heeled boots. I went into town earlier and had my nose pierced. I have wanted to do it for a while, and today seemed the perfect day to rebel just a little. I have my hair slicked back into a sleek ponytail, and I have on my hoop earrings. I feel sexy and beautiful.

I tried over the week to tell myself that I didn't care what Trent did with other girls; it didn't matter how Asher treated me, but as I looked at my reflection, I realized that I had been lying to myself. I only want Trent to myself, and I want my Asher back. This morning, I spoke to my grandpa about the mate bonds, and he agreed with Maddie. I likely have more than one mate, and I can't help but hope that Trent and Ash are two of them. I think I should talk to Asher and tell him the truth. Maybe I'll get the chance tonight. I guess I need to also have a conversation with Kalan. I also want to dance and enjoy myself with my girl and the new friends we're making.

"Girl, you look smoking hot! Those boys aren't going to know what to do with you!" Maddie exclaims as she enters my room.

I can't help the smile that graces my lips at her words. I also can't help the gasp that leaves them when I see what she's wearing. She's wearing a white mini skirt with a green tube top that seriously shows off her body. The outfit fits her personality so well, and it's not something she'd wear back home. She's wearing her hair up in curls on top of her head with a tiny tiara peeking through. My best friend, ladies, and gentlemen. Always the princess.

"Someone is trying to get lucky tonight.", I laugh.

Maddie blushes a deep crimson, but I know I just hit the nail on the head by the look in her eyes. I laugh again and pull her out of the room and down the stairs. When we reach the bottom, I hear my grandfather call my name. With a look at Maddie, who ensures me she'll wait right there, I head off toward where his voice came from. I walk down the hall to the open door. I haven't explored this far yet. It looks to be his office. He's sitting behind his desk reading over paperwork with a drink in hand.

As I enter, he looks up from his papers. "Wow, Little Bit, you look beautiful.", he says. "You must be headed to your first academy party."

"Yeah, Maddie and I were invited, and we thought it'd be a good idea to mingle.", I say. I'm waiting for him to tell me that I can't go, that it's not safe.

He surprises me by smiling and saying, "Ok, sweetheart, have fun. I just wanted to see you before I leave for a business trip in the morning. Be safe, yeah?" I give him a nod and turn to leave. "You know, you do look so much like your mom. She's so proud of you!" he gets up and kisses me on the forehead ushering me out the door. Wait, did he say my mom is proud of me? He must have misspoken.

Maddie is waiting at the front door with Kenneth when I get back to the foyer. He hugs me and then takes Maddie's hand. I hear a grunt behind me and see Rodriq standing in the hall; his eyes stuck on their joined hands. As I said, this is going to be interesting. Rodriq looks up then, and the hurt I see shining in his eyes makes me frown. He shakes his head, turns, and walks away. I genuinely feel sorry for him. I know he likes Maddie, but he's afraid to make any move. If he won't grow some balls, there's nothing I can do. We climb into Kenneth's Range Rover and head to Caleb's for the party. On the way, we pick up Kenneth's friend Mitchell. I think he said he was a puma shifter. He's a cute guy and a great conversationalist. It's a bit of a drive to the party, so Maddie decides to crank the music, and we sing along to the top of our lungs. We're all laughing and having a great time. I feel my phone vibrate in my pocket, so I check it. It's a text from Kalan.

Kalan: Hey beautiful. Sorry I haven't been in contact. I've been super busy.

Me: That's ok. Headed to a party with Mads. We'll talk later, yeah? I love you.

Kalan: With other guys? No. I forbid you to go!

Me: You what?! You can't forbid me to do anything, Kalan. I love you, but I won't be told what I can and can't do. I'm with Maddie, and I will have a good time. Goodnight!

With that, I shut my phone off. I huff out a breath of frustration and put my phone back in my pocket. A few minutes later, I hear Maddie's phone ring. She pulls it out, looks at it, and then looks at me. I know it's Kalan, and Maddie is probably wondering why he'd be calling her and not me. I shake my head at her, and she sends the call to voicemail. She then silences her phone and slips it back into her bag. Kalan has never shown possessiveness toward me. Is that the mate mark causing him to be that way? It can't be right. I'm not sitting over here wondering what he and Aldair are getting into, whom he's spending time with. What does this mean for the future if I have other mates out there and he's this jealous and possessive then? I just wanted to come out tonight and have a good time with Maddie. Now, with these thoughts running through my brain, I'm afraid I'll be a buzzkill. We stop at a little gas station to fill the car, and Maddie asks to see my phone. She powers it up and sees that I have 20 missed calls from Kalan and several text messages. She reads through them and then deletes them all. She's fuming mad when she's done.

"Maddie, why did you delete the messages without me seeing them?" I ask her. That's not like her at all trying to control my phone.

"Because my brother is an ass, and you don't need his negativity tonight. I texted him back and told him that when he got his head out of his ass, to call and not before. Now, we have a party to get to, fun to be had, and hot guys to ogle. Let's go!" she says excitedly. Her excitement is infectious, and before I know it, we are laughing again, and all thoughts of Kalan and his alpha-hole attitude are gone. In the back of my mind, my grandpa's words sit ruminating. *She's so proud of you.*

Another ten minutes later, we find ourselves driving up a mountain road. I can see tall pine trees and a forest on either side. As we reach what feels like the tip-top of this mountain, we come to our destination. There are cars parked everywhere.

The sound of music and laughter can be heard out here. We exit the vehicle, and I look at the house itself. It seems as if it is made specific to this area. It's massive, but it's got a cozy log cabin or lodge feel. The whole front is windows that look out into the forest. People are out here milling about with drinks in their hands. Through the windows, I can spot more people dancing and talking. Maddie has her arm linked through Kenneth's, and Mitchell offers me his. I smile at him and place my hand around his bicep as he leads me in.

15

REEGAN

As soon as I enter the house, a drink is placed in my hand. Mitchell quickly takes it from me and puts it on a side table. "Don't drink anything unless you pour it yourself or one of us gets it for you." He says, leaning down so I can hear him over the music. "Last year, a girl was raped. Someone slipped something in her drink.", he continues. I think I may be sick. Why would anyone want to do something like that?

"Thanks for looking out, Mitchell. That was sweet of you.", I tell him smiling. He grabs my hand, and we follow Maddie and Kenneth to what looks to be the kitchen. There are bottles of every kind of alcohol, some snacks, water, and soda. You name it, and it's probably sitting here. Both guys grab bottles of beer from an ice chest. Kenneth begins to mix Maddie a drink.

"What'll you have, Reegan?" Mitchell asks. I've never been much of a drinker, but tonight, I want to cut loose a little.

"You know what, surprise me," I tell him. He mixes me a concoction of what looks like vod- ka, rum, tequila, and gin with some other things mixed in. He tells me it's a Long Island Iced Tea. I take a sip and relish the flavor hitting my tongue. "Wow, this is delicious. I think you may have missed your calling as a bartender."

At this, he blushes and laughs. He is adorable in a kid-next-door kind of way. We've hit it off well. I could see him being an awesome friend in the future. I stand there talking to my friends and watching the people on the dance floor. I'm dying to get out there, but the song playing is a bit too slow to dance on my own, so I'm content to just watch for the moment. I see a cute petite blonde making her way over to us. I smile at her as she stops in front of Mitchell.

"Dance with me.", she says, grabbing his hand with her own.

He looks at me as if asking permission. I give him a huge smile and a nod. He blushes again but follows her to the dance floor. I take a minute to study them. She throws her arms around his shoulders and presses her body close to his. He places his hands around her waist, letting them settle with his fingers just above the swell of her ass. They are so in sync with each other's moves. If they aren't dating, they should be. They're cute together. Mitchell must be at least 6 feet tall, and she's tiny at maybe 5'2". I'll have to remember to ask him about her later.

I'm so lost in watching that I don't realize when the song changes to something more upbeat. Maddie grabs me and drags me to the dance floor. We go out and shake our asses and laugh as the music plays. When this song is over, a more sensual song starts to play. I don't recognize it, but it has an excellent beat, so I begin to sway my hips in rhythm to the song. I close my eyes and let the music take me. I may have spent half my life living in Elfame, but one of my favorite things about the human realm has always been music and dancing. We'd take lessons as kids when we spent our time here. I would practice still when we were home. It is another way to get out of my head and escape the crazy that has been my life for so long. I keep dancing. I feel hands on my hips and a body heating my back. I don't need to look to know it's Trent. I can tell by the smell of rain and electricity. I can tell by the shocks running through me wherever he touches me. He moves with me, keeping time with my movements until there's nothing but him, me, and the music. I don't know how long we dance like that, but the song finally changes to one I know. As "Perfect" by Ed Sheeran begins to play, Trent turns me in his arms. We sway together like this, his leg between both of mine.

He leans down with his lips close to my ear, "You've been avoiding me, Beauty." I try to look away, but he grabs my chin and turns me to face him. "Don't look away from me, Beauty. I'm done letting you avoid me. I've been dying all week not being able to be near you, to talk to you.", he says.

I can see the sincerity and hurt in his eyes. I never want to hurt him, but I'm still scared of what all these feelings mean. I don't want to make a mistake and trust the wrong person with my secrets. Most of all, I don't want to give my heart to the wrong person. I snuggle in closer and lay my head on his chest. He wraps me up in his arms, and we just dance. We dance through three more songs and then head to get drinks. As I approach, Mitchell is at the kitchen bar and hands me a water bottle. I smile as Trent grabs a beer.

The little petite girl from earlier comes over and introduces herself. "Hi. I'm Sam. You must be Reegan." I shake her offered hand, and then we talk about everything there is to do here in town. She asks what I've seen and what I want to see. While we're talking, we end up making plans to go to the amusement park next weekend. It sounds like it will be fun. "Well, I should probably be going. I have to work tomorrow.", she says. "Mitchell, did you need a ride?', she asks him.

"Oh, well, I came with Ken. Let me find him quickly and let him know. Reegan, you'll be ok if I go?" he asks me.

"Of course. Spend some time with Sam. We'll catch up on Monday, yeah?" I answer. With a nod and a smile, he's gone.

"Did you want to dance again?" Trent asks me. I didn't even realize we were still holding hands. He looks at me, full of hope.

"I need to find the restroom first.", I say. He smiles at me in his adorably sly way. I can see the thoughts running through his head. I'm not going to have dirty sex in a bathroom. And I'm not ready for that with anyone else yet. "I know what you're thinking, Trent, and it's not going to happen. I want to spend time with you and get to know you. I don't want to rush this, whatever this is.", I say pointedly.

He dramatically places his hand over his heart, "You wound me, Ms. Winthrope. I would never think of taking you upstairs and ravishing you in a bathroom of all places." I can see the amusement in his eyes, and I can't help but laugh. "My lady, the restroom is upstairs on the right. I'd be happy to escort you, but I'm afraid I'd come back without my balls if I tried." He laughs, and I join him shaking my head at his antics.

I'm still laughing as I make my way up the stairs. I'm not paying attention to anything. I stop at a

random door and turn the knob. What I find be–
hind the door has me frozen and nauseous. On the
bed is Asher with Calista riding him like he's one of
those mechanical bulls in the bars. Asher is lying
with his eyes closed, and he's not moving much.
I guess he's content to let Calista do all the work.
At that moment, Asher opens his eyes. He looks
directly at me. I'm locked in his stare. His eyes
widen as if coming out of some spell, and I think
I see guilt in them.

"Reegan," he breathes.

Calista must have heard him because she looks
over and screams at me, "Get out, creeper!"

With tear–filled eyes, I turn and run. Asher yells
after me, but I can't decipher the words over my
sobs. I keep running. I take a corner and run head–
first into a wall. Ok, not a wall, a person.

"I am so sorry.", I say with a sob. I look up to see
whom I've run into, only to be met with a pair of
sky–blue eyes.

"Watch where you're going, *princess!*" he hiss–
es at me. His eyes soften slightly when he sees
the tears streaming down my face. "Come on,
princess," he says, offering me his hand.

I reach for it, and when they connect, I feel the
electric tingles up my arm. I ignore them and let
Bentley help me up off the floor. He releases my
hand like it's on fire and leads me to a room further
down the corridor. I can't hear the music down–

stairs here, but some soft music is playing from a system in the corner. Bentley leads me to a balcony that overlooks the mountains, and I sit on the bench. Bentley sits beside me but stays completely silent, letting me wallow in my misery.

"You're not going to ask what's going on so you can laugh at my stupidity?" I ask him after several minutes of silence.

I'm not sure why I ask him this. Maybe because he comes across as a man who likes other people's misery. There's something dark inside him. I shouldn't want to be near this man, but I feel connected to him, like, maybe we're connected through our pain. I've heard stories about how his parents were murdered. The council never discovered who was responsible. His story is so like mine.

"I honestly couldn't care any less about your drama, princess. I don't like you. I don't trust you. I know what you are, and I truly can't stand you.", he says vehemently.

I get up, tears in my eyes again when he grabs me by the wrist and squeezes. "You're hurting me.", I cry.

"It's no less than you deserve. It's all your fault, and you will ruin us all." he spits at me.

"Let. Me. Go.", I grit. I feel a spark of something in my chest, like dynamite ready to explode. Bentley releases me, his eyes going wide. He takes a step back and then another, trying to create distance between us.

"It's not possible. The fates wouldn't be this cru el.", he mumbles.

He turns, ready to say something else when the door opens, and Trent and Jaymeson come through with drinks and snacks. They carry them over to the table in the corner. Jaymeson looks between Bentley and me.

"Everything ok here?" he asks, stepping closer to me as if he's going to protect me.

"I'm out.", Bentley states and then hauls ass out of the room.

"Want to tell us what just happened?" Trent asks me.

"Nothing. It's all good. Bentley was just being an ass. How did you know where we were?"

"Bent sent me a text. He said he found you crying in the hallway. Are you sure everything's okay?" Trent looks at me with concern.

"Absolutely!" I lie.

I paste a smile on my face. My wrist hurts, and I'm sure it will bruise. I'm just baffled about what Bentley said to me. Whom will I ruin? What's my fault? He doesn't know me. Is he jealous? Does he think I'll get between him and the guys? I'd never deliberately mess with their friendship. I can tell they're all close, and being the heirs to council seats, they probably grew up in the same circles.

You know what? Screw Bentley and his damn ego! Screw Asher and his whore! I will rock the next two years and learn all I can about what I am and where that leaves me. There's no way Bentley could know what I am, so why do I feel worried?

"Well, where's our fearless leader?", Jaymeson asks. "Are we waiting for him or getting this party started?" He opens the bottle of what I now can see is Vodka and begins pouring it into the cups. He reaches into his jacket pocket and removes some orange juice, which he mixes into one before handing it to me. I take a sip as he waits for the answer to his question.

"He's probably balls deep in Calista at this point. Let's just leave him to the viper, shall we?" Trent finally responds as he puts his arm around my waist and pulls me down in the chair beside him. I feel myself stiffen at his response, but I don't say anything. If Trent notices, he doesn't say anything about it. Instead, he says, "So Beauty, tell us all about you.",

"Oh, there's not much to tell. My parents died when I was five; I don't remember what happened to them. Hell, all I remember are my mom's kind grey eyes and my dad's smile. I don't remember any more details at all from back then. Marcus became my guardian, but with the Council and his other work, he couldn't keep me, so he sent me to live in Elfame. I was raised there by King Dain and Queen

Trina. I'm old enough now, so Marcus thought it was time that I come here to the Academy so I could be groomed for the Council.", I tell them.

"Hmmm. And the pretty boy prince? What's up with the two of you?" he responds.

"Oh, well, we grew up together, of course. He's several years older, so he was away a lot, doing the things that princes do.", I tell him with a wink. I don't want to tell Trent that Kalan is my mate. I need to, but it's not a conversation to be had in front of his friends. I may never be prepared to give him up. "That's enough about me. Tell me about you."

We sit and talk for the next bit, and I learn what I can about the guys. I know that Trent has a little sister and a little brother. Jaymeson grew up in a pack in Colorado, one of the largest in the States, and he is slated to become alpha. They tell me a little about Bentley and Ash. Trent hasn't said anything about my connection with Asher, and Jaymeson doesn't seem to know, so I keep my mouth shut. The less they know, the safer I am. The safer they are. I lose track of time; the next thing I know, Trent is carrying my half-asleep body down the hall.

"I can walk, Trent. Put me down.", I say sleepily.

"No can do, Beauty. I can't risk you falling down the stairs by falling asleep.", he chuckles. "I'll give you a lift home.

"I need to tell Ken and Maddie.", I tell him as I try to pull my phone out of my pocket.

"Already done. Kenneth is taking Maddie for food. She said to text her when you got to the house and let her know you're safe.", he says as he places a kiss on my forehead.

I just snuggle into his chest and wrap my arms around his neck. I hear Jaymeson chuckle behind us, but he doesn't say anything. When we get to the front porch, he does kiss me on the cheek and waves bye.

We make our way to Trent's car. It's dark, so I can't see all the details, but it looks like a sports car. He opens the door, and I slide into the passenger seat. The leather is buttery soft, and I feel myself melting into it. As we drive, I stare out the window. Trent reaches over and grabs my hand.

"What's going on in that beautiful head of yours?" he asks. I don't even know where to begin.

I must be tired because I tell him the first thing that comes to mind. "I like you." I blurt and then blush. "I like you, and I don't know what to do with that."

"Go out with me.", he says bluntly. "I know you heard me when I told Adeline that I don't date, but I want to be with you– for the first time in my life, I want to try." That brings a smile to my face. I believe him.

"Look, Trent, there's something I need to tell you. You may change your mind about dating me when you know. I.... Kalan and I.... we're mates; true mates." I sit and wait for what feels like forever for Trent to respond. He pulls the car off to the side of the road. He turns in his seat to face me better and then responds.

"How is that possible? True mates don't exist anymore. That's not possible, and if you were true mates, you wouldn't even look at me."

"True mates are rare, scarce, and I've been researching. Powerful female supernatural can have more than one mate. I think that could be why I am mated to Kalan but still feel things for others.", I tell him. I see him contemplating this. I reach down and lift the hem of my shirt where my mate mark rests on my ribs. Trent's eyes take in my side and widen with shock.

"Holy shit! You're serious. Does that mean?" he doesn't finish his thought. He pounces like a lion crashing his lips to mine. The kiss is fervent and possessive. His tongue invades my mouth, wrapping around mine in a war. He tastes like Vodka and the sea. The kiss ends much too soon, and we're both breathing hard. "Wait, is it possible that we could be mates too? And you said you feel things for others? Asher?" he asks.

"Asher and I are complicated, but yes, and possibly more. I honestly don't know.", I say quietly.

"I understand if that changes how you feel." Trent leans in, kissing me again. This time it's slower, more affectionate.

"This changes nothing. I want to be with you. That day I saw you in town at the taco stall, I knew there was something special about you, and I had to get to know you. I couldn't get you out of my mind. When you showed up at the Academy, I felt like something clicked into place for me. We can take this slow. I don't want to rush you." I could feel my heart melting with every word. I wanted to know everything about him and tell him everything about me, but that time would come. "I should probably get you home, huh? Let's do something next weekend."

"I have plans to go to the amusement park with some new friends on Saturday. Come with me?" I smile.

"Of course, I'll come, and then Sunday, can we spend some time with the guys?" he asks. He gives me these adorable puppy dog eyes as he asks, making me laugh.

"Yeah, that sounds perfect.", I say and then give him a light kiss.

He then pulls the car back on the road and heads toward my house. Well, Marcus' house. He places his hand on my knee and leaves it as he drives. He gets out and comes around when we pull up to the house. He offers his hands and pulls me out of the car. He then closes my door and pushes me back up against it. He kisses me again. This kiss is all-consuming, and it takes every ounce of energy I have not to jump him right here in the driveway. He grinds his groin into mine, and I gasp into his mouth. I can feel his hardness rubbing into me. I place my hand on his chest and give him a gentle push.

"Go, Beauty. I don't know how long I can control myself. Go inside and get some rest. I'll see you Monday.", he says. He sounds pained.

I give him a shy smile and turn towards the house. I walk in feeling like I'm walking on clouds. I make my way to my room. I can still feel Trent on my lips, on my body. I take a cold shower to calm my libido and then crawl into bed. As I drift off to sleep, I find myself in my favorite spot, my waterfall in Elfame.

16

ASHER

C reator, this is a mess. I'm lying in bed, the night's events repeatedly playing in my head. I don't know how long I sat there tonight watching Winnie. I saw her enter the party on Mitchell's arm. He's decent enough, but I'll cut off his hands if he touches what's mine. I watch her drink and laugh with her friends. And when she was on that dance floor, all I could imagine was her being in my arms. She seemed taken entirely with Trent.

I'm surprised I don't feel jealous at the thought of them together. No, I trust him with her. Being a dragon, I know more than most about mate bonds. Female dragons take on several mates as our numbers are dwindling. Most people think true mates don't exist anymore, but that's not the case. They're just super rare. But it does happen, and I wonder if my Winnie was meant for more than just me. Because with a clear head, I am confident she's mine. I don't know how I feel about that. I mean, if she's fated to be true mates with my brother, that I can handle, but if it were anyone else, just no. No, I'm not jealous. I'm upset that it's not me she danced with tonight. It wasn't my arms wrapped around her while she ground her ass on my cock. The more I watched her, the harder I got. I felt like I'd blow a load in my damn jeans. My view is taken over when a body stands before me and then plops down onto my lap.

"Oh, baby. You're already hard for me. Let's go upstairs, and I'll help you take care of that ache.", Calista whispers. If only she knew it wasn't her that got me aroused.

"Not right now, Cal. I'm enjoying sitting here listening to music. Besides, Bentley will be right back with my drink.", I say, not paying any attention to the pout she's sporting on her face.

She follows my gaze to where Trent is dancing with Winnie. He has one of his legs between hers, and if they weren't dressed, you'd think they were fucking right there on the dance floor. It's sexy as hell.

"Now, Asher!" She hisses while turning me to face her. "I don't know what's going on with you lately, but remember who you belong to." Then she whispers in my ear, "Come on baby, let me make you feel good."

Something in me changes with her tone of voice, and I let her drag me upstairs. My mind is telling me not to listen, but my body is doing something else. We go to the first empty room. She pushes me down onto the bed and begins to strip. I'll give it to her. She does have a nice body, but her personality sucks. When she climbs on top of me, she unbuttons my pants and pulls them down enough that my cock springs free. She doesn't waste any time straddling my waist and lowering herself onto me with a groan.

Not for the first time, I question what's going on with me. My body responds to Calista as if it belongs to her, but my mind remains detached from what's happening. In my mind, I know this is not something I want, but I can't stop her. I can't stop this. I only get any reprieve when I'm away from her and my dad, and I ignore their incessant calls. Until now, that is. My body may do what she wills, but with Reegan close, with my thoughts on her, my mind is clear. I try to make my body move, to throw Calista off me, but nothing works.

I've tried to tell my boys when my mind is clear, but my tongue gets tied, and the words won't come out. I'm alone, with little hope of stopping whatever spell Calista has cast on me. I'm cursed. My mind screams at me to tell the boys tonight, to pray that someone comes in and sees that I'm not into this whole mess, but that won't happen. Everyone is too busy getting drunk or high. And once this nightmare is over, I won't be able to tell my best friends that I am constantly being raped. I won't be able to tell anyone.

I close my eyes and see Reegan's face. I want to puke at what Calista does to me, but I can't show her anything different than she expects, so I picture my Winnie riding me. Thinking of her riding my cock, I begin to moan. I hear the door open, and there she stands as if my thoughts have conjured her. At once, the spell is over. I see so much emotion in her eyes that it rips my insides to shreds. I try to push Calista off me, but she sees Reegan at the door. She yells something at her, but all I can do is whisper her name. Reegan turns and runs. Calista looks back down at me and sneers,

"We aren't nearly finished here, Asher; now fuck me." I have no choice in the matter, so my body follows her orders.

I'm so disgusted with myself. Even if I can figure out a way to get out from under whatever spell Calista cast on me, I don't deserve Reegan. Hell, maybe I never did, but I vow here and now that if I do get away from Calista and her schemes, I will do everything I can to show Reegan how much I want to be with her. I will free myself from Calista's hold. For now, I'll stay away from her. I won't see her hurt anymore because of me. With that settled, I throw myself back on my pillows and close my eyes to let sleep take me.

I find myself in a familiar meadow below a familiar mountain. Sitting on the rocks overlooking the pool of pink water is Winnie. She seems sad. I can't help but take her in. She's so beautiful. She's wearing what I assume is a dress from Elfame, fit for a princess. Her long purple hair is lying in waves down her back. Her sapphire blue eyes are filled with tears. I suck in a sharp breath at the sight of those tears as they escape and leave trails down her cheeks. She must hear me because she looks up.

"What are you doing here, Asher?" she sounds dejected. "Why did you pull me into your dream?"

What? I've never been able to pull her into a dream. I always thought she was in charge of these. "I didn't know I could.", I tell her.

"Well, you must have because I damn sure didn't want to see you.", she hisses. My heart cracks into a million pieces as those words hit me. "Why don't you go back to your girl and fuck her some more."

I find myself angry at her words. "Winnie, you disappeared from my dreams a long time ago. I didn't even know you were real. Yes, I lived my life. Yes, I have fucked girls. But don't lay all the blame on me. The dreams are your gift, not mine!" I yell.

What does she want from me? I feel guilty as hell for what she saw tonight, but I want to lash out at her for being angry over circumstances beyond my control. Events that I can't tell her about.

"You're right, Asher. You aren't mine. Maybe you never were, and I don't know why the dreams ended. The creator knows that I never wanted them to. Those were the only times in my life, the only time I felt hope for the future, and you aren't the only one who lost them! I'm going, but before I do, you deserve much more than that snake you call a girlfriend. Love can make you do stupid things, but I'm done. I wasn't created to fix stupid. You know, you were the first boy I ever loved. My bad. I thought we had a future together, but you proved we don't. Next time you want to get your dick wet, lock the damn door!!!" she screams. And with that, she walks away.

I wake in a cold sweat, my breathing ragged, my face wet with tears. I didn't know I was capable of crying. My chest is heavy. I feel like I can't get a full breath. I stagger out of the room and make my way to the kitchen. Trent is sitting at the bar with a smile on his face. He loses it quickly when he sees me. He runs over just as I collapse to the floor.

"Dude, what the hell? You're burning up!" Trent exclaims.

He yells for the guys. I hear their footsteps pounding on the tiles, and everything goes black. I wake up hours later. My throat is dry and scratchy. My body is heavy. I open my eyes and see the guys camped around my bed. Jaymeson hands me a glass of water and some pain pills. I take them happily and then lay back and let my eyes fall closed. My chest has a tightness that's never been there before, and my dragon is growling inside my head.

"What the hell happened?" I ask anyone listening.

Bentley is the one that answers me, "We aren't sure. We were hoping you could fill us in. You staggered to the kitchen and collapsed. You were on fire, like your dragon was stuck, fighting to emerge. What the hell happened last night?"

"I don't know, honestly. After the party, I came home and went to bed. I remember waking up feeling weird and then collapsing on the floor.", I tell them. I don't tell them about the dream because I don't think Winnie wants anyone to know, and I don't know how to explain it anyway.

"Come on, Asher. It's time for some truths.", Bentley says to me knowingly. He always seems to know things.

"Like what the deal is with you and Reegan?" Trent asks. "Or how about what's going on with you and that vapid bitch?"

"I won't tell you Reegan's secrets. They're not mine to share.", I state. Bentley looks at me, and I see hatred in his eyes. Is this hate for Reegan or me? "And I don't know what to tell you about Calista other than she's my girlfriend, and we're getting married after graduation."

"What do you mean, you're getting married after graduation?", Jaymeson asks. "Is this your choice? Hers? Your dad's?"

I don't answer. I can't. Honestly, I don't even remember making the plan to be married. What the hell?

"Well, isn't that special? Do you remember tonight at all?" Trent sneers at me.

"I remember being at the party and then waking up here. Everything in between is foggy.", I tell him.

"That's convenient. So, you don't recall Reegan walking in on Calista riding your cock?", Jaymeson asks with an eyebrow raise.

"Shit!!!!! Motherfucker!!!! Please tell me you're joking." I cry. Reegan saw me and Calista. Why does knowing this make my heart bottom out?

"That's why she ran into me crying? Hmmm. Guess she'll learn to knock on doors before entering, huh?" Bentley cackles.

"You just stay the hell away from Reegan. You hurt her, and if it happens again, I won't be held responsible for what I do to you!" Trent says menacingly.

We all look at him with shock. Trent just stands there rubbing at the middle of his chest. I'd think he was about to have a heart attack if he weren't supernatural.

"Holy fuck!" Jaymeson says, "That's not even possible." He shakes his head. "Trent, why are you rubbing your chest?" he asks.

"I don't know. Hearing what Reegan went through last night just made sharp pains go through my chest.", he says.

"Dude is Reegan your mate?", Jaymeson asks with a look of awe and maybe jealousy.

"Um. Maybe." Trent answers sheepishly. "We talked about it a little when I took her home last night. Even if she is, we aren't rushing the bond. We're going to date and get to know each other better.", he says. His eyes are twinkling.

"Holy creator. You, dating? This is epic!", Jaymeson laughs.

You'd think I would be upset by the news, but it feels right. My dragon stirs a little at that and huffs his agreement. Is that what I'm feeling in my chest? I always thought she could be my mate, but then I started wondering if she was just a figment of my imagination, a wish my heart truly wanted.

"I'm done talking about that girl. She's not worth the time of day. Seriously, Trent, there are ways out of the bond. Take one.", Bentley says.

"Why would I do that? Bent, you know how special mate bonds are." Trent answers.

"Whatever, man.", Bentley says and storms out.

"What crawled up his ass?", Jaymeson muses. "I'd give anything for a true mate. I don't want to be stuck in a marriage of convenience with some bitch from my pack."

"Yeah. I don't think it's that, in any case. Bent has secrets, dude. We all know that. And he's a cranky bastard on a good day.", Trent laughs.

Yeah, Bent has secrets. Reegan has some. Hell, we all do, and when those secrets finally see the light of day, we may be royally fucked. Trent and Jaymeson leave the room with promises of ordering take-out. I get up and get in the shower. Trent's warning runs through my head. I don't plan on hurting Reegan. Right now, I need to keep my distance until I can break up with Calista. My dragon rumbles at the thought of not being around Reegan. I have to. I need to let my dragon out to fly. It's been so long. It feels like we're disjointed. Like we're separate. But we're not. We're two parts of a whole. When was the last time I let him fly? It takes me several minutes to realize that the last time I can remember spreading my wings was before Calista came into the picture.

17

REEGAN

Sunday flies by in a fit of physical and elemental training with some assigned reading Marcus wants me to have completed when he returns from his business trip. I didn't see Maddie all day or evening, so I haven't been able to tell her anything about what went down at the party or with Trent after. I'm just getting ready to make some dinner when my phone rings. The caller ID shows its Kalan, and I feel a mixture of emotions, the most significant being nervousness. I click the accept button and put him on speakerphone.

"Hey, baby. I miss you so much!" he exclaims.

"Hey yourself. I miss you too.", I answer. "What are you up to, my prince?"

"I just got done with a meeting, and I have another one to go to, but I wanted to take a second to call and tell you I love you.", he says. Kalan is the sweetest guy.

"I love you too. I was just getting ready to sit down and eat. I'm exhausted."

"Yeah. Marcus, have you working hard, huh? Hey, before I go and let you eat, I thought of coming to see you next weekend. Could we do something, just the two of us?", He says with a bit of mischief in his voice.

My body perks up at being alone with him, but I have plans with Sam and Mitchell on Saturday and with my guys on Sunday. *My guys.* What the hell am I thinking? Trent is my mate, but I don't know about the others.

"I have plans for the weekend, but I want to see you. We need to talk about some stuff, so maybe you could join us?" I ask hopefully.

"Plans with who?" he asks.

"Some friends from the academy. We're going to the amusement park on Saturday, and then I'm not entirely sure what we're doing Sunday.", I tell him. I don't want to talk to him about Trent or the guys over the phone.

"Will those guys from town be there? I know you've been spending time with them at school.", he says. I can hear the sneer in his voice. "You know what, just forget it. Have fun with your *friends.* I'll come another time."

"Wait!" I say, but it's too late. He's already hung up. I try to call him back, but it goes straight to voicemail. "Fuck!" I scream. As if I haven't had enough emotional shit to deal with this weekend.

I know Kalan is possessive but I've never seen him this jealous before.

"Woah, girl. What's going on?" Maddie asks as she enters the kitchen.

When I see her, it's too much, and I break down. I'm a sobbing mess as Maddie holds me rubbing my hair as I wail all my frustrations at her. When I'm calmer, I tell her everything. I tell her about the party, about Trent and Bentley. I even told her what an ass Kalan was to me on the phone.

"Ok, I'm going to kick my brother in the balls. As for Trent, I'm so happy for you, hon! I knew something was going on there. Now, Bentley knows what you are, which is tricky. Do you trust him?" She doesn't even breathe as she says this and begins asking questions.

"Surprisingly enough, yes, I do trust him. I trust all the guys. But Bentley hates me, and I don't know why. He's only known me for a week. How can you hate someone in a week?" I say

"I don't know, sweetheart. Maybe he's jealous. You're a catch. Who wouldn't be jealous they can't have you? Or maybe the rumors are true?" she asks with an eyebrow raise.

"What rumors?" we've been at the academy for a week, and she already knows all the news.

"I'll get to that. But let me ask you something serious. You said you trust all the guys. Does that include Asher? I know it hurts to see him with someone else. You knew him in your dreams, sweetie. Not the person he is, and he honestly comes across as an asshole of epic proportions.", she tells me.

"Yes. I've always trusted Asher, Maddie. I don't know what's going on now. It's been years since we've seen each other, and while it hurts to see him with someone else, what am I supposed to do? I feel that he and I are meant to be together, but I can't change what is. I don't plan on telling him any of my secrets. I don't trust Calista, and I feel she'll find out anything I would share with him. But I still want to be his friend. I don't think I can go through these next two years without him. I don't think I can go through life without having him in it in one way or another.", I explain.

I know Maddie sees my feelings better than anyone else, so she knows I'm being serious. She just nods her head. She gets it.

"Ok, well, leave my brother to me. He'll come around. Don't let him cause you any more stress than what you're already feeling. You deserve to be happy.", she tells me.

Hearing those words from her clicks some resolve into place inside me. I want to be happy. I don't know what I'm facing, but I know it will be hard, and I know these men are the key to helping me with this task. Later that night, while I lie in bed trying and failing to sleep, there's a knock on my door.

"Come in.", I call. Maddie enters with a pillow in her hand.

"Can I sleep in here tonight?" she asks. "I could hear you tossing and turning in here."

"Yeah, like when we were little?" I returned.

When we were young, anytime one of us couldn't sleep, we'd crawl into bed with the other, and it seemed the presence comforted us enough to sleep soundly. She pads over to the other side of the bed. I lift the covers, and she crawls in. We face each other, and she grabs my hand between us and lays them on the pillow.

"I miss this.", I tell her.

"Me too. So, what was it like kissing Trent? There are many rumors about him, you know. From what I hear, he's quite the lothario." she giggles and wags her eyebrows. "The only one that seems to not be constantly fucking someone is Bentley. From what a girl in my history class says, Jaymeson doesn't date anyone from the academy. He prefers humans. And while Asher is dating Calista, the consensus is that it's not by choice."

"What do you mean?" I ask her. "Everyone has a choice, Maddie."

"I don't know for certain, but some girls seem to think Calista has cast a spell on him. It's probably just jealousy. You've seen them together, and as far as I know, no spell can make someone love you."

I let that roll over in my mind for a minute. No, there isn't a spell that can do that, at least that I've heard of. And the rumor about Bentley, why do I feel a sense of pride in him that he doesn't seem to date?

"What did you mean when you said Bentley doesn't date? He's hot! There must have been some girls in that man's life.", I say.

"Maybe, but the girls at school think he's gay. Plenty of women would love to get a piece of him, but he always shoots them down. If he's dating outside the academy, it's a very well-kept secret."

Everyone has secrets, princess. That's what he said to me. Maybe he is gay. But that doesn't feel right. It just feels like he hates me, which makes my heart hurt for whatever reason.

"Hmmm. I don't think so. I mean, I could be wrong. He keeps everything so tightly held to his chest. He's such a mystery. I know he has secrets. He told me as much, but I don't think he's gay. Maybe he just wants to find the right girl to be with and share that intimacy with." I speak my thoughts.

"And let me guess, you want to be that girl. Hopeful thinking? Are you trying to add to your harem, sweet sister?" she snickers.

"Well, I can't say I'd mind." I laugh.

Maddie and I spend the next hours talking about everything that's happened since coming here. She tells me all about Kenneth, how sweet he is, and how she thinks he could be the one. My bestie is in love, and I am excited for her. She's changing but in a good way. I love seeing this confidence come out of her. She says I deserve happiness. If that's the case, then she deserves the world. If Kenneth is the one to help make all her dreams come true, so be it. But if he hurts her, I'll end him. Hell, maybe there's a harem out there for her as well. The creator knows that if she and Rodriq got their heads out of their asses, they'd be pure fire together.

We finally doze to sleep when the sun begins to rise. All too soon, my alarm is blaring. I think I slept for two hours. My and Maddie's hands are still linked together, so I'm careful not to wake her as I get up. I put on my workout clothes and head out for my morning run. I need caffeine in the worst way. I return to the house and am surprised to see a car sitting in the driveway. I'm even more surprised when Trent steps out of it.

"Hey, Beauty. I come bearing gifts.", he grins, holding up a tray with three cups of coffee and a bag of pastries in front of me. "I thought you and Maddie might like a lift to school this morning?" he says, though it sounds more like a question. He seems timid today as if he's afraid I'll say no. His eyes rake up and down my body. "Or I can give you a different kind of ride this morning, but we'll have to miss class." He wiggles his eyebrows lasciviously. *And he's back.*

I blush but shake my head at his antics. "Come on, Romeo, I need to shower and get dressed." He follows me into the house. I leave him in the kitchen while I make my way upstairs.

I take the quickest shower known to Fae-kind. Once I'm done, I head into my closet and put on a gauzy pink summer dress that hits me about mid-thigh and a pair of matching heels. I pull my hair up into a twist on the top of my head. I go light with my makeup. Looking at myself in the mirror, I think I look good. I go back downstairs and hear laughter coming from where I left Trent. I go into the kitchen and find Trent and Maddie laughing at something Rodriq has said. I stand leaning on the door frame for a minute, just taking in the scene. Trent looks so at home with my best friend and pseudo guardian. It brings a smile to my face.

"Wow, you look beautiful, Reegan.", Trent breathes. He's looking at me like I'm his world, and I want to be right now. I walk over and kiss him on the cheek.

"Thanks for breakfast. We should probably go if we don't wanna be late." I finish, taking a bite of a fruit-filled danish. "Oh creator, that is Heaven!" I exclaim. The danish is so good. It melts in my mouth, and the filling tastes fresh. I wonder if the berries had just been picked this morning.

"I'll be sure to tell my mom you approve.", Trent says with a laugh. "Ok, ladies, shall we?" he asks. I nod and turn to head toward the door. I feel Trent's hand on the bottom of my back as he leads us to the car. Once we make it outside, I noticed Maddie didn't follow. Trent opens the door for me, and I slide in. Maddie comes out as I'm snapping my seatbelt into place. She looks a little pissed. I wonder what Rodriq said or did to make her like this. Trent holds the door open for her, and she slides into the back with a slight huff.

"So, how many cars do you own?" I ask him, just now remembering he brought me home in a sports car Saturday night.

"Just the one you saw. This one is my mom's. Mine is being detailed. I also own a Ducati." he tells me.

"You own a Ducati?" Maddie squeals in excitement. Yes, my girl has a thing for bikes. What can I say? She has good taste. Trent doesn't scream biker to me, however. He seems a little too sophisticated in his designer jeans that hug his legs and his button-down shirt.

"Yeah, all the guys have bikes. We'll have to get together sometime, and all go for a ride.", he offers.

Maddie's whole face lights up at the idea, and she begins to ask question after question about the different models the guys have. Trent is patient with her telling her all about the guy's bikes, and it endears him to me a little more.

We arrive at school. Trent opens Maddie's door first and helps her out of the car. Kenneth sees her and makes his way over. He gives Maddie a sweet kiss, and they head off. Maddie turns and waves to us. I open my door, and Trent rushes to provide me with his hand to help me out. Once I'm up, he grabs my bag and throws it over his shoulder. He takes my hand in his as we walk into the school. I almost laugh at him trying to play the gentleman. We walk to class hand in hand. I can see people staring and hear the whispers. They all seem surprised that Trent would show anyone this much attention.

When we get to our Elemental studies class, Trent stops. He turns me to him and gives me a kiss that leaves me breathless. When he releases me, I stumble a little, and he chuckles. He turns me back around and gives me a little push in the door. We take our seats, and within minutes, Rodriq enters the room.

"Okay, class, we will do something a little different today. Instead of working individually on our elemental powers, we are going to do some elemental sparring.", he announces to everyone. There are some groans but even more cheers of excitement. "Now, if you all will follow me to the ring."

We get up and follow him outside to the ring. It's a vast circle surrounded by some sort of magic that won't let our abilities leave the area. He tells us to spread out around the ring when we arrive.

"The point of this exercise is to see what we need to work on this semester. Ok, ground rules. Number one: No killing or maiming blows. Number two: The sparring will stop when one opponent withdraws or if they are pinned. We are going to mix physical and elemental sparring to create what you will all face in two months at the trials.", he explains the rules.

"What are the trials?" I hear myself asking.

"I'll explain them to you later, Beauty.", Trent answers.

"Thanks for volunteering, Reegan and Trent. Since you guys seem full of energy this morning, you're up first.", Rodriq says with a devilish smile. "You may want to lose the heels, sweetheart. They won't help you here.", he laughs.

"You're such an ass.", I tell him.

Again, he just laughs at me. I take off my shoes and lay them on the edge of the barrier. I then meet Trent in the middle of the circle. He's removed his button-down and stands in a black tee-shirt that leaves nothing to the imagination. I can even see his adonis belt through the fabric. Damn. Now I'm drooling. I don't want to spar with him. I want to lick every groove of his abs. I can see some ink peaking below his sleeves. I want him to take his shirt off and show me the artwork on his body. I can feel his elemental abilities' power, and I don't know if I'm a match for him, even with the extra training I've had to put in. Now that additional training makes sense.

"See something you like?" he asks me. I'm blushing again. "Come on, Beauty, show me whatcha got."

"Wait." I hear a tinkling voice day behind me. I turn to see who's talking, and my eyes meet Sa rina's. Here you go, Reegan. You shouldn't have to mess up that beautiful dress." She holds out a pair of short shorts and a tank for me. I take them gratefully, if not a little reluctantly. I look around and realize there's nowhere to hide to change.

"I'm not changing in front of all these people.", I say

"No worries. I can hide you.", she says as she starts creating shadows. They wrap around us to where I can't see anything but her and the clothes she gave me. I hurry and change, and then she releases the shadows.

"Thanks. I bet that ability comes in handy", I tell her.

She answers with a nod and a smile. I walk back into the ring and prepare myself for whatever attack Trent will use. I know his elemental ability is water, and he also has an affinity for electricity. He doesn't know what kind of elemental I am. No one does– yet. I guess they're about to find out. Trent is staring at me slack-jawed. It takes me a second to realize it's because these clothes are just a tad revealing. My breasts are about to pop out of the tank, and I know if I turned around, he'd be able to see my ass cheeks.

"See something you like, Trent?" I tease, throwing his words back at him.

"More than you know, Beauty.", he winks. "Now, let's give these people a good show, shall we?"

Trent and I circle each other, trying to get a read on what the other will do. Trent raises his hands, and a ball of water begins to form. It gets larger and larger until he throws it at me. I let my hand shoot out. A gust of wind turns his water back on him, and he is soaked. I can't help but laugh at the look on his face. He looks like a drowned rat.

"Oh, babe. You look a little wet there. Need to dry off?" I ask as I send another heavy dose of wind in his direction. He lets it hit him, but he stands his ground instead of knocking him off his feet, as I expected.

He gives me a sinister smile, and the laugh catches in my throat. "It's so on now, Beauty."

I hear the sizzle before it comes, and I duck out of the way of the bolt of lightning. The next thing I know, I'm on the other side of the ring opposite where I was standing, with no clue how I got there.

"You have a spiritual affinity?" Trent asks. I hear an audible gasp from the other students, and Trent stands there in shock. I knew I had the affinity, but I'd never been able to use it before. Cool.

"Worried now, sweetie?" I ask him. I hear the challenge in my voice, and he must, too, because the next thing I know, he's spraying me with water. Now he's the one laughing.

I just use the wind to dry myself off and wait for his next move. He pools the water around my feet before freezing them to the ground. I look down and then look up at him with a smile. I bend down and touch the ice making it melt with fire. I then shoot a small ball of fire at him, making him roll out of the way. I take that moment to pounce. I have him on his back with my knees in his shoulders so he can't move. He looks at me with awe. But that look quickly becomes a look of hunger, and I realize that I have placed my crotch in his face. His tongue slips out, and he licks his lips looking at me.

"Now, this is the type of sparring I can get behi nd.", he says.

I quickly backpedal and place my knees on his lower arms. He wraps his legs around me and flips us so I am on my back with him straddling me.

"Mm. Just how you should be. On your back and underneath me. Creator! You don't even know what you're doing to me. If we didn't have an audience...." he trails off.

I give him a sweet smile as I kick up a gust of wind, knocking him back on his ass. I take advantage and freeze his hands and feet to the ground, effectively making it where he can't get up. I give him a small smile and pull a fireball into my hand.

"I give!" he yells out.

I release him from the ice, and he hops up, coming over and taking me into his arms. He spins me around, causing me to laugh. "My girl is a badass!" he yells.

I feel a slight twinge in my heart at the words, *my girl*. We take our places outside the ring, and Rodriq has another couple enter. I notice he's writing something on his clipboard, and it has me curiously looking at him. He raises his eyes to mine and gives me a slight smile and a nod. I did well.

I keep getting looks from my classmates, but they all seem happily surprised at my abilities. No one appears scared, which I take as a good sign. I'm still thinking about the spiritual affinity that peeked through during our match. No matter how hard I've tried, I haven't been able to use it. Why now? I guess that's another mystery for me to solve.

18

REEGAN

The rest of the morning passes quickly, and we head to lunch. Trent retakes my hand and beams at anyone who comes up to me, telling me what a great job I did during our sparring sessions this morning. I put my head down. I don't like all this attention. When you're supposed to hide what you are, isn't it best not to draw attention to yourself?

Rodriq reassured me that it was a good thing as it kept my true nature hidden. He also thinks solidifying the bond with Kalan has strengthened me and made my abilities easier to reach. That makes sense and goes along with Maddie's research on mate bonds.

"You're quiet. Are you alright?" Trent asks. He looks genuinely concerned. "You know you were awesome this morning. You don't like the attention of others thinking your kickass?"

"I'm not used to it at all, and I'm not anything special, Trent," I say. "Let's forget it. Ok."

"Bullshit, Beauty. You are exceptional. You kicked ass today. Your abilities are out of this world. I knew you were strong, but I didn't realize how strong. Don't let me hear you down yourself again, clear?" he chastises. My mouth opens and closes several times before I get my barings back. A scolding Trent is so sexy. "Besides, you have to be special. Only someone extraordinary could be my mate.", he says. At that, I laugh. "There she is.", he says.

He gives me a light kiss, and we continue to the dining hall. We don't talk anymore about how special I am. Trent grabs me from behind. When we reach the door, he kisses my neck just below my ear. "One of these days, you're gonna trust me with those secrets of yours.", he whispers. Then he opens the door and pulls me in.

"I need to change before we head in.", I tell him while pulling him toward the women's bathroom.

"Please don't. You look hot as fuck with those little shorts and a tank top."

He proves how hot he thinks I am as he backs me into the wall. He reaches around to grab my ass as he kisses me like he's dying of thirst and I'm his life-saving water. He grinds his hips to mine and lets out a low groan. I can feel his hardness; it takes everything in me not to jump up and wrap my legs around him. We're supposed to be taking things slow.

I push him away, but there's no force behind it. "Everyone can see us.", I say.

"So, let them. I want everyone to know you're mine.", he returns. *Swoon!*

I'm getting ready with a comeback when my stomach growls loudly. "Come on, Beauty, let's get you fed." he chuckles and reluctantly lets me go.

When I get to the line, the guy I helped last week is waiting. He offers to make my tray and carry it for me. "I got it, man.", Trent tells him. "Thanks for taking care of my girl, in any case. I appreciate it." Trent offers his hand. The guy, Matt, takes Trent's hand and shakes it.

Matt looks at me," No one has ever stood up for me before. If you ever need anything, I've got your back, princess.", he says and walks away.

"Damn. Look at you making friends. Seriously though. You're different. You stood up for him when everyone else would have laughed and walked away. I have a feeling you're going to turn this academy on its head.", Trent says quietly. He gives me a small kiss and turns back to the line.

Trent grabs his tray, and we pile them both with food. He takes mine from me and carries it over to the guy's table. I see Maddie walk in with Kenneth. I motion for them to join us. I know one of the seats at the table is meant for Asher, so I pull two chairs from another table and place them at ours so my friends can sit. Jaymeson and Bentley join us first. Jaymeson kisses my cheek as he passes, and Bentley scoffs and takes his seat. They each sit and begin to chat about their day. Maddie and Kenneth join us, and I introduce him to the guys. He and Jaymeson seem to hit it off well as they start talking about computers. Bentley just sits there and eats. I can feel him look at me every once and a while, but when I look up, he's already looking away. Trent reaches over and snatches one of my french fries off my plate.

"Dude, I will cut a bitch over my food.", I tell him in all seriousness.

His eyes go wide, but he's quick with a comeback. "Sharing is caring, baby." he beams at me. "I'll even share the burger you've been eyeing since we sat down.

I huff a laugh as he steals another. I'm seriously about to stab him with my fork when a high-pitched whine attempts to deafen me. God, her voice is grating.

"Why is *she* sitting here? I thought we made ourselves pretty clear about these seats being taken.", Calista sneers. "Trash belongs in the bins, not at the table of the Elites." Asher takes his seat and pulls her down to his lap. Adeline stands there glaring at me. I look away and feed Trent a fry.

The next thing I know, Trent has lifted me from my seat and placed me on his lap. "There. Problem solved.", he says.

Bentley lets out a bark of laughter that seems to surprise everyone. I look over and see him looking at me. The look is sinister. I go back to my food. "Babe, can I get around you for a sec to take a bite?" Trent asks me.

I see that look in his eyes. He wants to play some games. I'm down. I take my fork and cut off a piece of the chicken that Trent chose. I turn in his lap and offer him a bite. He leans forward and wraps his mouth around the food, never breaking eye contact. Then he moans like it's the best damn thing he's ever put in his mouth. I can't help the small laugh that leaves me.

"I knew you wanted to fuck her but seriously? You even let her kick your ass in the ring this morning. Is that what you're resorting to now to get laid? That's so beneath you when there are plenty of girls that won't make you work so hard.", Adeline says with a sniff. "And what the fuck are you wearing? Did you have to wear your trashy clothes today to ensure everyone knows you're a whore? News flash, they already know." she screeches at me.

I can't help but laugh full-bellied now. I've had about enough of this bitch. "Oh yes, he's so pathetic. Do you even hear yourself? You just admitted to being a skank. You don't make a man work to get in your panties, huh? Damn girl. I thought one of the viper's minions would have more respect for herself. News flash, sidekicks went out of style in the '80s," I retort snarkily.

I'm still laughing, but now so is everyone else at the table, including Asher, though his laugh is quiet. The only way I know he's laughing is the shake of his shoulders. The laughter dies down after a minute, but the smile remains on my face. It feels good to stand up for myself.

"You're just going to let her talk to my friend like that?" Calista nearly screams at Asher.

"I don't control Reegan or Adeline, for that matter. Maybe she shouldn't dish it if she can't take it.", he responds.

Calista leans down and whispers something in his ear. His face completely changes to an impartial mask, and he stays quiet. Wow. She has him whipped, doesn't she?

"So, this is new," Jaymeson says, trying to change the subject. "When did you two hook up?"

"We didn't *hook up*," Trent tells him. "We're dating, taking things slow." Trent looks at me for backup. I look at Jaymeson and nod.

"Well, congratulations.", Jaymeson says.

I know he knows about Trent and me because of the look on his face, and while I think he was trying to take the attention away from Asher, I also think a part of him is just as spiteful as the other guys and wants to rub it in just a little. The rest of the lunch is eaten in silence. When the first bell rings, signaling the end of lunch, Trent lifts me from his lap. Jaymes offers to take our trays and get rid of the garbage. Asher just gets up and walks off with Calista by his side.

"I have to go to meet Rebecca. A new student is coming in. Will you be ok?" Trent asks.

"I'll walk her to class. I have to go that way anyway.", Bentley offers.

"Ok, I'll meet you after classes?" Trent asks while kissing me.

"Well, duh. You are my ride after all.", I tell him and give him another kiss before he exits.

Bentley leads the way out of the dining hall and toward my next class. I don't understand why he offered. Bentley hates me. Maybe this is a truce thing between us. As we round the corner, he grabs me and pulls me into an alcove where no one can see us. He wraps his hand around my throat and squeezes. Guess I was wrong about the truce. I should be scared, but honestly, while I am a little, I'm also a little turned on by it. Creator, what is wrong with me?

"I don't know what game you're playing at *Wea ver*.", he hisses in a whisper. "Leave the guys alone, or your secrets won't be secret for long. Mate or not, I will take you down." he squeezes my throat again and then turns and stomps down the hall. *Mate?* I am so fucked!

I make my way to Supernatural Politics with my
hand around my throat and his threats weighing
heavy on my mind. I keep trying to give meaning to
his words. Maybe he meant he didn't care if I was
Trent's mate. That has to be it. *Right?* I head in and
take my seat. I detest this class. I don't pay attention to anyone as I sit there reviewing my reaction
to Bentley's touch. When the professor enters, he
begins his lecture. I spend the next two hours taking notes. I'm packed up and ready to leave when
the professor releases us.

As I stand, the professor calls out to me. "Ms.
Winthrope, a moment, please?" I make my way up
to his desk. He waits until the room is cleared to
speak again. "I wanted to tell you that I admire
your dedication to note-taking in class, but I need
to see more participation from you. If you're to take
a council seat in the future, you must be willing to
participate in discussions with your fellow supernatural. As such, I am assigning you to the debate
team. This will, of course, be for extra credit."

I'm ready to interrupt him when he lifts his hand
to stop me. "I have already spoken to your grandfather, and he agrees. Your bookwork and quizzes
last week showed that you have a clear understanding of how our world works, even though it is
my understanding that you weren't raised among
us. This will give you a leg up in this area. At the
end of the term, there will be a debate competition

in front of the council before your trials. You will need to complete both to pass. These outline everything you need to know, including your speech topic for the debate and presentation."

"Yes, Professor Morley." I turn to go when it hits me. "Wait, you're Bentley's uncle?" I am shocked by the realization.

"That I am. I'm surprised it took you a week to put that together.", he laughs. "I'm sure my boy can be a great help to you on this assignment, as could all the other boys. They are, after all, the next in line to council seats. Take my advice. Stay away from Calista. She'd love nothing more than to see you fail, as would her father." he winks and shoos me on my way.

Calista isn't the only one that would love to see me fail. I think Bentley would be the one to push me off a tall building, given half a chance. He's so not going to be willing to help me. I doubt Ash will help, either. That leaves Trent and Jaymeson. I'll ask them about it later.

My last class of the day is herbology. I know I excel in this area. I grew up with Fae and learned from the best. Our semester project is to cultivate and grow four plants that are special to us. I chose Lavender because it reminds me of my mom. Orchids because they've always been my favorite flower. Turmeric for its healing properties, and instead of choosing one more, I decided to cultivate the spices used in Chai. I spend the class mapping out my planting spot and making a list of all the supplies I need for my plants to grow successfully. The goal is not to use our abilities but the things humans would use. I get lost in my methods and am surprised when class ends. I'm kind of sad when it does. I can get lost in any nature. This class may well become the one thing that can keep me sane in this place.

I head down to meet Trent at the car. Maddie is waiting to tell me that she and Kenneth are having dinner in town before she heads home. I slip into the car with Trent, taking off toward my home. Trent is super quiet on the drive, and while I want to ask him what's bothering him, I feel like he won't answer, so I let it go. When we pull into the driveway, I see an unfamiliar car sitting in the drive. Trent gets out and helps me out of the car, but instead of keeping hold of my hand, he releases it. I feel cold from the loss of his touch. He'll talk to me when he's ready. I head in with him following. We make our way to the sitting room where voices are coming from. As I walk through the doorway, I see Alita, Aldair, and Kalan sitting with Rodriq and Rebecca, chatting. At the noise of my heels, the conversation stills. Alita looks up and beams a huge smile. She almost knocks me over with her exuberance as she hugs me tight.

"Oh, my sweet girl. You look amazing! We've missed you.", she says excitedly.

"I've missed you too. Is father here as well?" I can't help but ask.

"Not this trip, but he sends his apologies. Where's my other daughter?" she asks.

"Oh, Maddie is having dinner with a... friend.", I tell her. She gets a twinkle in her eye, but Aldair looks murderous.

"What friend?", Aldair asks. "Please tell me my baby sister is out with some girls."

"No, actually, she's out with a lovely guy named Kenneth, and you, Aldair, will not ruin this for her.", I tell him pointedly.

He pouts at me. Pouts. It's kind of cute. Aldair has been an awesome big brother in my life. And he's super protective of both Maddie and me. It was cute when we were little girls, but not so much now. Especially since we know how many women he's snuck into the castle over the years.

"No, hello for your mate?" Kalan asks. He's seething and glaring at Trent like he's gum stuck to the bottom of his shoes.

"Hello, Kalan.", I say. "Mother, may I introduce Trenton Strong? He is next in line to the council seat representing Elementals. Trent, meet Trina, Queen of Elfame and Aldair second in line to the throne.", I say, ignoring the look of loathing Kalan is giving me.

"Your majesty," Trent bows. "It is a pleasure to meet you, but I think I should leave you to it.", He asks, "Do you need a ride to school tomorrow?"

"I think I am capable of getting *my mate* to school in the morning.", Kalan says.

"Trent, I would love a ride.", I counter. "Let me walk you out."

I make my excuses and follow Trent back out to his car. "Hey, are we ok?" I ask Trent.

"I don't know, Reegan. Your prince and his broth-er made it clear that they didn't want me near you. I may be an Elite, but I can't compete with a prince.", he says sadly. "I know we're mates. I can feel it in my soul, but I don't want to cause you any pain. I'm afraid if I stay in the picture, you'll be the one hurt."

"Wait a minute. It's not a competition. I won't lose you, Trent. I won't lose Kalan either, but if he wants to be a dick, he can take his ass back to Elfame until he sees reason. You are my mate as well, and that's that. I'll work it out.", I promise.

Trent goes to get in his car, but I forcefully grab him, turn him around, and kiss him. I kiss him until there can be no doubt of my feelings for him. I put all my hopes and promises in that kiss, and he returned it a hundred times stronger. He weaves one hand through my hair, and with the other, he grabs my ass and turns me until my back slams into the car. He lifts me so that my legs wrap around his waist. He doesn't release me for several moments, and he rests his forehead on mine when he does.

"I won't lose you either. I'll fight with all I am and all that I have for you, Beauty if that's what you want.", he says.

"I'll handle this. Pick me up in the morning?" I ask.

"Absolutely. I'll even bring more coffee and pastries.", he says with a smile.

"I look forward to it. I might like those pastries more than I like you", I tease with a wink. And with that, he kisses me once more and gets in his car to head home.

I get back to the sitting where everyone is still congregating. "Who wants to tell me what's going on? Kalan said he couldn't get away until the weekend."

Aldair looks at Rodriq as if trying to decide which one should speak. Decision made, Rodriq comes over and sits next to me. "I may have told Marcus about the sparring sessions this morning. We didn't realize how quickly your powers would manifest and grow. Since your mate bonds with Kalan, your powers are stronger. And with the manifestation of your spirit ability, we don't know what to expect, so we thought we'd call in backup. Aldair has enrolled in the academy and will help me to train you. As one of the strongest Fae, he can help you hone your elemental abilities. My job will be to draw out your other abilities, whatever they may be, and help you master them all."

"Uh, ok. What do you know about mate bonds? Besides that, they are very rare?" I ask, changing the subject.

Everyone looks at me with confusion, but Kalan looks at me with a bit of fear. I figure I should tell them what Maddie and I have learned. I guess one of my secrets is coming out now. I wish Maddie were here to offer me strength. As if I summoned her, she comes breezing into the room. She hugs her mother and Aldair but completely ignores Kalan, other than giving him a look that says she's going to kick his ass. She takes a seat on my other side.

"Trent called me." that's all she says, but I know she dropped her date to be here. "So, I heard talk of mate bonds."

"I was just getting ready to talk about that," I tell Maddie. She squeezes my hand and gives me a slight nod. "So, here's the thing. When I was twelve, I started having dreams. Not just dreams, but I could control someone else's dreams.", I begin. I see Kalan step forward to say something, but I stop him. "Let me finish, please. Anyway, I started dreaming. All my dreams took place at the waterfall. One night, A boy joined me in those dreams. I didn't know if I created him as part of my imagination because I was lonely or if it was something else. He started joining my dreams almost every night for two years. We talked about everything, including our future together. At some point, the dreams stopped. It took a little while, but I got over not seeing him every night, and then the dreams became a thing of the past. I chalked it up to the overactive imagination of a lonely child."

"What's this to do with mates?", Aldair asks. He looks like he's honestly curious.

"We were always taught that true mates didn't exist anymore, but I would've sworn that the boy from my dreams was just that. Then Kalan and I got together and found out we were true mates. When we were in town the first day we arrived, Maddie and I ran into a couple of guys at a food stand. One of those boys recognized me. I freaked out when I realized who it was and that the boy that had shown up in my dreams for those two years was real. But it wasn't just him. I had a weird feeling around the other boy, Trent, like my heart was calling out to him. I didn't know what to do with that, and I didn't want to hurt you." I direct that last sentiment to Kalan. "Maddie noticed something, so she started doing some research. I'll let her tell you what she discovered."

"Wait, can I interrupt quickly?', Aldair asks. When I give him the go-ahead, he says, "So, you can control dreams. Can we go back to that for a minute? Tell us how you came to discover that."

"The first time I controlled a dream was when I was twelve. Maddie was having some sort of nightmare. I don't remember what it was about, but I remember going to wake her. When I touched her, I was kind of sucked into her dream. I thought about how I wanted her to sleep peacefully, and then her dream changed to whatever I was thinking of. Honestly, I thought the dreams stopped altogether, but I had one on Saturday night."

"Back to the mate thing.", Maddie says, taking over the conversation. "I decided to research after noticing Reegan and Trent acting weird. I can't explain what it was, but I knew I had to find as much information as possible; what I found rocked me. So, while true mates are rare, they do happen, more so with strong supernatural females. The stronger the female, the more mates she can have. The feeling that Reegan has in her chest is fate trying to make the connection with her true mates. She wouldn't have noticed it with Kalan so much because they've known and been around each other their whole lives, but now that their bond has formed, fate wants to forge the others. As she takes a mate, her powers will get stronger, and she will likely take on aspects of her other mates like more strength, better hearing, and vision, etc."

"So, what effects did Kalan's mate bond have?", Aldair asks.

"I'm not entirely sure other than that her abilities seem stronger.", Rodriq replies.

"I think the mate bond with Kalan opened up my spirit ability. I used it today for the first time. I also think that my wind ability is twice as strong as it was.", I say. At that, I see Kalan puff his chest with pride. He comes toward me, but I make him stop. "I'm not done with you, Kalan. We have more to discuss in private.", To Alduir, I said, "And you, stay out of mine and Kalan's business. I love that you're here to support me, but don't get involved until you know both sides of a story." Aldair looks properly chastised, so I get up and hug him. "Thank you for caring.", I whisper to him. I go back and take my seat.

"So, Trent, the boy we just met, is one of your mates?" Alita asks me. She has a soft smile on her face.

"Yeah, he is. But we're taking things slowly. He has a bit of a reputation, so he wants me to be able to trust him.", I tell her. "And I'm pretty sure that Asher, the boy from my dreams, is also one of my mates, but he has a girlfriend, and we've stayed away from each other. He and I have many issues to work through, but I can't answer the questions he may ask because I don't trust the girl he's with. I don't trust him with my secrets so long as she's in the picture."

"Hmmm. What if you just got him alone for a bit and mated?", Aldair asks with a toothy smile.

"I won't force the bond on him or anyone, Aldair. He should have a choice in the matter. It's his life too.", I say to him. He is now laughing at me.

"You're too pure for your own damn good, princess.", he laughs.

"Not as pure as you think.", Kalan says under his breath. I look at him in horror. He did not just say that. Now everyone is laughing. I'm mortified. My face looks like a cherry. I try to hide, but Maddie won't let me.

"Ah, come on, sis. We knew it was only a matter of time before you and Kalan were going to get busy.", she laughs.

"Oh, my creator, please stop!" I shriek.

"Okay, enough children. I have to head back to Elfame tomorrow, so I'd like to have dinner with you all before. Any ideas?" Alita finally says, putting an end to my embarrassment.

"Ken told me about this amazing restaurant on the outskirts of town. We should check it out. I'll call him and have him meet us there.", Maddie says, smiling.

She takes off out of the room. Now I'm the one laughing at the horror on the boys' faces thinking about having to meet Maddie's guy and behave themselves. I get up to go freshen up while Alita makes us a reservation for dinner.

"Reegan, can we please talk?" Kalan asks me.

"Later. I'm not ready to talk to you yet.", I tell him.

I walk away. I go upstairs, change back into my dress, and fix my hair. I know it's a mess after sparring with Trent today. Once I do that, I refresh my mascara and lip gloss. My phone dings.

Trent: Everything ok? It was a little tense before I left.

Me: Yeah, it's good. I haven't talked to Kalan yet, but everything will be fine. We're getting ready to go for dinner. Oh, and thanks for calling my back-up.

Trent: I wish I could join you. I'm going to have dinner with the guys tonight. I'll see you in the morning, though—Goodnight. Sweetheart. XOXO

Me: XOXO

19

KALAN

Reegan looks beautiful as she storms out of the room. I seriously fucked up; I know. But I can't help it. Possessiveness is part of my nature as a Fae, and not only that but why should I have to share my mate? I had her first. I loved her first, dammit! Now, I'm told I have to share her, not with just one man, but possibly multiple others. This isn't fair. I know I sound like an ass. As I said, I can't help it. Let's just hope she forgives me.

"What's got you looking like you just sucked on a lemon?", Aldair asks.

"Nothing, man. Just...." I let the thought trail off.

"It sucks being in the doghouse, huh? It sucks to be you. And you won't be getting sucked anytime soon.", He laughs. As he heads out of the room, I grab a pillow from the bed and fling it onto his head. It hits its mark. "What the hell, bro? I'm going to tell Reegan you're being mean to me." he threatens and takes off.

I catch up to him right outside of Reegan's room. I tackle him as he goes to knock, and the door opens. All three of us end up in a heap on the floor.

"Reegan, Kalan is picking on me. Protect and save me, Princess." he whines pitifully while snorting to hold back his laughter.

"I'm sure whatever it is, you deserved it, Aldi.", she responds, using the nickname she called him as a child.

"Oh, that's it," he says, trying his damndest to keep a straight face.

He begins to tickle Reegan mercilessly. As she writhes on the floor trying to get him off her, I see a flash of pink panties that makes me drool. Aldair isn't letting up on the tickle war.

"Stop! I have to pee!" she screams.

When Aldair finally lets her up, she rises off the floor and turns toward the bathroom. The next thing I know, Aldair and I are both drenched from head to toe in the water.

"Reegan, dry us off this instant.", I say. She just laughs and walks away. From the security of the bathroom, I hear her laugh.

"Guess we better get dried off and changed or Mom is gonna have our hides.", Aldair says.

I had hoped I'd be sharing a room with Reegan, but I didn't want to push her too far. I need her forgiveness, not to piss her off even more. After getting dressed and ready to go, I head downstairs

to meet everyone. We should be leaving in just a few
minutes. Rodriq calls me over, and we walk outside
together.

"Look, I know this situation is tough, but you
must support Reegan. While you're getting pissy
about the possibility of sharing her, she's dealing
with years of spells to keep her powers and memories contained. She's dealing with being the key
to saving not only this world but all of them. She
needs to concentrate on that and grow into her
powers, whatever they are, not on her first love acting like a two-year-old that lost his favorite toy.",
he admonishes.

I know he makes a good point, and it's still hard
to reconcile the Reegan I understand to the one that
is meant to save the world. A week ago, she was
just the love of my life. Now she's the difference
between a bright future and one full of darkness.
I just hold my head down, knowing that Rodriq is
right, and I vow to myself and the Creator that I
will do better. Rodriq smacks me on the back, and
I get into the car. Everyone joins us, and within
minutes, we're headed to this restaurant that my
baby sister heard of from her... boyfriend? When
we arrive, Rodriq parks, and we head in. There's
a pretty little hostess standing at the front of the
restaurant waiting to seat patrons.

"Professor Rodriq, how nice to see you.", she says.
"Kenneth is already here waiting. Right, this way."

She leads us toward the middle of the restaurant to a table that could seat twelve. Maddie hurries to the guy's side and kisses him on the cheek as he pulls her chair out. He's an attractive guy. I'll give him that. He seems nerdy, but it's tough to tell with supernaturals. Reegan sits next to Maddie, allowing her to see the door and most of the restaurant. I accept the chair opposite her, and she frowns. The next thing I know, her face lights up. I look to where her gaze is drawn and see four guys enter. One of those guys is Trent. I wonder if one of them could be the *dream boy*.

"Excuse me for a minute. Kalan, if the waitress comes, could you order me a sweet tea with lemon and a glass of ice water, please?" she smiles and walks toward the guys.

She reaches the guy with ash blonde hair first. He looks pleased to see her as he kisses her on the cheek and gives her a hug that lifts her off the ground. She then looks at a big guy with ice-blue eyes. He looks murderous. Trent grabs her and kisses her. The fourth guy ignores her. He's the one that she met in her dreams. She talks to them for a minute and heads back, following them.

"Everyone, this is Asher, Jaymeson, and Bentley. You already met Trent. I thought they could join u s.", she says, pointing to each guy as she introduces them.

We all shift to make room for the new guys. I take a seat next to Reegan this time. We introduce ourselves to the newcomers, who seem intrigued that Rodriq would join us.

"Professor?" I think Jaymeson asks. "Didn't expect to see you here consorting with students."

"Oh, Rodriq and Reegan go way back.", Trent answers. "He's been her tutor for years."

Rodriq laughs, "Yes, I have."

A server comes to take our drink orders and hurries them to the back to fill them, giving us time to look over the menu. We all get into a conversation on Reegan's last week at the academy, and when we get to the part where she beat Trent's ass in the ring, I feel a swell of pride for my girl in my chest. These guys, surprisingly, don't seem too bad. Bentley doesn't seem to like Reegan and sneers at her a lot. It takes everything in me not to call him out on it, but if Reegan is willing to ignore it, so am I.

"This place is bustling. Shouldn't the waitress have come to take our orders already?" Maddie asks.

"This is pretty normal. It will probably be a few more minutes. I'll go to the back and see if I can rush them up a bit.", Trent says.

"Trent, can we talk for a minute?" I ask him.

"Sure.", he answers hesitantly. "Follow me."

Reegan looks like she's about to follow, but I stop her. "It's ok, love. We won't be too long. Sit and enjoy your time with your.... friends." I tell her. I give her a quick kiss before Trent and I head away.

We get to the back, and Trent directs me into an office. "Is it ok we're back here?" I ask him while looking around.

"Yeah, my mom owns this place.", Trent tells me.

To say I'm surprised is an understatement. With him being a council heir, I imagined his parents holding high-ranking jobs within the community. To each their own, though, right?

"So, um, what did you wanna talk about?" Trent asks as he takes a seat in what I'm assuming is mom's chair. He gestures for me to take the one on the side of the desk.

"Look, I just wanted to apologize for this afternoon. I was an asshole, and I shouldn't have been.", I say. "But I need you to understand that it's a hard situation to know that I'm not enough for Reegan."

"Did you ever consider that Reegan has so much love in her heart that she needs more people to share it with?" he asks me. He isn't being sarcastic. He's genuine, and it honestly makes me feel more ashamed of my behavior. "I'm not going to try to steal her from you, but I won't give her up either. I have liked her since I first saw her at the taco truck. If it makes you feel better, she and I decided to take

things slow and get to know each other. I have a bit
of reputation for breaking hearts and all that."

"That won't be an issue for Reegan. Before her, I
had my fair share of lovers. If she were bothered,
she would have left Elfame long ago." I tell him
seriously. "Anyway, I just wanted to say I was sorry
and see if we could work at being friends."

"Yeah, I think that would be cool. Have you
thought about whether there are others?"

"I haven't been able to think of much else since
she told me about the mate thing earlier. She's sure
Asher is one of her mates, but she says there are
complications."

"Oh yeah, only one. And it's huge. Her name is
Calista, and she's a royal bitch that thinks everything should be handed to her. She's been with Ash
for like two years. All the guys hate her, but he
doesn't seem to care. Reegan needs to tread care-
fully with that one. Her dad is dangerous as hell,
as is Asher's."

All I can do is grunt a response. At that moment,
the door opens, and a beautiful woman with jet
black hair and eyes walks in. "Trenton, what are
you doing here? Is everything alright?"

"Yeah, mom. Everything is fine. The guys and I
came in for dinner and ran into some other friends.
I was coming back to find you. We've been waiting
for a while, and no one has come to take orders. I
thought you might like to know you have royalty in

attendance tonight.", he says as he kisses her on the cheek.

"Oh my. Well, I'll have Pearl come out right now to take care of you all," she says as she scampers away.

I can't help but laugh as we make our way back to the table. Trent takes his seat, and I see him grab Reegan's hand and give it a light squeeze. Some have switched seats leaving one empty on Reegan's other side. I sit down and kiss Reegan to let her know everything is well.

20

REEGAN

If the waitress doesn't take our orders soon, my stomach will start eating on itself. Having the guys show up here seems to have been a good thing. Everyone seems to be in good spirits except for Bentley. *Grumpy bastard.* I ignore him the best I can by thinking about what Trent and Kalan could be talking about. While talking to Jaymeson about my assignment in Supernatural Politics, the boys show back up. Trent sits down, grabs my hand, and squeezes it while Kalan kisses me and sits.

"So, what did we miss?" Trent asks.

"We were discussing an assignment Prof. Morley gave me today. My grandfather feels I should participate in the debate the council holds before the trials. I have been given a speaking assignment, and the professor told me that you guys could be a great help.", I explain. "Jaymeson was just agreeing to help me."

"I'll help as much as I can.", Asher says but then goes back to talking to Aldair as if I'm not even in the room. Trent looks to Bentley, who in turn just scowls but grunts an approval.

"Awesome. We'll have to set up some study dates, and I'm sure Kalan, as the prince of Elfame, will also be a great help to you. We can even video call while he's back there.", Trent offers.

I smile at the guys in thanks. At this point, a couple of servers come over to the table. They're both gorgeous, but one of them is a little on the shy side. Aldair just stares at her while everyone else gives the menu one more look.

"What can I get you boys tonight?" one waitress asks the guys with a sultry voice.

It's like she's offering herself up to them instead of the food. Excuse me, but these boys won't be eating anyone except me. Wait, what? Where has this possessiveness come from? She goes around all the guys and flirts.

When she gets to Asher, she leans down and whispers in his ear loud enough for us all to hear, "If you want, I can be available for dessert." Oh, hell no! Kalan grabs my leg and squeezes it while Trent holds the other. That's the only thing that keeps me rooted to my seat.

While she continues to make googly eyes at him, the other girl comes over to take the orders on my side of the table. She is super sweet and courteous. "Pearl! You know this is my table. I'll take the orders." the other waitress says bitchily. I'm about fed up. That's when her eyes realize who is sitting at this table. "Oh, my Creator! You're the prince of Fae! Can I get your number? Maybe we can meet up later?" She asks lustily.

At this, even the guy's hands on my thighs can't keep me from jumping up from my seat. "Excuse me?" I ask. "Are you serious right now?"

"Yeah, why not?" She shrugs. "These guys are hot," she says with a smirk. This bitch must be daft. I'm about to jump over the table and rip her eyes out of her head.

"Is there a problem here, Juliet?" a middle-aged woman asks as she walks over to the table. She's beautiful, and she looks familiar. Juliet doesn't answer. "Juliet, I asked you a question."

"Nothing Reegan can't handle, mom.", Trent says from beside me. Oh shit. This beautiful woman is his mom. This is the first time she's ever seen me, and I just made an ass of myself. Could this night get any worse? "Reegan was just sending Juliet back to her station. We'd much prefer Pearl to handle our table." I try to hide behind Kalan, but he won't let me for some reason.

Trent grabs my hand and lifts me from my seat. "Mom, may I present Reegan Winthrope? Also, may I present Alita, queen of Elfame, and her children Maddie, Aldair, and Kalan.", he introduces.

"It is an honor to have you in my establishment. Anything you want, just let Pearl know." his mother gushes. She walks over to me and wraps me in a hug. "Now I know who the coffee and pastries were for. It's nice to meet and put a face to the woman that was able to beat my son in the ring. He's been undefeated there for years. It's about time he met his match, and a match you are."

We continue exchanging pleasantries while Pearl gets everyone's orders, and then Trent's mom, whom I learned is called Meredith, takes Pearl and our orders back to the kitchen. While we wait for our food to arrive, we all talk and joke, exchanging stories of life in Elfame and the human realm. When the food comes, conversation silences as we all dig into the best meal I think has ever graced my mouth. Once we are all stuffed, I am surprised when Bentley takes the check and refuses to let us pay. He leaves, telling the guys he has to get home. We all walk out, and Jaymeson gives me a big hug. Trent then takes my hand and leads me to the car.

He helps me in and kisses me. When the kiss ends, I notice Asher staring with a longing look. The look flashes away much too quickly for me to be sure. I let the feeling in my heart go and looked away from him. Once everyone is loaded, we head home. When we arrive, I give my goodnights and love to Alita since she'll be gone before we wake, and I head to my room.

I've just snuggled up in my covers when I hear a soft knock on my door. Kalan comes in a moment later and sits on the edge of the bed.

"Baby, I'm sorry. I am. I was an ass, and I should have talked to you before I let my temper get away with me. I apologized to Trent, and he does seem like a good guy. I support you, and I love you. If that means I have to share you, so be it. As long as I get a part of that big heart of yours, I can handle that.", he says lovingly.

I lean over and give him a small kiss. "You're forgiven.", I tell him.

I wrap my arms around his neck and kiss him again. This time he takes over and kisses me deeply. He runs his hands up and down my spine, eliciting shivers all over my body. I crawl into his lap and straddle him. I can feel his hardness between my thighs, and while I would love nothing more than for him to pound the shit out of me, I have other ideas. I drop to the floor on my knees and undo the snap of his jeans. I pull, and he lifts his hips to help me remove his pants and boxers. I grab his cock in my hand. The skin is so soft, and I can see a drop of precum beading on the tip. I lean down and lick it off him. He tastes salty and a little sour, but I like the taste. I lick him from base to tip, circling my tongue around the end as I pump him with my hand.

I close my eyes and take him into my mouth as far as I can. I have to use my hand at the base, he's so long, and I don't want to gag. I bob up and down, making sure the flat of my tongue runs up the underside of his cock. Kalan gently wraps my long hair around his fist to keep it out of my face. I look up at him from under my eyelashes and see him, eyes closed with a look of pure ecstasy on his face.

"Yes, baby. Right there." he groans. Before long, he grabs my head to hold me steadily as he fucks my mouth. I hollow out my cheeks and take him as far as I can. He proves me wrong when I think I can't take any more of his length. The noises he makes have me so wet, I'm dripping. I can feel him tensing and know he's about to cum. "Move, Reegan. I don't want to come in your mouth. I want that pussy."

I do as I'm told and lift my mouth off his cock. He stands, pulling me with him. He slowly removes my clothes like he's unwrapping a precious gift. When my bra hits the floor, he takes one nipple into his mouth and sucks. He then kisses my breast and nibbles on the flesh. I'm a writhing mess, and my legs try to give out on me. He picks me up and throws me on the bed. I let out a squeak.

"Get on your hands and knees, ass in the air for me, baby." Once I'm in the position, he tells me, "Grab the headboard and don't let go.

Again, I do as I'm told. I can feel him moving around behind me. He enters me with one thrust. I cry out in surprise and pleasure, feeling so full. He begins to drive hard and fast. I can feel his balls hitting my clit in this position, and it feels so good. He pounds into me repeatedly. I come, screaming his name, and he follows with three more pumps of his hips. We both collapse into a boneless mess. It takes forever for me to come down from this high.

"Mm, makeup sex is the best sex.", he laughs. I giggle with him, trying to keep my eyes open. Kalan notices and tells me, "Get some sleep, baby. Your alarm is set, and I'll ensure you get up in the morning." I'm asleep before the final words leave his mouth.

21

REEGAN

I wake up the following day to my alarm blaring Demi Lovato's, *Confident*. Kalan is still sleeping beside me. I get up gingerly so I don't wake him and make my way to the shower. After cleaning the mess Kalan made me last night, I plug in the hairdryer. I look in the mirror and notice a hickey on my breast. *Seriously. He fucking marked me!* I'm mad but also find the mark hot in a way. At least it's in an area no one will see.

I blow out my hair, do my makeup, and get dressed. Today I go for a more casual look of black yoga pants and an oversized beige sweater. I feel pretty but understated. When I leave the bathroom, I notice that the bed is empty. Kalan must have gone down for coffee. I search for him and find him in the kitchen with Aldair and Trent. When Kalan looks at me, I can't help but blush. I feel like everyone can look at me and see exactly how our night ended.

"Good morning, baby. Trent brought you coffee and a cinnamon roll.", Kalan says as he kisses me. He keeps it short, which I'm honestly thankful for. To Trent, he says, "Dude, your mom's cooking seriously rocks."

I take a drink of this life-giving elixir and moan my approval. "Kalan's right. It is amazing."

"Man, why didn't you bring me any?", Aldair whines. "I'm the pretty one."

"Yeah, you aren't my type, though, sweetheart. You might have better luck with Bent.", Trent says.

"Yeah, you aren't my type either though I don't mind a little swordplay every once in a while, but that waitress last night, damn. Could you get me her number?", Aldair asks seriously.

"You can't be serious, bro. Did you not notice that Reegan was about to kick her ass last night, and you want to fuck her?" Kalan asks.

"Not that whore. The other one. The quiet one. Pearl, I think.", Aldair answers.

"Nah, man, I don't mess with my mom's employees like that.", Trent says. "Besides, she goes to school at the academy. You can just ask her yourself.

"Wait, go back. The rumors are true. Bent is gay?" I ask. Why does that thought seriously disappoint me?

"No, Creator, no. He's bisexual. You know we don't live by the same constraints as humans, and it's in his demon nature anyway.", Trent tries to explain. Of course, I know that we don't constrain ourselves, but Bentley comes across as too manly. "He doesn't talk about it much, but his dad was an Incubus. He kind of picked up some of those traits."

Well then. That's news to me. Maybe that's why I'm so drawn to him. I don't want to think he could be one of my mates. He hates me far too much for that. I can just see how that will work out. I have enough on my plate without worrying about constant fights with him.

"And on that note, it's time for you to leave for school. Have a good day, baby. I'll see you this af ternoon.", Kalan tells me as he ushers us out.

I'm pleasantly surprised to see Trent has his car today. I learned his car is a Bugatti, one of the most expensive on the market. I was shocked to discover that his family is wealthy, beyond rich. His mom owns and operates the restaurant as a passion project. Twice a week, they feed the homeless humans in the city, not leftovers or cheap things like grilled cheese and soup, but expensive meals. Trent helps when he can. When he doesn't have other business or homework to attend to, he spends the time helping me study. The more I learn about him, the more I like him. He even asks me to come with him the next time he goes to serve food. Humans don't know about the supernatural anymore, but

the good ones among us try to make life a little
better for them.

School goes by quickly, and Asher is absent from
lunch. Jaymeson joked that he was probably off
with Calista getting his dick sucked. I almost puked
after hearing that, and the food in my stomach felt
like lead for the rest of the day. Aldair found Pearl,
so they had lunch together. We planned to have our
first study session on Sunday evening after our
outing, which Trent still won't give me any clues
about. When school finally ends for the day, Trent
takes me home, and I ask him to stay and hang out.
He agrees, and he, Kalan, and I go swimming in
the pool. Thank goodness it's heated because September in Tennessee is chilly. We all splash around,
having a good time. The cook makes us up some
snacks and brings them out to the patio along with
some drinks. The guys jump out and head over to
grab a beer while I swim a couple of laps on my
own. I get out and saunter over to Trent and grab a
towel.

"Damn, Beauty. You wet in that bikini will be
running through my dreams tonight for sure.", he
tells me as he wraps me up.

He dries me off and then helps me into a robe.
He takes his seat and pulls me into his lap. His
fingers skim my skin beneath my robe, and I'm
now shivering for reasons other than being cold.

"I'll give you guys a bit to be alone.", Kalan says.

"You don't have to. You can stay and hang out.", Trent tells him.

"Nah, I'm good, man. I'm going to go put on some dry clothes and call dad.", Kalan says. He fist-bumps Trent as he walks by. I snuggle deeper into Trent's hold and relax.

"Should I go? I know you only have the week with Kalan, and I don't want to intrude on that." Trent sighs.

"No. I'll have time with him tonight. Right now, I'm enjoying being in your arms.", I say

"Really? I can think of other things we could do.", he responds

"I bet you could, Trent, but we're taking things slow, remember." I laugh

He groans, "I know. I know. But when you're sitting here and smelling so good, I can't help myself. It's hard to hold back."

I get up from his lap and sit next to him instead. He pouts at me like a little boy, but I don't want him to be uncomfortable. It's also hard to hold myself back when this pesky feeling in my chest won't ease up.

"Look, I know this is hard for you. You're used to girls being ready and willing. I'm willing, Trent, but I'm not ready. I need to know with certainty that I can trust you. There are so many things I want to tell you that I can't, and I won't make the bond concrete until I know for certain I can trust you with everything.", I tell him quietly.

"Beauty, it's fine. I know. I want to know everything about you, but I know you aren't ready to share that with me. Just know, I'm not going anywhere, and I'll be here when you are ready.", he tells me.

He's so genuine that it's hard not to blurt it out to him right now. But I can't. As much as I want to, I know it's not the right time. I need to know he doesn't just want to be with me because I'm a Winthrope or because of the bond. I need to know he truly likes me.

We sit there until the sun goes down, talking and being together. I learn so much about him that it begins to feel like we've known each other forever, but the conversation is one-sided. I don't have anything but shoddy memories from before I was five, and I have many blank spots. It's like I'm in that movie where they use a neurolizer on witnesses to keep the aliens a secret.

Kalan comes back out as we're getting ready to head in, and I stop in my tracks at the look on his face. "I have to go back to Elfame.", he tells me.

"What? When?" I ask him.

"Tonight. Now. I've been summoned. Something about the King of the Unseelie Fae requesting a meeting with dad and me: Dad tried to postpone, but Belfour wasn't willing. I am so sorry, baby. I'll be back as soon as I can. I love you.", he says as he packs his bags.

We say our goodbyes, and he leaves with Rodriq to the portal. Trent goes soon after with a promise to pick me up for classes in the morning. With nothing else to do, I make my way upstairs and pull out my Kindle. I find a rom-com to read for the night. I snuggle into my blankets and lay there for a while, just reading. I don't know when I fell asleep, but I can tell I'm in a dream when I open my eyes. Well, more so a memory since I'm a little girl again. I don't know where I am, but I can hear mommy and daddy frantically trying to find me.

"Winnie, where are you, baby girl? Please come out for daddy." I hear, but I can't see him. I'm in a beautiful meadow surrounded by orchids in every color of the rainbow. "Reegan Esmerelda Winthrope, get your butt out here right now, young lady." Daddy sounds mad.

I look around and see a beautiful woman with blue hair approaching me. When she gets closer, I realize she also has eyes like sapphires. It's almost like I'm looking in the mirror except for the hair color.

"Reegan?" she asks, looking directly at me. "You must remember."

"Remember what? Where am I? Who are you?" I ask her.

"You are in purgatory where you used to come and play when you were a small child. You always loved the orchids. I am Neveah. I am the original weaver. I am here because I need you to remember everything. Your childhood, your powers, all of it."

"All my powers haven't manifested yet.", I try to tell her.

"Oh, sweet child. You were born with your powers. I instructed your parents to mask them, and the same with Marcus when your parents disappeared. You weren't ready for them. Now you have to be. You are in danger. I don't know where the threat comes from, but I feel it."

"Yeah, from Lilith. I am supposed to restore balance; if I don't, it will all burn."

"Lilith isn't the threat yet. This is more closely tied to you and the academy.", she says.

With that, she lays her hand on my cheek, whispers, "Remember." and then disappears.

I can't think of anything but what she said about my parents. She said they had disappeared, but that's not right. They were murdered. I was there. "Remember.", I repeat to myself over and over. And then I do remember everything.

22

REEGAN

I wake up in a sweaty mess when my alarm goes off and I burst into tears. The memories keep flashing in my mind. I remember what my parents look like. I remember their smiles and love for me. They'd do anything to protect me. I also remember the night they were taken from me. Neveah didn't lie. My parents weren't killed that night, at least I don't think so. When Marcus got there, they were just gone. I remember him putting me in his car and taking me away from the beautiful house I loved. I remember the tire swing dad hung in the old oak tree in the backyard. I even remember the stuffed unicorn I refused to sleep without. There are so many memories. Marcus locked them all away in my mind so I wouldn't remember. I feel so betrayed.

The memory I keep holding onto is the little boy with ice-blue eyes I used to play with. He was older than me, but we were friends. *Bentley and I were friends.* With that realization comes another. It's no wonder he hates me. I remember that night so clearly now. I don't want to relive it, but I think I have to. Mom and dad were arguing. The Morleys were the historians for the supernatural council, and they had discovered the prophecy and what I am. The night my parents disappeared, Bentley's parents were allegedly killed. My parents had put them in danger to protect me. I had put them in danger. My existence put them in danger. My parents had received the call an hour earlier about Mr. and Mrs. Morley's deaths. They were terrified because my powers were so strong. More potent than they thought they should be, they needed to hide me. Mom had called Marcus and made me believe we were playing a game of hide and seek.

I had just gotten myself sealed into my hiding spot when I heard a loud bang like the front door had blown up. I listen to mom's screams as she's dragged up the stairs. I can't hear dad anywhere.

"Just tell me where she is, Esme.", I hear a man say. I don't recognize his voice, but it's one I'll never forget.

"Go to hell, *Councilman*.", mom hisses at him. "You will never get your hands on her."

"Oh, I will, Esme. I will. And when I do, I'll knock Marcus off the council throne and take over. Supernatural will answer to me and only me.", the man says. Then I hear a smack.

"You think so highly of yourself, don't you? The Weaver can't be controlled, and her job isn't to work for you. She will rule, and she'll keep Lilith locked up where she belongs.", mom says.

"We shall see.", the man responds.

After that, I hear a pop. I realize now it was a gunshot. I then hear footsteps rush down the stairs, and all goes silent. I don't know how long I lay there before I fell asleep. The next thing I remember is Marcus getting me out of my hiding spot and taking me away. He never mentioned that night to me, and I never asked. I just lay in my bed crying for the loss of my what? My parents? My childhood? It's just too much. I don't know how long I'm stuck in this crying fit, but eventually, the sobs stop, and while the tears keep coming, they are silent. I'm lost in my memories. So lost that I don't hear my bedroom door open or someone enter.

"Beauty. Maddie says you hadn't come down yet. Is everything ok? Trent asks. I can hear him coming around the bed to face me. "Beauty? Shit, what's wrong?" he is now on his knees, looking at me. "Tell me why you're crying?" he asks.

"I...... I can't." I start sobbing again. "It's too much." He climbs up on the bed and draws me into his arms. He doesn't ask any more questions. He just holds me. "I need Kalan." I can feel him tense. I can't even be bothered that I just hurt his feelings like he isn't enough, but Kalan has been there since the beginning.

"What the actual fuck." I hear him breathe. I think he's pissed off at me until I hear his following comment, "Beauty, are we in Elfame?"

I jolt up and force my eyes open. We are, in fact, in Elfame. "Holy shit!" I exclaim. I take off out the door to find Kalan, Trent on my heels.

"Beauty, tell me what's going on. How are we here?" Trent yells from behind me.

I run around a corner and smack into a hard chest. Hands reach out to grab me. I look into the eyes of the only dad I've ever really known. The sobs come again. Dain hugs me tight to his chest.

"What are you doing here, sweetheart? What's going on?" Dain asks with concern.

Right then, Trent rounds the corner. Dain looks at Trent, then at the tears streaming down my face, and a look of pure rage takes him over.

"Stop. I'm not upset at Trent. Where's Kalan? We all need to talk.", I tell Dain, hugging him close to me.

"You're damn right we do. Reegan, how did we get here without a portal?" Trent asks.

"What did you just say?" Dain asks. A servant is coming down the hall but freezes when she sees us. "Please tell Kalan I need to see him. It's urgent. We'll be in the library.", he tells her. She hauls ass to do as she was bid.

Dain takes off toward the library, and we follow. He offers us a drink, which I gladly accept. This is going to take some liquid courage. It's only moments before Kalan shows up and notices me sitting there.

"Baby, I just left last night. Did you miss me so much you skipped out on classes?" he jokes with a smile. That smile quickly dissolves when he gets a good look at my face. "What the hell is going on here?"

"Kalan, calm yourself and let Reegan speak. If I'm correct in my thinking, she has a lot to tell us.", Dain rebukes.

Kalan comes over and takes a seat beside me. He patiently waits for me to get my jumbled thoughts together.

"I had a dream. This one was different. I met the original Weaver. I know how that sounds, but it's true. Anyway, she told me I had to remember. She said I was in danger and had to remember to protect myself. And just like that, it was like a dam burst open, and I could remember everything.", I say, looking at Dain.

"That still doesn't explain how we ended up here, Beauty.", Trent says matter of factly.

"What do you mean, ended up here? You came through a portal, dumbass.", Kalan says, defending me.

"We didn't. One minute we were in Reegan's room, and the next we were here.", Trent responds.

"I guess with the memories came my powers. Marcus had hidden my memories and powers with some spell to protect me.", I tell them. "Look, Trent, I shouldn't be saying any of this in front of you. I should have tried to prevent teleporting. We aren't mated, and I need to know I can trust you. If you tell anyone, it puts me in more danger and you and the guys by association."

"You left out the yet in that comment, Beauty. We aren't mated yet. And you can trust me. I'd never do anything to harm you or my brothers.", Trent tells me. I can see the look in his eyes. He's offended that I would even think such a thing.

"So, what other powers do you have?" Kalan asks.

"Honestly, I'm not entirely sure. I remember some, but the prophecy was lost the night Marcus rescued me. Dain, is there any way my parents survived that night? Neveah said they disappeared."

"Why would your grandfather lie about something like that?" Dane asks. I watch his eyes shift. He can't meet my gaze.

"Dain spill it. You know something, and I deserve to know what. They're my parents!" I scream at him.

"I can't. I physically can't. I made a blood oath all those years ago. The only one that can answer those questions is Marcus.", he states sadly.

"That's answer enough. That son of a bitch has been lying to me my whole life. Not anymore. I am going to string him up and get answers.", I say vehemently. "Dain, can I speak to Kalan and Trent alone, please? I need to tell them more, but I'm sure you already know."

"Sure, sweetheart. Take the day, and then I expect you back at that academy tomorrow.", he orders as he comes to hug me. "Never doubt that you are my child, Reegan. In all the ways that matter, you are mine and Alita's child, and we love you.", he says to me where only I can hear. With that, he heads out.

The boys look at me expectantly. I know they're waiting on an explanation, but I don't want to have the rest of this conversation here where anyone can hear us. "Let's take a walk?" I ask them. They nod. Kalan gets up and leads the way. He knows where we're headed. It was always my special place. Trent holds my hand as we walk through the property toward my favorite place. When we reach our destination, I walk over to the cave and place my hand down on the ground. Within seconds moss shoots up from the stone, creating a seating area. I take a seat close to the rock wall. It's smooth and chilled, but it's comfortable. I can feel the magic surrounding this area and know it's safe.

"Wow, this place is amazing!" Trent exclaims as he looks around.

"Thank you. It's mine.", I tell him with pride.

"I'd claim this place as well if I lived here. It seems super peaceful."

"No. I didn't claim it. Well, I did, but I created it."

"What? That's not possible.", Trent eventually says, looking at Kalan for confirmation.

"She did. I remember that day. Reegan always liked the beach, but she kept saying something about missing home and the mountains. She and Maddie joked about a rainbow waterfall with a pink pool at the bottom and a cave where they could hide from doing their chores. The next thing we know, this massive mountain rose with all the details the girls talked about.", Kalan laughs. "Marcus had to wipe everyone's memories so they would think the mountain had always been there. He was pissed because he realized that his spells to dampen Reegan had not worked. To you, it just feels like extra magic floating around, but those of us who know Reegan well can tell it's her magic that keeps this place here."

"So, I was right the other day when I said you were badass.", Trent jokes. That brings a slight smile, but knowing what I have to share next keeps it in check.

"I knew Bentley when we were kids. We were friends. He was older, but I remember his parents coming to our house. He would push me on the tire swing. I'm the reason his parents were killed. But, if my parents disappeared, I wonder if that could be the case with his as well.". I tell them.

"Magic identified the bodies, Beauty. His parents are gone, and you were just a little girl. It wasn't your fault.", Trent says.

"Tell that to Bentley. He told me it was my fault. There's something else. The night my parents disappeared, the man that broke into our home was a councilman.", I tell Kalan. "If a spell identified the bodies of Bentley's parents, is it possible they had cast some sort of spell that made the bodies seem like theirs?" I say, thinking aloud. "Trent, do you know the details of that night? I know you were young."

"No, all I remember is us guys having a sleepover at my house when we got the news. My mom might know, though, or maybe Professor Morley.", he muses. "I know Bentley's never been the same, but he doesn't talk about that night, and we never push him to."

"I want to go back to what you said about a councilman. Did you know him?" Kalan asks.

"No, I never saw him from my hiding place, but I remember his voice.", I say. "I'm done remembering today."

Trent gets up and comes over. He squeezes himself in behind me and wraps me in his arms. As he rubs tiny circles up and down my arms, I relax. He kisses me behind my ear, and I can't help but tilt my head to give him access to my neck. He trails kisses all up and down the side of my neck. His hand leaves my arms and begins kneading my breasts. My eyes meet Kalan's, and I see the hunger shining through.

I close my eyes and concentrate on the sensations running through my body from Trent's touch. "Let me make you feel good, Beauty."

I can't answer with words, so I nod. He rises and lifts me. He carries me over and places me between Kalan's legs. He grips my night shorts and begins drawing them down my legs. While he does that, Kalan lifts my shirt over my head. He then unsnaps my bra and pulls it from my arms. Trent meets Kalan's gaze, and when he gets a nod of approval, he leans in and takes a nipple into his mouth. He suckles it as Kalan kisses down my neck and kneads the other breast. Trent kisses down my chest and stomach, stopping to pay attention to my belly button. He grabs my thighs and pulls me down a little so he can lift my hips. He lays on his belly and wraps his muscular arm over my hips to keep me in place. He takes his finger and runs it through my folds. My hips buck, but he holds me in place. He continues to tease me, never touching me where I need him.

"You're so wet, Beauty. It's the most beautiful th ing.", he says in awe.

"Stop teasing me, Trent.", I say.

As soon as the words leave my mouth, he wraps his lips around my clit and sucks. *Oh, creator!!!* He sucks and licks at my clit like it's an ice cream cone. Then he moves to lick up and down my folds. He repeatedly spears me with his tongue, and when I think it's not enough, he inserts two fingers into my pussy and curves them, hitting that bundle of nerves that takes me over the edge. Even when I orgasmed, he didn't relent. He continues for what feels like hours. I cum repeatedly until I can no longer move. I'm entirely listless and sated, and whatever other words describe it. More than that, though, I'm happy. Being between these two men and having their sole attention on me is Heaven. I can feel Kalan's bulge pressing against me and see Trent straining against his jeans. I want nothing more than to take care of them both.

"No love. I can see those thoughts running through your mind. This was about you. We'll take care of ourselves later.", Kalan tells me. "Let's rest a few minutes and then show Trent Elfame.", Kalan suggests.

We spend the rest of the day frolicking around Elfame. We play in the ocean, and Trent collects the most beautiful shells. We shop in town, ending quickly when the females refuse to stop flirting with my men. Margo treats us to a delicious dinner which Trent declares is even better than his mom's cooking. When the day ends, Trent and I take the portal back to Earth, so we don't draw too much attention. Trent's phone begins to go off as soon as we make it to the other side.

"Shit. I have like twenty messages from the guys and a voicemail from my mom.", Trent says. "I need to call them back."

"Go ahead. I'll make sure your phone is spelled so you can receive calls and messages in the future.", I say.

While he calls his mom and the guys, I order a car to take us back to my house. When the vehicle arrives, we hop in. Once back at the house, Trent has to leave to head home himself. He kisses me deeply and tells me he must take care of his blue balls. I laugh at him. I feel like I'm always smiling and laughing when we're together. I see why he will make a good mate. While Kalan is my rock, my ground, Trent is the fresh air I need to survive in my life's messed-up chaos.

23

TRENT

The guys are pissed when I get home. Mom wasn't thrilled either, but I explained that Reegan needed me, which seemed to nullify her a little. It helped that I promised to bring her by for dinner one night next week. I haven't gotten through the door before Asher is in my face.

"Where the hell have you been, man? We've been worried sick," he spits.

"Reegan needed me. She's going through some stuff, and I wasn't going to leave her alone." I explain.

"So, that means you have to disappear. No one knew where you were. You didn't respond to any of us. Maddie and Aldair were searching for Reegan all damn day.", Bentley says.

"We were fine. She just needed to get away for a bit.", I tell them.

"So, you needed to get your dick wet and couldn't tell your brothers that?" Asher seethes.

"Careful, Ash. You sound a little jealous over there, and you Bentley, get off your high horse. Either fix whatever issues you have with her or get the fuck over it!" I say.

"She's going to be the end of us.", Bentley says quietly.

Jaymeson has been quiet up to this point. As he watches from his perch on the sofa, I don't know what he thinks, ever the papa bear to us all. I walk away before I do something I'll regret, like punch the big bastard in the nose. I make my way to my room. I can still taste Reegan on my tongue, and I refuse to let the two assholes ruin what we shared today. I don't know why I initiated oral sex with her, but once I tasted Reegan, I knew I could live off eating her for the rest of my life.

There's so much about her that I love. *Wait. Love?* I can't love her already, can I? It has to be the mate bond I'm feeling. I know there are other things she needs to tell me, but my heart swells when I think of how much trust she has in me that she would share even a few of her secrets. I still don't know what a *Weaver* is, but I'll ask Reegan about that later. Right now, I want to jump in the shower and jerk off until I get rid of this buildup. I hear a knock on the door. I guess my shower will have to wait.

"Hey man.", Jaymeson says as he enters.

"Hey.", I respond. "If you're here to give me shit, you can forget it. It won't change anything. I don't regret being with Reegan today."

"I wouldn't either. I had a question.", he says. I wait for a minute for him to ask. "I don't know how to breach this subject, but what would you say if I told you I think Reegan is my mate too?"

"There wouldn't be anything to say. Better you, my brother, than some outsider I don't know.", I tell him. "Besides, I figured there'd be more than Kalan and me."

"I don't know what to do, man. My wolf constantly howls at me to claim her, but I can't. I'm afraid she'll deny me. What happens if she denies me?" he asks in a panic.

"Dude, chill. Reegan would never deny you, but I'd take things slow. Let her get to know you and your wolf first before you breach the topic of mates. She doesn't trust easily, and she has secrets, man.", I explain.

"I take it you know some of those secrets.", he says matter-of-factly.

"Yeah, I do, but I won't share them. They're her secrets, dude.", I tell him.

He nods, "I understand, and I would never betray her trust by expecting you to. So, take things slow. Let's hope my wolf is on par with that idea, or I'm fucked because I don't know what he'll do."

"I'm going to take a shower and crash, bro. I'm wiped.", I tell him.

"Hmmm. Make sure you brush your teeth. I can smell her on you. I hope you had fun today, man. And I'm glad you were there for her." he laughs as he exits.

I can't help but laugh as well. No wonder Asher was crazed. If Jaymes' wolf can scent her, Ash's dragon can. I bet he's giving him hell. I find myself laughing again as I make my way into the shower. The hot water flowing over me relaxes my muscles, and the sound of the shower spray helps me think. The main thought running through my mind is that I have jerked off too much to a certain sapphire-eyed girl. *Take things slowly,* I tell myself. But damn, I'm not a saint. I need to be between her legs like I need my next breath. My cock jumps at the thought. *Yeah, buddy, we're on the same page.* My cock jumps again like it's some sentient being that fully understands my words.

I grip my shaft and squeeze, trying to ease some of the pain from being hard for several hours; no little blue pill is needed. All I need, is amethyst hair and the most gorgeous blue eyes I've ever seen. I was so caught up in the moment earlier that I didn't fully take in her body. When the pain gets to be too much, I begin to stroke. It isn't long before I come. I'm like a prepubescent kid. My dick only softens a fraction, so I turn the spray to cold.

This isn't helping either, so I start thinking mundane thoughts like sports statistics. When that doesn't work, I think about dad and mom and the noises that come from their room when I stay there. Yep, that'll do it. I go flaccid quickly. Now maybe I can go to sleep. I don't even search for clothes. I just climb into bed naked. I watch some TikTok videos on my phone. Humans do the funniest things.

The rest of the week flies by. I spend what time I'm not in a class with my girl. We talk, and she tells me more and more of her secrets. I learned more about the weaver and am thrilled with how our relationship is building. Jaymeson comes to hang out a couple of times; he and Reegan seem to have hit it off. Bentley remains his crabby self, and Asher opts to spend all his days and nights with Calista.

I'm not sure what's going on there, but something's fishy. He doesn't talk to any of us. He has lunch away from the dining hall. We get quick texts about where he is, and that's it. I can see the toll it's taking on Reegan. She hates that he is ignoring her. She filled me in on their history. I still can't wrap my head around everything she can do, but the more I learn, the more enamored I am.

Wednesday night, we have dinner with Maddie and Kenneth. Conversation flows as Maddie regales us with stories of her and Reegan's childhood.

We avoid the topic of Reegan's past and what she is. It's been a well-guarded secret. Reegan didn't even know until they came here for the academy.

Marcus calls and says he'll be gone another week which seriously irritates the hell out of Reegan. She wants answers. As I hold her at night, she tells me what she remembers of her and Bentley's parents. She talks about how Bentley was back then, and we both say how much we wished he'd open up about everything he keeps so tightly held inside himself. Reegan spells my phone so that it will work any-where within the realms, citing that if I'm to be her mate, I need to be able to communicate no matter where I am. Nights are spent watching Netflix. Reegan likes the shows *Lucifer* and *The Walking Dead.* Zombies aren't real, but it's a fun show, and while I don't see Lucifer as a bar owner when he walked the earth, who knows what that man got up to.

Saturday rolled around, and we planned to go to the amusement park, but it decided to rain, so those plans got canceled. Reegan invites everyone to her house for a little get-together. She wanted to plan a full menu of stuff for everyone, but I talked her into ordering some pizzas and Chinese food to keep things simple. We take off to the store for drinks and snacks. She and I peruse the aisles, deciding what to get. She wants to make a good impression, and I love her for that, but I tell her the guys are simple.

"Get some chips and dip, and we'll grab some cheese and crackers. It doesn't have to be fancy, Beauty. No one will care."

"If you say so. But if this turns out bad, I'm blaming you.", she says.

"Please. We're guys. Give us hot girls, video games, and beer. That's the extent of things to make us happy.", I tease.

I kiss her and take over the shopping. We end up leaving the store with every different flavor of potato chip available, some chunks of cheese with meats and crackers, and beer for the guys. Reegan opted for wine coolers for the girls. We get back just before everyone shows up. Jaymeson has his arms laden down with video games and consoles. Maddie points him in the direction of the game room. We all follow. Reegan and I get to work setting up the food and drinks. I'm floored when I finally take a second to look around the room. So is Jaymes.

"This may be the biggest television I've ever seen. Can I move in?" he asks Reegan. Reegan giggles, but I see a slight blush take over their faces. "Alright, the systems are hooked up. Reegan, do you want to choose the game?" he asks her.

"No, I've never played before. I wouldn't know what to do. You guys go ahead.", she answers.

"You've never played? I could teach you if you want.", he says shyly.

"Maybe another time. You guys play. I want to see Trent kick all your asses.", she laughs.

"I'll take that bet.", Asher tells her with a challenge in his eyes. "Winner gets a lap dance."

"What?" she asks. Asher hasn't said one word to her all week, and now he wants to bet a lap dance. *Fucker.* I guess I better kick some serious ass because I can see that while Reegan is confused, she isn't going to back down, either. "Oh, Ash. You're on. If Trent wins, you give me a lap dance."

"And if Trent loses, you give me one.", he says haughtily. "Anyone else wanting in on this?"

Everyone shakes their heads. No one wants any part of this, and I'm pretty sure I could get a lap dance anytime I like. We all grab a drink and take seats around the room. Maddie snuggles on a loveseat with Kenneth. Sam and Mitchell take a seat side by side on the floor. The guys all take seats on the sofa. The only seat left is the oversized chair. I sit down, and Reegan goes to sit on the floor between my legs. Instead, I pull her into my lap.

"Sit your tight ass down right here, Beauty. You're going to be my good luck charm."

Jaymeson puts in Call of Duty and sets up a free-for-all match with a 30-minute limit. The player with the best score at the end of that time wins. Aldair saunters in and takes a seat. As we start playing, it's clear that we're all competitive as hell. The others start cheering us on like this is a spectator sport. Reegan keeps looking at my score and cringing. I'm seriously getting my ass beat. It probably wasn't the best idea to have her warm ass sitting on my crotch while I needed to concentrate. When the time limit is up, I am the clear loser, and Asher beats us all.

"So, Reegan, about that lap dance.", he starts. I look at Reegan and see the fire in her eyes. While she's not happy, she plans to follow through.

"The stereo is in the corner. Pick a song.", she tells him with her head held high. She makes her way over to him and straddles his lap. He leans in and whispers, but we can all hear him.

"Oh no, baby. I don't want it right now. I want a private lap dance later.", he says with a smug smile.

I'm ready to pummel his ass as I watch Reegan shiver. I can't see her face to know if that shiver is fear or something else.

"Fine. Whatever. A bet's a bet, right?" she says as she gets up and returns to me.

"Alright. Trent and Bentley, you're out. Let's get Kenneth and Mitchell in and see if they can do any better than these assholes.", Jaymeson says. They switch places. Reegan excuses herself to order dinner.

"Aldair, take my place, man. I got to piss.", Bentley says.

He gets up and leaves the room. I sit there watching the guys play. I look at Asher repeatedly and see a secret smile on his lips. What's he up to?

24

REEGAN

I go to the kitchen and pull out the menus to order dinner. Instead of doing Chinese, I decided just to do pizza with breadsticks. It's easier than trying to take individual orders from everyone. Once the order is placed, I sit at the bar and nurse a bottle of water. While I'm sitting there, Bentley comes in.

"Um, could I get a bottle of water?" he asks.

"Sure. Help yourself." I motion toward the fridge.

"Thanks.", he says, exiting the way he came.

Half an hour later, the food arrives, and we all dig in. After we're all stuffed, the guys play one more game before we decide to watch a movie. We pile pillows onto the floor, and everyone settles in. Asher takes the chair Trent vacated as he and Jaymeson join me on the sofa. I curl myself into Trent with my legs bent and my feet resting on Jaymeson's lap. Maddie and Kenneth remain on the loveseat, but she covers their laps with a blanket. Bentley gets the movie started. After a few minutes, Maddie gets up.

"Does anybody need anything?" she asks us all.

"Popcorn?" Kenneth asks.

"With Reese Pieces!" Ash and I say at the same time. When I look over at him, he's smiling and winks at me.

"Well, I'll be damned. You remembered." Asher says with a laugh.

"I haven't eaten it any other way since you told me about it.", I tell him.

"I thought you two just met when you started the academy.", Kenneth says, confused.

"It's complicated.", I say and look away.

"It doesn't have to be.", Ash mumbles.

My heart fractures a little at his comment. No, it doesn't have to be, but I can't have him how I want, how I'm meant to, so why should I share anything with him? And the fact is, it is complicated. My whole life is. I don't know that there will ever be a time again that won't be. Maddie comes back with the cook in tow. Popcorn is spread around, but I realize Maddie only made one bowl with Reese's.

"Jaymeson and Asher will have to switch places if you both wanna eat that gross display of popco rn.", she says, scrunching her nose.

Jaymeson gets up and trades places with Ash. I sit up long enough to share some popcorn. When I'm done, I snuggle back up to Trent but keep my feet away from the other end of the sofa. The next thing I knew, Asher grabbed them and pulled them into his lap.

"Relax.", he whispers.

I do as I'm told, enjoying being close to him again. He absentmindedly starts rubbing my feet, and I soon fall asleep. I don't know how long I doze, but I wake up, and everyone's gone except my pillow and footrest. I've been covered in a blanket. I keep my eyes closed because I can hear them speaking quietly. I'm too curious to interrupt their conversation.

"What's your deal, man? You're a complete asshole to Reegan most of the time, and then you decide to be nice and rub her feet.", I hear Trent say quietly.

"As she said, it's complicated. I can't share her secrets with you, even if you are my best friend.", Ash answers.

"I appreciate that, and I know she would as well, but I know about the dreams, bro."

"So, she shares her secrets with you but won't share shit with me? Dude, she was my everything back in the day. I couldn't fucking wait until bedtime because I knew I'd get to see her.", Ash says with such emotion that it breaks me.

"Look, I don't know all the details, but you can't expect her to come to you willingly when that bitch you call girlfriend gives her hell, and you don't say shit. Not only that, but you have completely ignored Reegan this week and spent every second up Calista's ass! Why should Reegan make herself vulnerable when you have no intention of leaving Calista?"

"I know. But my heart and head are warring with each other. I'm being pulled in so many different directions. Then there's my dragon. He wants Reegan just as badly as he did when we were kids. Did you know my dragon emerged early? A whole fucking year early, and it was because of Reegan. I know she was the cause."

"Then why are you not fighting for her? Why are you still with Calista?" Trent asks.

"It's complicated."

"Yeah, it seems everything with you is complicated. Let me make it simple for you. Leave Reegan alone, if you truly care about her the way you claim. Let her be happy. Be her friend but stop this hot and cold bullshit you keep pulling. At least until you get your head on straight. You are my best friend, but she's my mate, man. I won't see her hurt if I can help it. A lot is going on that I can't tell you, but please trust me. She needs you. She needs all of us.", Trent says.

After a long moment of silence, Asher answers, "Yeah. Ok. I'll try. That's all I can promise."

I've had enough of eavesdropping, so I stretch myself out to let the guys know I'm awake.

"Where is everyone?" I ask them looking around.

"The pool.", they answer simultaneously.

"Did you want to join them?" Trent asks.

"Hell yeah! Let me go get changed.", I say as I jump up and head to my room. Trent's laughter follows me.

I'm dressed in record time. I chose a black and hot pink string bikini that hints at my ass cheeks but shows off my breasts amazingly. I opt for no cover-up. When I exit, all the guys' eyes are on me. Even Aldair does a double-take.

"Damn. If you weren't my brother's mate, I'd steal you away!" he exclaims. While everyone laughs, I hear a distinct growl come from Asher. I walk by, patting his cheek.

"The view's even better from the back."
, Jaymeson whispers.

"Yeah, it is.", Trent states proudly.

I dive into the heated water, staying under as long as possible before breaking the surface. Then I start doing laps. When I get to the end of the pool, I look up to see all the guys have removed their shirts. I can't breathe. *Damn!* I take the time to look at them, starting with Trent. He's built well. He has a six-pack with that beautiful V.

His tattoos start at his shoulders and wrap around his back across his shoulders. I can't make out the design, but my mouth waters thinking about tracing those designs with my tongue. Jaymeson has more of a swimmer's build with a washboard stomach. I can see the blonde hair that trails down to his swim trunks. I don't look any lower than that, afraid I won't be able to control myself.

My Ash is next. I've seen him shirtless before when we were teens but seeing him now doesn't compare. He has impressive abs, and his V is deep around his waist. He has tattoos on both arms, but they aren't sleeves. I see one peeking out of his swim shorts, but I don't know what it is. When he turns around, I see an entire backpiece, and I gasp. It's my mountain. Every detail is perfection, from the trees to the rainbow waterfall. It's amazing!

Bentley is stacked! That's the only way to explain him. He is built like a fucking tank. He has arms the size of tree trunks, an eight-pack, and pecs that I want to lick and suck. What surprises me the most are his tats. He is covered from the elbow up to his shoulders. He has one on his left pec and some on his legs. Some look like runes. Others I can't make out from a distance. I don't know why I'm surprised by them. Maybe because he comes across as strait-laced in his jeans or slacks and button-downs. I haven't seen him wear a tee shirt at all. He's always in long sleeves.

"Like what you see, Beauty?" Trent asks.

"Very much.", I respond and immediately blush and dunk my head under the water. I can't believe I said that.

The next thing I know, we're all participating in a game of chicken. Somehow, I end up on Bentley's enormous shoulders. We take out all our competition except for Trent and Ash. As we face off with them, Trent and I against each other, while the other two hold us up, I can feel the heat from Bentley's hands dig into my thighs.

"Never thought I'd see the day where big bad Bentley had a beautiful girl with her thighs wrapped around his shoulders and him not take advantage.", Jaymeson jokes from the side of the pool.

Bentley grabs me and throws me off into the water. I come up spluttering.

"What the hell, dude!" I scream at him while still trying to catch my breath. "What was that for? Are you for real that intimidated by me, Bentley? I should just kick you in the balls."

"You're more naive than I thought if you believe you will ever get anywhere near my balls.", he smirks. "I'm out.

He stalks away, leaving me pissed. I'm fuming. "Playtime is over, guys.", I say as I make my way to the steps and exit the pool.

I grab my towel, wrap myself up, and head inside after saying bye to everyone. Asher hugs me, and Jaymeson kisses my cheek, telling me, "Don't let Bentley bother you. He'll come around."

Trent doesn't leave with everyone. Instead, he follows me inside. When we get to my room, I try to head to the shower. Trent doesn't let me get far. He snatches my hand and pulls me into his body. He backs me into the door and starts kissing me. This kiss is different. It's full of hunger and desperation. He reaches down and pulls my towel away. He steps back long enough to look at me, then he's back, kissing me again, slower and more passionately than I've ever felt. He snakes his hand down into my bikini bottoms and rubs my clit with his palm. I start to roll my hips riding his hands, chasing my orgasm. Before I can cum, he removes his hand. I cry out in frustration.

He pushes my bikini top up, and my breasts fall out. He cups them in his hand like he's feeling their weight before he leans in and kisses them. He takes one nipple in his mouth and sucks. He releases it with a pop and then does the same to the other. He gets down on his knees. He grabs the strings on either side of my bottoms and releases them. They float to the floor. He then takes one leg and lifts it onto his shoulder. He licks me from ass to clit in one motion causing me to moan. He does this several times before he begins sucking on my clit. My hips buck and roll.

"That's it, love. Take what you need. Use me. Ride my face.", he says.

I do. I ride his face as he inserts two fingers into my pussy. I'm over the moon. I come with a scream. He holds me there as I come down. When he places my foot back on the floor and rises, I think he's done. I am so wrong. He bends at the waist and lifts me over his shoulder. As he carries me to the bed, he smacks my ass and squeezes. I moan again. I didn't know being spanked could be such a turn-on.

Trent chuckles, "You liked me spanking that tight ass, huh?" he asks and does it again.

When he reaches the side of my bed, he lowers me back to the floor. With a slight push to my chest, I'm on the bed. I lie back, preparing myself for whatever comes next. Trent reaches down and pushes his swim trunks down his long legs. As his cock springs free, I start to drool. Most wouldn't describe a cock as beautiful, but Trent's is.

"I'm glad you think so.", he chuckles. Dammit, I said that out loud.

He's already hard. His cock is long and thick, bigger than Kalan's, and I can't wait to have that inside me. He chuckles again; I know I said that out loud. I can't even be embarrassed by it. I think I'm still high from the orgasm I had.

"Scoot up on the bed and put your hands above your head.", he instructs. I do as I'm told, and once I'm in position, he says, "Don't move your hands. If you do, I'll have to punish you."

"Ok," I say as he makes his way up the bed and places his shoulders between my thighs. He licks me again, and my hands automatically come down to his head. He stops and looks up at me.

"I told you not to move. Put your hands back up there." I do, and then I feel ice lock my hands in place. "Now, don't melt it, and don't move. If you do, I stop, and you won't get to come."

"Yes, sir.", I say with an eye roll.

He smacks my inner thigh and laughs, "You like being a bad girl, Beauty. Will you force me to punish you and not let you come again? I can work you up over and over, and when you're right on the cusp of coming undone, I can stop and leave you wanting."

"No, please don't. I'll behave.", I tell him seriously.

He removes the ice from my wrists and replaces it with vines. "There, now you won't be tempted to melt it."

"You're an earth elemental as well as water?" I ask.

"Later. Right now, I'm starving.", he complains.

When he brings his tongue back to my clit, it's cold. He's made his tongue cold like the ice that shackled my wrists. I have no words, so I just moan and cry out. I cum two more times on his tongue. When he's done, he moves up my body and kisses me. I can taste myself on his tongue.

"Do you know how beautiful you are? You are magnificent." he breathes. "Do we need a condom?" Supernatural can't catch STDs, but we can get pregnant.

"No. I'm on birth control", I tell him. Birth control is a spell that has to be placed every year or so.

He lines up with my entrance and enters me inch by inch. I can feel myself stretching to accommodate his size. It stings at first, and I cringe, but after a minute, it feels good. It feels right. He stays still for a moment, and I need him to move, so I wrap my legs around him and kick him in the ass to get him going. He starts slowly, allowing me to get used to his size, and then he speeds up. He pounds me into the mattress.

"Fuck. You're so tight.", he says as he pumps in and out of me.

I come again. This orgasm hit me so hard that I think I blacked out for a second. Trent puts his arm behind me and lifts me so he can get even deeper. I can feel him everywhere.

"Come for me again, Beauty.", he implores.

"I don't think I can.", I tell him.

"Of course, you can."

He continues pumping into me while circling my clit with his thumb. Even though I had my doubts, he coaxed one more orgasm from me. When I cum this time, he joins me. We're both sweaty as we lay there together in my bed. Right now, I don't want to be anywhere else.

"I know we said we were gonna take it slow, but after having you snuggled up to me all evening and then seeing you in that tiny bikini, I couldn't help myself.", he tells me with a bit of fear in his voice.

"It's ok. I'm done with taking things slowly with you, Trenton Strong. I trust you.", I say and kiss him. "Can you stay tonight?"

"I'm not going anywhere, Beauty."

We snuggle back down in the bed with my head resting on his chest. We only last a few minutes before we head to the shower, where Trent cleans me to eventually dirty me up again, over and over. It's not so bad when Trent gets my mark and vice versa. There on his hip, my mark burns into his skin. His ends up on the opposite side of Kalan's on my ribs. The elemental sign for water and earth is entwined into a unique design. After Trent falls asleep, I lie awake for hours tracing the mark with my fingers. There's a fullness in my heart, and if I close my eyes, I can see the two individual strings of my mate bonds. Trent's string is a vibrant green, while Kalan's is a beautiful yellow. I tug on the yellow one and send my love down it. Within minutes my phone dings.

Kalan: I love you too. I can feel you. It's amazing. What are you doing awake?

Me: Thinking of you.

Kalan: Something's up. I know you.

Me: I may have cemented the bond with Trent tonight.

Kalan: I knew you wouldn't last long. LOL. Were you worried I'd be upset? I'm not. Believe it or not, I like the guy. He's good for you.

Me: I love you so much.

Kalan: I love you too, baby. Get some rest. I'll call you tomorrow evening.

I lay back down. Trent grabs me from behind and pulls me into his body with my back to his front. He kisses my hair but doesn't say anything. I fall asleep happy and content. I don't think of anything other than my two mates, and when I dream, it's happy memories from my childhood before everything changed.

25

TRENT

I wake up before dawn and look over at Reegan. She looks so beautiful, with her hair fanning around her face. A small smile graces her lips, and I can't help the love that spreads throughout my heart looking at her. Our bond is cemented. I didn't plan for that, but I couldn't hold back. I have to get up and get plans going for our outing today. Before I go, I leave a note on the pillow beside her head, letting her know that she needs to be ready and what to wear. I set the alarm on her phone, and it's still open to her text conversation with Kalan. I don't mean to be nosey, but I scroll through regardless. I smile when I see his response, and he's right. I can feel Reegan in my heart. I can tell she's content. It's a fantastic feeling to be on this level with someone. I give Reegan a light kiss on the forehead and leave.

I go home and get everything ready for the day. I wake the guys so they can get prepared, too—Asher's back to being cold today. I don't know what's going on with him, but he should seriously check his attitude. I meant what I told him. He may be my best friend, but if he hurts Reegan, I will kick his ass. Jaymeson is like an excited puppy as we get all our supplies together. He and I leave with Bentley and Asher, saying they'd meet us there. We stop at the store and grab everything we need to grill at the lake. We then borrow my dad's truck and the jet skis. I can't wait to see Reegan out on the water. I hope she likes the surprise. She thinks it will just be the guys and her, but I asked everyone else to come. I'm hoping for a fantastic day.

On our way to the lake, we stop at Reegan's house with coffee from Mom's shop. Reegan doesn't know that mom owns a shop and a restaurant. I'll have to share that with her soon. I walk up and knock on the door. Someone I don't know answers. I ask for Reegan and Maddie, and both girls come running down the stairs. Reegan jumps into my arms and wraps her legs around my waist. She almost knocks me over.

"You left. I thought you'd be here when I woke up.", she pouts.

"What?" Maddie screeches. She pulls Reegan out of my arms and starts lifting her shirt. Once she spots my mark on her ribs, she lets out a squeal that I'm sure is about to break all the glass within a three-mile radius. "You did it? God, I'm so jealous!"

Reegan and I laugh. "Come on, Beauty and the Jealous, let's go."

I turn around, and Reegan launches herself on my back. I catch her, wrapping those long legs around me, and take off down the long driveway. Reegan reaches down and smacks my ass.

"Come on, noble steed. Away!!!" she laughs.

Maddie just shakes her head with a smile. When she sees me looking, she mouths a thank you. I'm not sure what she's thanking me for. I give her a confused look, and she mouths later. I can't help but laugh at Reegan's antics as she continues smacking my ass.

"Yes, my lady, but fair warning, turnaround is fair play."

Reegan groans, and I laugh again. We make it the rest of the way to the truck without any more spankings, and when Reegan sees who's standing there, she gives him a bright smile.

"Jaymes!" she yells and throws her arms around his neck.

He hugs her tightly and says, "Hey, gorgeous. We brought you coffee, but I don't think you need it with all that energy."

"Do not deny me, Jaymeson Matthews.", she fusses.

"Yes, ma'am."

"Hmmm. I like the sound of that.", Reegan responds.

Jaymeson grabs the girls' bags and places them in the back of the car, giving me a look as he passes. The look says, "What have I gotten myself into?"

Jaymeson returns and lifts Reegan into the truck in the front passenger seat. He then helps Maddie climb into the back. We may have to get a ladder for that one. When we reach the lake, the other guys are already there. They have the grill set up and blankets laid out across the bank. Chairs have been set up around a fire pit they dug for when the sun goes down. We unload the truck, and I hand out breakfast sandwiches I had Mom make for everyone. We chow down, and when we're done, Asher goes over and starts unloading the water skis. I notice that Mitchell has brought a set as well.

"We should wait just a little while for the water to warm up before we go out on it.", Mitchell says.

"Yeah, I agree.", I respond to him. I hold Reegan close.

We sit comfortably for a while when a familiar car pulls up.

"Fuck.", Jaymeson says.

I look over and see Calista and Adeline making their way over to us. "What the fuck, dude?" I direct to Asher. "I told you to keep that bitch away from Reegan."

"I didn't fucking invite her, Trent. I don't even remember telling her we'd be here when we talked last night.", he tells me. He honestly looks perplexed by the fact that she's here.

Bentley looks at both of us with concentration. His eyes take on a look of understanding. "What are you doing here, Calista?" Bentley asks her.

"Asher invited me, silly. And you know I just can't say no to my fiancé.," she says directly to Reegan.

"I don't see a ring on your finger." is Bentley's comeback.

"Oh, that's only a formality. Daddy and Senior have already drawn up the contract. Isn't that right, baby?" she responds as she puts her hand on Asher's chest.

Ash has the decency to just grunt. Calista sits down, but while there's plenty of room on the blanket, she sits right in Asher's lap, and Adeline comes over and sits right next to me. Reegan is over by Maddie, and it looks like the latter is trying to talk the other down. Reegan gets up and storms away. She goes around to the swing hanging from the tree and sits down.

"Oh, was it something I said?" Calista feigns innocence.

I'm just about to get up when Bentley grunts and gets up. I let him go. They have many issues to get through, so I sit there and start talking to Maddie and Kenneth. I glance over toward Reegan and see Bentley pushing her on the swing. They're talking, which is a vast improvement over the past couple of weeks.

"Asher, baby. Take me out on the lake?" Calista asks.

Ash nods, and she gets up. They head out. Maddie and the others follow, leaving me alone with Adeline. I put some distance between us on the blanket, but she doesn't take the hint and just moves closer. When she gets within reaching distance, she removes her top. She's wearing a one-piece swimsuit with what looks to be cutouts all over it. Her boobs are practically bursting out of it. I know she wore it on purpose to try to get my attention, but it isn't going to work.

"Trent, would you be a gentleman and put some sunscreen on me?" she asks and puts her hand on my arm.

"Don't touch me, Adeline; you don't need sunscreen. You can't burn."

"Is this about that girl? You know you want me, Trent. You always have."

"I wouldn't want you if you were the last woman on Earth or any other realm.", I tell her and walk away.

She huffs and curses me but notices Aldair standing by the grill, filling it with charcoal, and diverts her attention to him. She's barking up the wrong tree if she thinks he'll give her the time of day after hearing her talk about Reegan that way.

He comes across as a male whore, but I know he cares about Maddie and Reegan. He's majorly protective of them both.

"Give me one minute.", I hear him tell Adeline. "I just need to ask Trent something about lunch."

He walks over to me and says, "I'm going to have some fun with bimbo barbie. She needs to be knocked down a peg or two. I mean, she can't act this way with the princess of Elfame and get away with it."

"Absolutely. But you know if the girls don't know what you're doing, they're going to be pissed at you for giving her the time of day.", I tell him.

"Nah, man, they'll get it tomorrow. Let them be mad now. It makes it look more authentic." he laughs and heads back to where he left Adeline.

I snicker under my breath at his plan and turn back toward my girl and one of my brothers. When Bentley sees me, he walks away.

"Everything ok, Beauty?" I ask her.

"Yes and no.", She sighs.

"Want to talk about it?"

"No, I want to forget about it and enjoy the water. What's going on there?" she asks, gesturing toward Aldair and Adeline, who are now laughing together.

"Probably just trying to get his dick sucked.", I say. "Creator knows she'd give it up to anyone.", I joke.

"Ew! I do not need that visual." she scrunches her nose.

I kiss the tip of her nose and lead her to my jet ski.
I push it into the water as she removes her clothes.
My heart rate kicks up at the sight of her in a black
two-piece with a high waistline accentuating her
hips, and the top has a crisscross pattern across
her chest and back. She looks sexy as fuck, like one
of those pin-up models. Even in a ponytail, her hair
reaches just above her ass, and I want to grip it
in my fist and force her to her knees so she can
worship my cock. I sneakily try to readjust myself
in my shorts, but she catches me. She gives me a
sly smile and winks. She knows exactly what she's
doing to me.

"Do you want to drive?" I ask her

Her whole face lights up, "Seriously? Fuck yeah!"

We climb on with her in front of me. I tighten
my thighs around her hips for stability, tell her how
to turn it on and steer, and we're off. We weave
through the water. She hauls ass, laughing and
squealing as the water sprays up around us. We
don't notice the other ski coming until it's too late.
I grab the handles away from Reegan and jerk
them sharply to the right. I realize it's Asher's ski,
and Calista is driving. She turns into us as I grab
Reegan and throw us both off.

The handlebar hits her in the head, and she goes
under. I dive under and grab her, pulling her to the
surface. She's knocked out cold. Asher is next to us
in seconds and holds Reegan from the other side.

We swim her to shore, and I start chest compressions. Reegan starts coughing up water, but it takes a few minutes for her to wake up.

"What happened out there?" Maddie screams as tears trail down her face.

"That's a good question.", Bentley says. "Calista, what the fuck were you thinking?"

"What? I didn't do it on purpose. She was going too fast, and I couldn't get out of the way.", she defends.

"Bullshit. I saw you turn into us. You did that shit on purpose!" I scream.

"Asher, get your bitch out of here before I do something you'll regret.", I tell my friend. "I fucking warned you, man. Keep your bitch on a leash, or I'll make sure she's fucking euthanized.", I seethe.

Ash looks scared shitless, scared for Calista or Reegan, I can't be sure. But as he looks down at Reegan, I see the concern etched in his features. Whether he wants to admit it or not, his heart belongs to her just as much as mine does.

"Calista, maybe you should go. Let things calm down.", he says.

"You're not coming with me?" she asks and then looks down at Reegan like she's gum on the bottom of her shoe.

"No. I need to make sure she's ok and that she isn't planning on retaliation. If she snitches to her grandfather, it'll mean a severe punishment for y ou.", he tells her.

She screeches like a fucking banshee and high-tails it out of there, even leaving Adeline behind. Maddie is now down on her knees by Reegan. She gingerly puts Reegan's head on her lap. I can see the cut is already healing. Reegan begins to stir, and she looks at me when she opens her eyes. Then she takes in the damage to the jet skis.

"What happened? I'm so sorry about the jet skis. I'll pay to replace them.", she says to me. She's still groggy, and when she gets up, she falls back down. I grab her in my arms and carry her over to a chair. I sit with her on my lap.

"You'll do no such thing, Beauty. Calista did this. Not you.", I tell her. "You're ok, and that's all that matters. Do you want me to take you home?"

"No. I want to enjoy the rest of the day. I'm okay, and I won't let that bitch ruin it." She looks around like she's trying to find the bitch in question.

"She left. We're supposed to be talking you out of snitching to your grandfather, at least according to Asher, but if you wanna tell him, I've got your back."

"I'm not a child, and I can handle Calista. She'll get hers."

"That's my girl. Now shall we grill some food and talk politics? We should have a study session at some point today after all."

"Ugg. Fine. Whatever. I guess I need to know this shit, right? I mean, will I ever see a council seat? Isn't Marcus ancient or some shit?"

"Yeah, he is, but he doesn't have to die for you to take the seat. He could retire.", I tell her laughing at her snark.

We spend the rest of the evening talking about the council around the fire and watching Aldair flirt with Adeline. I was right. The girls are pissed. I can't wait until they see her face tomorrow. At some point, Adeline talks Aldair into taking her home for a drink. Asher leaves shortly after. The rest of us sit and continue our conversation until it gets late, and the girls fall asleep by the fire. It gives me the idea to go camping sometime. I carry Reegan to the car, and Kenneth brings Maddie. Once we have them safely buckled, we head home. I wake Reegan with a kiss and tell her I'll see her in the morning. As much as I want to stay, I can't. I will have to explain the jet ski damage to my dad and hope he's not pissed.

26

REEGAN

After Trent dropped us off, I tried my damnd-est to fall asleep, but every time I closed my eyes, I only heard the conversation with Bentley earlier. I was sitting on the swing, pissed that Calista and her cronies had shown up. I don't know if I believe that Asher didn't tell her. He had to have, but all of a sudden, he had memory loss. I'm not buying it.

"You ok, princess?" Bentley asks.

"Do you care?"

"Not really, but I do care about Trent, and since you're pissed off, so is he."

He starts pushing the swing I'm in, bringing back so many memories. It takes everything in me to hold back the tears. I don't know that I believe all the arguments that he doesn't care about me. I don't know what to think anymore.

"I remember when you used to do this at my house.", I say softly.

"I don't care. This doesn't make us friends. I still hate you, Weaver, and that will never change. I'm only over here to appease Trent. You mated him, didn't you?"

"That's none of your business."

"It is. Trent is my brother in every way but blood, and I won't see him hurt because of you."

"I would never hurt Trent."

"Everywhere you go, destruction follows. My parents died because of you. Your parents died because of you. Who's next?"

He has a point, but my parents aren't dead. They went missing. I'm about to tell him when he notices Trent coming our way. He takes off and grabs a beer. I have to stop thinking about that conversation. I snuggle down into my pillow and close my eyes, wishing for sleep to claim me. I find myself back in that beautiful meadow with Neveah when it does. She sits among the flowers, and I see them lean into her as I watch. She talks to them, and I can see them blossom and grow from the air she breathes on them.

"You came.", she says, looking up at me. "Sit with me."

"I suppose I did.", I respond.

"You also took another mate. What of the others?"

"Others?" I question.

"Yes, The dragon, the shifter, and the grumpy hybrid. You did know they were your mates as well?"

"I had a feeling, but it's complicated.

"So, uncomplicate it. You're a strong girl, and you'll only get stronger with each mate you take."

"That would be easy, but one of my *mates* is engaged."

"To that vapid girl, Calista. She's a sneaky one. She's a half-vampire, half-witch hybrid, and daddy runs her. Pay close attention to her and Asher when he's with her. I think you'll notice something."

"Am I supposed to know what you're talking about?" I ask snarkily.

"Maybe. Maybe not. But pay attention either way. I'm glad you remember, finally. And you teleported!"

"Yeah, I remember. Why did my grandfather have to hide the memories of my parents and that night?"

"Oh, sweetheart. You were all in so much danger. We all did what we thought was best."

"What about Bentley's parents? He blames me for their deaths. And where are my parents?"

"I can't answer those questions. The answers will reveal themselves in time."

"In time?" I asked with frustration.

"That's not important right now. What is important are the trials. There are only so many weeks until you compete, and you must do well to pass. Now, here's what you need to know. The trials are meant to test you mentally and physically. It's a free-for-all. You can use the powers that the academy knows about."

"So, my elemental powers?"

"Yes, including your spirit powers. You need to practice with these. They will allow you to hide here in purgatory if needed. You can also call on spirits to help navigate the course and distract your competitors."

"So, others will be doing the same thing?"

"Not at all, silly girl. You are the only spirit elemental at the academy. Do you think the creator bestowed that gift to just anyone? No, only the strongest elementals hold that power, and there are only a couple dozen in all the realms." she looks at me like I'm daft.

"Wouldn't that be considered an unfair advantage?"

"No more than vampire compulsion, which does not affect you, by the way. You're welcome."

She sits with me for hours, explaining the ins and outs of the trials and my powers, along with what to expect from my debate. She warns me that some are not too happy that Marcus has an heir, and she finds that hilarious. I try to breach the subject of the prophecy, but she ensures me that I need not worry about that and again tells me that all will be revealed in time. She urges me to cement my bonds with the other guys to make myself stronger and more balanced. I tell her I need more time. She says that after the life I've led, she understands my inability to trust easily but to look at more than their pasts and seek out their hearts.

"Now, it's time for you to wake up, sweetheart. Do me a favor, though?" Neveah asks.

"Yeah, sure.", I respond.

"If you talk to your grandfather, tell him to come to see me. We need to chat, and I'm getting bored with his constant disappearing act."

"Ok, and about the chat, take a number. He owes me answers.", I tell her.

She nods, and my mind goes black. I wake up with a headache from hell. Only Lucifer could curse me in such a manner. It feels like somebody is taking a hammer to my skull. I feel fragile as I make my way to the shower. The cut on my head has healed. Maybe I have a concussion. Can supernatural creatures even get a concussion?

I turn the spray to the hottest setting and climb in. After showering, I throw on a pair of cropped jeans and a cold shoulder top with booties. I may feel like shit, but I don't have to look like it. My makeup is a little heavier today, and I take the time to add curls to my hair. When I'm done, I make my way downstairs. Like every day recently, Trent is waiting for me with coffee and a pastry. I kiss him in thanks and take a big drink. I notice Jaymeson sitting on the other side of the bar.

"He insisted on coming with me this morning to ensure you were ok," Trent explains his presence.

"I'm fine. I have a bit of a headache but nothing I can't handle.", I tell them both. "Thanks for looking out, though."

"So, a little birdie told me that today is your birthday. Have dinner with me tonight?" Trent pleads.

"Shit, is it today. I forgot.", I say. "I don't celebrate it."

"We aren't celebrating. We're having dinner.", he tells me.

"Fine." I groan, drawing a laugh from both guys.

"Uh, Reegan. There's a gift waiting for you outs ide.", Maddie calls from the porch.

I get up to look, and my breath catches at the vision in front of me. Sitting right there in the driveway is a vintage 1968 Dodge Challenger. It's beautiful, and it's purple. It's been fully restored, and the seats are black with purple trim. I squeal when I see it. Of course, the sight of my dream car would take my headache away. There's only one person that could have gotten this for me. He's the only person who knows of my fascination with vintage rides, particularly this baby.

"Maddie, I need a phone.", I say excitedly.

Maddie hands me her phone, and I dial Kalan. He answers on the first ring.

"Happy Birthday, baby. I take it you got your gift," he laughs, "Do you like it?"

"Yes!!! How did you do this, Kalan?" I ask.

"I've been working on it for months. When we found out you'd be staying, I changed the delivery so the car would be there when you woke up on your birthday. Do you like it?

"I love it so much. Thank you, baby. I wish you were here so I could thank you properly."

"I'll be there Saturday to celebrate with you, and you can thank me then.", he says huskily.

"Deal. I have to go so I won't be late. I love you.", I tell him.

"I love you too, baby. I'll see you soon.", he responds and then hangs up.

"Please tell me we can take that to the academy.", Jaymeson says.

I laugh, "Of course."

"I don't think I can beat that with dinner.", Trent grumbles.

I grab his face in my hands and kiss him, "There's nothing to beat. It's the thought that counts in gift-giving, and I wasn't expecting anything anyway.", I say sincerely. "Now let's go. I wanna show this baby off."

"Shotgun!" Maddie calls.

We lift the back seats for the guys, and it's hilarious to see Jaymeson squeeze into the back. When we reach campus, everyone stares. We all split off for class. I have a pep in my step all morning. When lunch arrives, I'm still riding the high of having my dream car. I take a seat at the table surrounded by my friends. My circle has grown, and now even Sam and Mitchell join us. We're all happily chatting when Asher and Queen Bitch join us. Adeline isn't far behind. She, of course, takes the empty seat beside Aldair. I made sure there were separate seats for Asher and Calista today. There's now no need for her to sit in his lap.

"Asher, I thought I told you to keep the bitch away from Reegan," Trent says as Asher sits down.

"You can't be serious. Yesterday was an acciden t.", Asher answers.

"What the fuck is wrong with you, man? You were there. She did that shit deliberately, and Reegan was hurt. It could have ended a lot worse.", Trent seethes.

"If Calista says it was an accident, it was an accident. End of.", Asher responds.

"Bullshit, if it's the end of the story.", Trent says.

"It's ok, baby. Let her stay.", I tell him, grabbing his arm to gain his attention. "Trust me?"

"Fine, but one word out of her mouth, and I'll drown her in her own bodily fluids where she si ts.", he tells me.

We sit there and eat, and I surreptitiously spy on Asher and Calista. Neveah was correct; something is off there. Asher glances at me, but Calista whispers to him when he does, and his whole demeanor changes. I have some theories, but I don't want to speculate yet.

I notice Adeline trying to get close to Aldair. She tries to touch him, but he brushes her off. Was the blowjob subpar? Of course, it was. It was Adeline, after all.

"What's wrong, baby?" she asks him.

"What's wrong is your desperation.", he answers with a laugh. "You are so desperate for attention; you would even take it from someone that clearly doesn't like you."

"You didn't act like this last night. What is it? All of you want Reegan," she giggles, "I bet she's still a virgin," she says.

"You want to talk about last night? I pushed you off when you tried everything to get me to let you ride my dick. I knocked your ass on the floor, and you took it as an invitation to suck my cock. If I were a gigolo getting paid, I wouldn't whip it out for you."

"As for the question of Reegan's virginity, not that it's any of your business, but I can guarantee she's not. And while I assume your pussy is so loose, a man would need breadcrumbs to find his way out, Reegan's is tight as hell. I'd stay buried balls deep in her all fucking day. Hell, I spent the night before last exactly that way.", Trent adds.

The entire room erupts into laughter. Adeline
storms out to catcalls of "Loosey-Goosey." The
whole place has turned into a group of nasty
teenagers. Aldair isn't finished and turns his attention to Calista.

"And you. I don't care what your boyfriend says,
you deliberately hurt the future queen of Elfame
yesterday. Do you fear Marcus Withrope's wrath?
How about King Dain's? You should be more worried about incurring mine or Kalan's. See, we have
nothing to lose. I could kill you where you sit, and
your precious council would do nothing. They're
here to control the supernatural of Earth. Well, I'm
not from Earth, and you'd be smart to remember
that.", he tells her.

Calista's eyes go wide but narrow as if she's concentrating, then widen again in surprise.

"Don't test me, witch. You can't read me. I'm
much too strong for that. And your compulsion
won't work either, so don't even try.", he tells her as
he sits back in his chair.

I somewhat feel sorry for Adeline in a way. She's
friends with Calista, and I can't help but wonder if
trying to keep up with the queen bee has caused her
to become the monster she keeps showing us all.

The bell rings for class, and I empty my tray. As
I'm walking back toward Trent, Calista bumps me
and whispers, "You better watch your back. Your
protector can't be with you all the time."

She grabs Asher's hand and walks away. Ash looks like he wants to say something, but when he opens his mouth, no words come out. Curiouser and curiouser. The rest of the day goes smoothly, though one of the guys walks me to and from class.

Maddie takes off with Kenneth when classes let out. Trent and Jaymeson ride home with me since the former left his car this morning. Trent graciously takes the back seat so that Jaymeson isn't scrunched up though it's a tight fit for him. Trent tosses his keys to Jaymeson and tells him he'll catch a ride home with me after dinner. Jaymeson takes off as we head into the house. I make a beeline for the kitchen and gulp down a bottle of water.

"Did you need to change before dinner?" Trent asks me.

"I don't know. Are you taking me somewhere fancy?" I ask.

"No, what you have on is fine. I just thought I'd give you the option."

"I'm good. Were you ready to go?"

"Yeah, if you are. Can I drive?"

"Sure. Since you know where we're going." I laugh.

We leave and head out of town. We follow several winding roads until we reach a gorgeous home set in the mountain. It looks like it grew there. It's all wood and reminds me of a cabin, but it's much too big to be called that.

"Are we having dinner here? Where are we anyway?" I inquire.

"We are at my parent's place and having dinner here."

I'm a little taken aback and a lot nervous. I only met his mom briefly, and I've never met his father. Do they know we're mates? Will they care? Trent comes around and opens my door for me. He takes my hand and helps me out of the car. When we reach the door, he just opens it and enters.

"Mom. Dad. We're here.", he calls out.

A beautiful man comes out of a room to the right. I can tell right away that he's Trent's dad. I'll be an extremely fortunate woman if Trent looks this good in twenty years. He hugs his son and then turns to me, offering his hand.

"You must be Reegan. Trent did not do you justice when he described how beautiful you are.", he says as he places a kiss on my knuckles.

"Now, Peter, don't make the poor girl uncomfortable.", Trent's mom says and pulls me into a hug.

"Thank you for having me over, Mr. and Mrs. Strong.", I say.

"Please, it's Peter and Meridith, dear.", she tells me. "And it's our pleasure. Happy birthday, sweetheart. I hope you like pot roast."

"It's my favorite.", I happily inform her.

"Great. Well, follow me. Trent, you can set the table.", she tells her son.

Trent grumbles a bit but does as he's told. Their home is beautiful. I'd almost call it minimal but homey. I love it. As we go toward the dining room, I stop every so often to look at pictures. I enjoyed seeing Trent as he grew up. One photo stops me in my tracks. Meridith notices and backtracks to my side.

"You knew my parents?" I ask.

"Oh, yes. We were groomed at the academy together. She was one of my dearest friends. I was distraught when the news came that she and your father were killed.", she responds.

In the picture, my father stands with his arms wrapped around my mom, and Darius does the same with Martha.

"I wish we would've known sooner that you had survived. We would have done anything to help you grow up and take your rightful place on the council. But Marcus didn't tell any of us. We thought you were lost with your parents.", she explains. "I think I have a copy of that picture if you'd like it."

"That would be wonderful. I don't have any pictures of them.", I tell her.

She puts her arm around my shoulders and leads me into the dining room, where a massive spread of food is waiting. There's pot roast, roasted potatoes, honeyed carrots, some sort of greens, and home-made rolls. I dig in. The food is divine! After every-one has had their fill, we all head to the den to talk. Martha excuses herself, carrying a giant chocolate cake when she returns. They sing *Happy Birthday* to me. I tear up a little.

"Oh, sweetheart. What's wrong?" Meredith pauses in her serving and asks.

"Nothing. I just haven't celebrated since my mom and dad. This means a lot to me that you would do this. You don't even know me.", I say.

"Let me tell you what I know. I've heard what's been happening to you with Calista and how strong you are. I heard you stood up for a boy you didn't know on your first day at the academy. I know you have a loving heart. I also know you are my son's mate. Fated at that. And if I didn't know those things, knowing you make my son happy is enough. I don't need to know more about you to know that you deserve happiness, and if we can be a little part of that, even better.", she tells me.

Now she has tears in her eyes as she comes over and hugs me tightly. For the first time since my parents disappeared, I am happy to have celebrat-ed, and I love Trent and his parents for doing this for me.

27

REEGAN

T he rest of September passes in a blur. Kalan, true to his word, came on the Saturday after my birthday with Alita and Dain in tow to celebrate. Of course, they decided to take me to Meredith's restaurant for dinner. Meredith doted on me the whole night and even joined us for a while. Trent declined the offer to join us, saying it was a family event and he didn't want to intrude.

The rest of the month and all of October were spent in a whirlwind of training for the trials and the debate. It was also spent dodging attacks from Calista. She tried to hex me several times, but each one was minor compared to what I'm sure she truly wanted. Like, she hit me with one that resembled food poisoning but only gave me an upset stomach for all of five minutes. Aldair was able to pick up on the foreign magic and removed it even though it didn't cause much harm. She set up a trap in my locker that would have dyed my skin blue. Luckily, I could redirect the dye with my wind power, so I didn't have to walk around looking like a smurf for days.

I wasn't worried about Calista. The only thing she was doing was pissing me off. I held myself in check the best I could so my secret powers didn't show themselves. She and her cronies would throw out snide comments at me. She has many cronies, or she enlisted the help of those that she scared and bullied before. I was called a slut, a whore, and my favorite was slimy cunt. That one had me laughing so hard. I keep walking by with my head held high and a smile on my face. It doesn't matter what these bitches think of me. Calista is a jealous bitch that feels threatened by me. She has no idea how threatened she should feel.

It's Halloween, my least favorite holiday. Also known as Devil's night, it's the one night of the year when Supernaturals are free to let their true natures come out. *Let your freak flag fly.* Whoever thought up that idea must be lacking brain cells. There's some party at a club downtown that all the guys want to go to, so I am getting dressed in this sexy dark angel costume.

It's made from a grey gauzy material and sequins between my breasts that are about to pop out. It laces up the back and has the same color grey in the wings that are also gauzy. I paired it with a pair of sexy black combat boots. I gave myself an overdone smokey eye with thick black eyeliner that fans out and deep red lipstick. I pulled my hair up on the top of my head and added ringlets. The only jewelry I wear is my nose ring which I got a couple of weeks ago. My eyes have a glow that isn't usually there, and I'm hoping it passes off as a pair of contacts.

As an elemental, no distinguishing features mark me as a supernatural creature except my eyes. Shifters can't shift into their other form since they can't communicate with anyone but pack members. Not just that, but could you imagine how the humans would react to seeing a massive wolf or even a dragon taking to the sky? Demons get to let their true skin show. Some have fun colors like blue or red. Fun fact: demons on Earth don't have horns. They only get them with much time spent in hell. That's too bad. I bet Bentley would look sexy as hell with horns. Another fun fact: Fae, while they have more pointed ears, do not have wings. That was a sore spot for Maddie as a child. She wanted wings so badly. So, while some of us can't show our actual forms, we can still let our natural inclinations free.

Maddie comes in looking like the fae she is. Her ears aren't masked, so the point is evident. She's used her earth ability to wrap delicate vines up and around her arms, and I can tell her little dress is made from real leaves.

"You look hot!" she tells me with a saucy wink.

"Thank you. You don't look so bad yourself."

"Yeah? You like it?" she asks, giving a little twirl. "I feel like it's missing something."

I already know where she's going with this, so I say, "Come here and turn around. Do not get your hopes up, and do not get pissed if it doesn't work."

"If what doesn't work?"

"Just get over here.", I tell her.

She comes over and gives me her back. I place my hand right in the middle of her shoulder blades. I close my eyes and picture a set of amazing wings. They are light and airy and sparkle when the light hits them. I imagine them as butterfly wings but more transparent. When I open my eyes, I see the wings first. The next is Trent standing in my doorway with a look of awe.

"Wow, Beauty. Your eyes." he breathes. I look in the mirror and see that my eyes are no longer sapphire blue but molten silver.

"Oh, my Creator! You did it, Reegan! You gave me wings!" Maddie yells excitedly. "And your eyes are amazing. Is that part of your abilities, you think?" she asks with a tilt of her head.

"I don't know. Do you think they're stuck like this?" I ask.

"Nope, I see the blue coming back in them.", Maddie says.

She's right. In a matter of seconds, my eyes are back to normal. Maddie is standing in front of the mirror, admiring her wings. I wish she could keep them, but I'll have to take them away at the end of the night to not draw attention to her or my ability. She rushes over and throws her arms around my neck. I hug her back, and she's out the door. I'm assuming she will show the wings off to Kalan and Aldair. I'm left alone with Trent, who looks super sexy in his suit. It must have been specially made for him.

"Damn beauty. That outfit makes me want to do all kinds of dirty things to you.", he growls.

"I would be down for that over this ridiculous holiday any other time, but Maddie is super excited, so don't start something we can't finish.", I say, batting his hands away from my body.

"We could get a quickie in.", he says seriously.

"Oh no, Romeo. Not happening.", I say as I pass him. "I'll let you do whatever you want to me later, though.", I whisper in his ear. I then bite it.

I'm rewarded with a slap on the ass as I slip out the door. When I get to where Kalan is, I take him in. He looks like a fae prince with a gold and jewel-encrusted crown on his head. His suit is grey and fits snugly to his body. He hands a crown to Trent, and I see it's also jewel-encrusted but dark silver in color. They stand side by side. Trent is a couple of inches taller than Kalan, and they are the opposite of each other. Where Kalan is light-haired and fair-skinned, Trent is all dark and handsome with his tan skin, dark hair, and eyes. Both carry themselves regally, but Kalan has seriousness to him while Trent has a playful look in his eye.

"The others should be here any minute. Are you ready to go?" Kalan asks.

"As ready as I'll ever be.", I respond.

"You look beautiful, by the way.", Kalan tells me as he kisses me on the forehead.

"Why couldn't the beautiful angel fall in love with me instead?", Aldair whines.

"Because you'd need another twenty or thirty angels to keep you satisfied.", I laugh.

"Oh, do we want to compare harems, dear Reegan?"

"Nope. I'm good, dear brother-to-be." I blush.

Aldair has been in a bit of a mood lately. Pearl refuses to talk to him, and Aldair isn't used to being rejected for anything, especially pussy. He's never been challenged, and he doesn't like it. I think it's good for him. Maybe she'll finally make him grow up a little. I mean, if he isn't just after a quick fuck, but she doesn't seem like that type of girl.

The doorbell rings, and the others are led to the sitting room. Aldair pours us all shots and tells everyone it's a new tradition that we all drink before heading out. We do as we're told. The liquor goes down smoothly. Jaymeson brought his car this time. I think I should call it a tank. It has three rows of seats. Asher climbs in the back seat. I end up in the next row, sandwiched between Trent and

Kalan, and Bentley rides shotgun while Jaymeson hops behind the wheel. Maddie rides with Kenneth and his crew. Aldair opts to drive on his own, citing the need for his ride should he meet a hot piece of ass to go home with.

It takes less than twenty minutes to reach the club. It's called something glow. I can't hear the music from outside, but the music is pumping once we're ushered in. The place is packed. There's a large dance floor in the middle surrounded by four-top tables. There are massive booths along three walls and a bar that runs the length of the fourth. I see a stairway off a hallway in the back that leads up to a couple of balconies overlooking everything. Asher leads the way over to the stairs and up. We're taken into one of the rooms when we reach the top.

Inside there's another dance floor and a bar. There are booths up here as well. I walk to the balcony and look down at all the bodies writhing on the dance floor. It's hard to tell who's human and who's not. Arms wrap around me from behind. By the smell of the ocean, I can tell it's Trent.

"You want a drink, Beauty?" he asks me.

"Yes, please. A Long Island Iced Tea would be great.", I answer.

Trent leaves me, and another set of arms takes their place. Kalan presses a kiss below my ear. "If we weren't in this bar, I'd be fucking you right now."

"Would you now?" I ask as I turn in his arms. He leans down as I tilt my head and kisses me.

"Oh yeah, most definitely. You are sexy as hell as a dark angel."

"Mm. And you are the perfect fae prince."

"You know you made Maddie's whole world tonight, right?"

"I know. She's wanted wings for as long as I can remember. I'm glad that for one night, I could give her that."

"She's going to expect you to make them for her every year now, right?" he laughs.

Yes, she definitely will. And I'm strangely ok with that. I see her swaying in Kenneth's arms on the small dance floor. She looks so happy, and it's not just the wings bringing that smile to her lips. Trent comes back over with my drink, and I take it grate- fully. I drink it slowly, knowing it packs a punch.

"Dance with me, Beauty?" Trent asks, extending his hand for me to take.

I look to Kalan. He gives me a small smile and a nod. I take Trent's hand. Instead of stopping at the small dance floor, he leads me down to the main one, where all the people are. Kalan keeps his gaze on us as we make our way between the bodies and begin grinding on each other. As we dance, Trent herds me toward a corner. When he gets me there, he turns me to where I'm facing him and grabs my ass, grinding his pelvis into mine. He then turns us to where his back is to the wall, and my back is to his front. He grabs my hips and grinds my ass on his cock. I can feel how hard he is, and I'm getting turned on.

"Should we give Kalan a show, Beauty?" he whispers in my ear.

I don't answer. Instead, I seek out Kalan and see him staring at me from the balcony. It's not his eyes that hold me captive, however. It's Asher standing a little away, staring at me with a hardness in his eyes. I feel a slight pinch on my side.

"Answer me, Reegan.", Trent growls.

"Yes." I breathe.

Once he has my permission, I feel his hand snake down to my thigh. He spreads them a little while grinding his hips into my ass. His hand slowly makes its way up my thigh and under the skirt of my costume. He slides my panties out of the way and runs his finger over my folds. I groan out and press back harder into him.

"Keep still, Beauty, or everyone here will get a show. I have no issue throwing you over the table and fucking you from behind."

I stiffen in his arms until he runs his fingers down me again. I gasp at the feel. When two of his fingers enter me, I'm lost. I close my eyes to the sensations.

"Keep your eyes open. Don't close them. Let them see what I do to you.", Trent chastises.

So, he knows Asher is watching. I meet Asher's eyes again and see only hunger instead of hardness. Trent repeatedly pumps his fingers in and out of me while rubbing my clit with his palm. I come. Hard. Trent removes his fingers, looks up at the balcony, and sucks his fingers clean.

I look up again to see Asher storm away. Kalan still stands there with a cocky smirk on his face. Trent turns me, and his lips crash on mine. He kisses me for what could be hours, for all I know. When he breaks the kiss, I have to catch my breath. He leads me back to the balcony area.

During our sexscapade on the dance floor, Calista and Adeline showed up. They're both dressed as what's supposed to be sexy cats. Their fangs are prominent tonight. Instead of looking sexy, they just look slutty. I ignore them both as I sit in one of the booths. Trent comes over with another drink for me and a glass filled with Brandy for Kalan. It isn't long before Jaymeson and Bentley join us with their drinks. We sit for a while, just enjoying the music.

Eventually, Jaymeson asks me to dance, and I agree. We make our way over to the small dance floor. He wraps his arms around my waist and pulls me close. I have to crane my neck to look at him. He takes the lead swaying me and twirling me. When he twirls me out and brings me back in, I throw my head back and laugh.

"You look beautiful when you laugh like that.", he says softly. A slight blush comes into his cheeks.

"Thank you. You look good yourself.", I tell him, which causes another blush.

Jaymeson is extremely good-looking, and his idea to be a mad scientist tonight fits him perfectly. He's got this geeky C.E.O. aura about him that is such a turn-on. We dance for another two songs before he leads me back to the table. We squeeze back in. This time I end up beside Asher.

"Did you enjoy the show?" I whisper to him. "Where'd your girlfriend get off to? I was certain she'd try to pull some bullshit tonight."

Asher doesn't so much as grunt, but he looks at me with a hostile expression. *Ooh. I must have hit a nerve.* Jaymeson pulls me into a conversation about Halloween past. I laugh at the stories, especially about the four dressing up as *Ghostbusters*. It's endearing to hear all these stories of their childhood, and I can't help but wish I had grown up like that. Don't get me wrong. I loved growing up in Elfame, but the royals were the only people I had. I didn't have friends outside of them. I had Asher once, didn't I? It's hard to see him as that gangly teen that made me laugh and kissed away my sadness. Now all I see is a man that seems to loathe me. Then there are times when I get a tiny peek at the Asher I remember, and it breaks my heart all over again when he inevitably grows cold again.

"Excuse me. You're in my seat.", Calista says. The look on her face is one of pure hatred.

"Oh. I'm so sorry. By all means, have it. Asher is such a grumpy Gus tonight anyway.", I reply as I get up.

"Maddie, I need to use the lady's room.", I say.

Maddie and Sam both go with me to the restroom. That second drink went straight to my bladder. Once I'm done, and my hands are washed, we head out of the bathroom. *Sweet, but Psycho* is blaring from the speakers, and Maddie grabs Sam and me and hauls us to the dance floor. We shake our asses, hands in the air to the song. I'm ready to head off the floor when that one ends, but *The Git Up* starts. When in Tennessee, am I right? We all get in a line and dance to the song. The movements come naturally to me.

The song bleeds into another one and then another. We stay here on the floor, having a blast. As I dance with my girls, I feel a set of hands grasp my hips. They aren't the hands of my guys. I feel his hot breath on my neck when he wraps his body around mine. My brain is screaming danger. Before I can get so much as move, my vision is distorted, and everything around me is a smokey black.

"You are coming with me, sexy.", his smoky voice says.

"Thanks, but no thanks. I came here with my friends, and I'll be leaving the same way.", I respond, trying to turn to look at him.

He wraps one arm around me, and the other holds my chin, effectively caging me. I can't move. Everything around me goes darker. I can't move my body as shadows lock me in place.

"The more you fight, the tighter the shadows will get. I don't mind taking care of you here, but I was hoping to have some fun with you first.", he says as he covers my mouth with his large hand and begins to drag me away.

I can't teleport because I'm afraid it will carry him with me. I try to use my elemental powers, but they won't answer me. I need to calm myself. *Think Reegan.* I look inside myself and find the strings of my bond. I tug on them hard, sending my fear to my guys. I hope they can follow our bond to find me. Once he has me outside, he releases the shadows. I look around and realize we're in the back alley of the club. On one end is a brick wall and on the other stands a group of seven men looking at me menacingly.

"If you try to run. My friends inside will kill your little red-haired friend," he threatens.

I don't move. I lock up my entire body. I may not run away, but I will not go willingly. Just as he goes to grab me, the men at the end of the alley come our way. I look at them all and realize they're all demons. I'm trapped in a stinky dark alley with a group of monsters, and I don't even want to know what this sticky substance I'm standing in is.

"She doesn't look so intimidating.", one man growls.

"Yeah, well, looks can be deceiving. Calista said we needed to be careful with her. Our job is to make her disappear, right? But we get to do what we want to her before then?" another man says as he runs a finger down my throat and across the swell of my breasts. I shiver with disgust. Of course, Calista would orchestrate this.

"There will be time for that later. Right now, we need to get out of here before her friends show up.", my captor says. "Come now, Princess. Be a good girl, or I'll torture you before getting rid of you."

"Release these shadows holding me, and I'll show you a good girl.", I hiss at him. I'm scared shitless, but my power lurks beneath my skin, begging to be released.

At that moment, there's a loud crash at the door to the club. When it breaks free, I see a giant black wolf with white tips on his feet and ears. At first, I think it's coming out to eat me until its eyes meet mine. They're steel grey, but there's a glow to them.

Jaymeson. His wolf is close to 5 feet tall. He's beautiful, I think, as he leaps in the air and snaps the head right off the demon that touched me. He spits its head out, and I watch it roll until it hits the boots of my captor. His eyes widen in fear as Jaymes stalks forward.

His buddies all congregate in front of him, and he stands straighter. He'll let them all die to save himself. Jaymes lets out a howl, and the next thing I know, all the guys are exiting the building, even Asher. They all take one look at me and jump into the fray. As they fight the demons, my captor tries to grab me again. I'm not sure what he's planning, but I refuse to go down without a fight. Aldair reaches us and takes in the shadows. Within seconds, the shadows are gone. Did I mention one of his badass powers is dispelling magic? Once the shadows are gone, I take a second to get my bearings. Aldair is corning my captor, but I can't have that.

"Aldi, he's mine.", I call. To my captor, who cares what his name is, he won't live long enough to hear it called again. I say, "I told you I'd show you a good girl. Did you want to play with me? Let's play."

He tries to use his shadows on me immediately. I use my wind to blow them away. He tries to throw his demon magic my way, but I dispel it quickly. He even tries to barrel around me at one point, but I blast him with wind and knock him back.

"I don't think so. I'm not done with you yet." I snicker.

When he comes at me, I use enough force with my wind to knock him into the brick wall. He goes down in a heap. He gets up quickly and runs at me again—this time, I let him come. With my hand behind my back, I get a fireball ready. When he gets close, I launch it. It hits him in the chest. He lets out an anguished cry. I douse him with water to put the fire out.

"Did your mommy never teach you to stop, drop, and roll? The next time you decide to take someone, do your homework. Now, I want to know what you were offered and if Calista was the only person involved.", I say

I let another fireball grow in my hand. I put it close to his face. He doesn't open his mouth to answer my questions.

"Seriously, you're willing to die for her?" I ask him.

"It's not her I'm worried about. She's a puppet with a wet pussy to stick my dick in. It's the one's pulling her ropes you need to be worried about, little girl.", he hisses. "But I'll never tell you who it is."

"Well, I guess we're done here then" those are the last words he hears as I launch the next fireball directly at his head and use my ice to keep him there.

Kalan grabs me and crushes me into a hug. I'm then passed around from guy to guy.

"What did that demon say to you?", Jaymeson asks me.

"Nothing important.", I answer, not ready to spill anything. "Where's Asher?"

"He left with Calista once the other demons were handled.", Trent tells me.

"Of course he did. And Maddie and Sam?" I inquire.

"They're safe, Princess." Bentley tells me, hugging me close again." I'm glad you're ok. I may hate you, but I don't want you dead."

"You know what I think? I think that you don't hate me at all. You may want to, but you don't. When you're ready to talk, I'm here. There are some things you need to know.", I whisper for only him to hear, and I gain a small laugh from him.

I'm exhausted, and my legs choose to give out on me now. Bentley catches me before hitting the ground and lifts me in his arms, bridal style. He carries me to the car and climbs into the middle seat, holding me in his lap and letting me use his chest as a pillow.

28

REEGAN

I wake up the following day and see Bentley standing by my dresser.

"You won't find the secrets to the universe inside those drawers.", I laugh. "Shit, what time is it?"

"Noonish. You slept a long time.", he replies.

"Fuck, I have to get to class." I struggle with the sheet that seems to be attacking me.

"You're excused from classes today."

"Where's the rest of the guys?"

"They're all downstairs playing video games. We've been taking turns checking on you. It was my turn."

"Oh, well, let me get up, and I'll join you guys."

"Not so fast, Princess. You said we needed to talk. There's no time like the present.", he says haughtily. Now he's pacing.

"Fine, but can you sit down? You're making me dizzy."

He looks around the room for a place to sit, and when he sees the only options are a window seat

or the bed, he looks mortified. Yeah, big boy, you'll
have to sit next to me for this conversation. He
hesitates before sitting on the edge of the bed, his
spine ramrod straight.

"Are we going to talk about what happened last
night?" he asks quietly.

"Not yet. That's a conversation for when we're
all together. I wanted to talk about what happened
seventeen years ago."

"No. Absolutely not.", he says with a raised voice.

"Stop. Just, please listen."

"Fine, but it won't change anything."

"What if your parents didn't die that night?" He
looks ready to bolt. "Just.. give me a minute. I didn't
know who you were when I first met you here. You
know what I am. My grandfather hid me in Elfame
and buried my memories of everything before that
night to protect me. I believe my parents didn't die
that night but disappeared instead. I think maybe
that's what happened to your parents as well."

"My uncle told me what happened, Princess. He
told me he saw the bodies. He was there when they
were identified.", he explains.

"Or, he lied to protect your parents, to protect you.
I don't have all the answers. Marcus keeps doing
his disappearing act, so I can't get them from him.
The only answer is that it wasn't a rogue witch that
did all this to us. It was a councilman."

"That's not possible."

"I remember it, Bent! I remember the voices I could hear coming from mom's bedroom. I remember her calling him a councilman. I remember what his voice sounded like."

"Let's say I believe you. There is nothing that would have kept my parents away from me for so long. They would've come back!" he all but screams at me.

"Would they? Your parents knew what I was, what we would be. Why wouldn't they stay gone, let you take a council seat, and follow your destiny? If they had come back, it would have spelled your death and theirs."

"This conversation is over. It's still your fault they're gone. It's your fault I had to grow up without them. I still hate you, Princess. That's not going to change no matter what stories you tell me." he jumps up from the bed and storms out of the room.

I lay there for a few more minutes and then get up with a sigh. I throw on a pair of sweats and a tank and go down to see the guys. When I get to the den, I crawl into Kalan's lap. We don't say anything. I'm content to just feel him with me. Every so often, he places a kiss on the top of my head and goes back to his game. Bentley doesn't return. Hours later, Jaymeson leaves, and Kalan puts on a movie. We sit in silence for a while. My stomach begins rumbling.

"Alright, pause the movie. Our girl needs nouri shment.", Trent says as he places his hand on my thigh.

Kalan grabs the remote and stops the movie, "Come on, baby. Let's see what the cook left us to‐ day."

He grabs my hand and helps me up from the sofa. We hurry into the kitchen, where Kalan throws open the refrigerator.

"We have a pasta sauce, some fresh pasta, and stuff for a salad.", he grumbles. "Why couldn't it all be cooked already?"

I got this man.", Trent says.

He grabs the sauce and gets a pot of water to boil the pasta. While we wait for the water to boil, he cuts the veggies to make a salad. He even looks back in the fridge and grabs ingredients to make a homemade dressing. When everything is done, he plates it up, and we head over to the little breakfast nook to eat. There's no need to use the dining room with it, just the three of us.

"So, you ready to talk about last night? We've been patient, but we need to know what happened .", Kalan says with regalness.

I sigh, "Not much to tell. Calista hired them to get rid of me, but apparently, she hired them under someone else's orders." I shrug.

"Whose orders?" Trent growls.

"He wouldn't tell me. All he said was that I should be afraid of the man that held Calista's s trings.", I tell them both.

"Ok, change of subject. What's up between you and Bentley?" Kalan hedges.

"I'm not going there, Kalan." I shake my head.

"Come on. We're opening up about things, so open up.", he responds.

"Fine. Bentley knew me before. Like our parents were friends, they used to come to our house for dinner and shit. His parents died the same night as mine though I don't think they died. I think they disappeared into hiding to keep us safe. Regardless, Bentley hates me. He blames me for taking his parents away from him.", I try to explain.

"I don't think Bentley hates you, Beauty. I see how he watches you, and it's most definitely not with hate in his eyes.", Trent offers.

"Yeah, well, tell him that because according to what he told me upstairs earlier, he hates me, and nothing will change that. Why couldn't I be a normal girl with a mundane life?" I whine.

"You couldn't stand a mundane life, baby. Admit it. You like the drama." Kalan laughs.

"No, your brother likes drama. I could do without it.", I reply.

Maddie and Aldair come home later, and Kalan fills them in on what went down last night. Aldair has the brilliant idea to get drunk to forget all about it and the man or men trying to kill me. That sounds like an excellent idea to me, so I throw myself into the challenge. Unfortunately, Trent decides to be my conscience and won't let me get too inebriated.

"We have class tomorrow. You don't wanna show up with a hangover or worse, still drunk.", he tells me as he takes the bottle of Tequila away.

"But of course, I would. Wouldn't that be fun?" I giggle.

"No, what would be fun is if I were to take you upstairs and finish what we started on that dance floor last night.", he whispers.

"Yeah. I could see where that would be loads of fun.", I whisper huskily.

Trent grabs me and throws me over his shoulder, taking off toward the stairs. I laugh, "If you don't hear from me in a few hours, come check to make sure I haven't died from orgasms!" I yell.

Trent takes the stairs two at a time. My face smashes into his ass as I bounce around on his shoulder. I grab his waist to steady myself. His ass looks bitable, so I decide to give it a try.

"Ow! You're going to pay for that Beauty.", he laughs.

"Why? It's not my fault you have a bitable ass." I laugh.

"You're drunker than I thought, Beauty. Now behave, or there will be no orgasms."

"Not fair. You promised."

"I did no such thing."

We finally reach my room. Trent pushes the door open and then kicks it shut with his foot. He walks over to the bed and throws me down on it. I bounce a couple of times, and then he's there, on top of me, his body weight pressing me into the mattress. I lock myself around him like one of those adorable koala bears. I latch my mouth to his. His tongue jets out to battle with mine. I moan and try to move my hips to get friction. With his weight, it's difficult, but I don't stop trying. Is he as aroused as I am?

"Tell me what you want.", he whispers as he nips my ear.

"You.", I answer silkily.

"I know you want me, Beauty. Tell me what you want me to do to you."

"Fuck me. I need you inside me. I need to feel you moving in and out of me."

Trent raises up and lifts me to a sitting position. He removes my tank, and his eyes glaze over at the sight of me braless. He then pushes me back down and pulls off my sweats. Now, his eyes show hunger as he takes in my bare pussy.

"You are a naughty girl, Beauty. Walking around here with no underwear. You wanted to be fucked, huh? Were you hoping for Kalan or me? Or would you have liked it to be Jaymeson or Bentley?" he asks. "Ahhh, you'd go for any of us. Or all of us? I can see your eyes light up at the thought. You're dripping wet, love."

He removes his clothes in record time and, without hesitation, lines up and surges in. I cry out. He pumps in and out a few times when we hear the door open. Kalan stands there for a few seconds.

"Did you come to watch?" I asked him breathlessly. Trent hasn't stopped fucking me, but he has slowed his thrusts.

"For now.", he says. He walks over to the window seat and sits.

Trent hasn't stopped his thrusts, and it feels so good. I look at him, but he turns my head away.

"Look at Kalan, Beauty.", he says. "Show him how beautifully you fall apart for me."

Kalan has his pants unbuttoned and his cock in his hand. He's stroking it to the timing of Trent's thrusts. Watching him while being fucked by Trent sends me over the edge. I come, hard.

"Fuck! I love feeling your pussy clamp down on my dick." Trent groans loudly. He pulls out, and I whimper in protest. "Rollover for me. Ass in the air."

I do as I'm told. He rubs his cock along me. "Kalan, come over here. Get on the bed in front of her.", he commands.

Kalan comes over, stripping as he does. He climbs onto the bed, and his cock is now right in my face. I dart my tongue out and lick the tip. He hisses.

"That's it, Beauty. You're going to suck his cock while I fuck you.", Trent says from behind me.

I take Kalan into my mouth and begin licking his shaft. Trent enters me again with a forceful thrust which pushes me further onto Kalan. Kalan grabs my hair in his hand and guides my head. They set a bruising pace. Trent fucks me from behind while Kalan fucks my mouth. It's not long before I cum again. I slip off Kalan's cock, so I don't bite him, and I bury my face in the sheets. When I come down a little, Kalan guides me back to him.

I don't know how long they have used me like this, but I'm not complaining. They both come simultaneously, and we all collapse into a heap, my face in Kalan's lap and Trent across my back, still buried deep inside me. He only pulls out when he's gone completely soft. As he does, he pulls me with him.

"That was hot as hell, but I need a shower," I say as I stretch.

"I'll go get some snacks and water.", Kalan says as he pulls his sweats back on. "But don't get too comfortable. We're not nearly done yet."

After my shower and snackage, they show me how not done we are. That night, I fall asleep between them both, Trent at my back and my head resting on Kalan's shou arm.

29

TRENT

I wake up with the most delicious feeling between my legs. I have died and gone to Heav-
en. Reegan's warm mouth is around my cock, and
she's sucking and licking like it's her favorite damn
lollipop. I barely open my eyes to take in the view
and realize that while she's sucking me, she's using
her other hand to stroke Kalan. He's also awake
and looking at her.

I snatch her head off my cock with a pop. "While
I love being woken up to a good blowjob, we have to
go to class today."

"Uh-huh. But we have time.", she says, rising on
the bed and straddling my hips. She sinks down on
my cock, and we both groan. She begins to ride me,
all while still stroking Kalan's cock in her hand.

Kalan gets up and straddles my legs behind her.
He uses his hands to tweak her nipples while she
rides me. He takes one of her hands and pulls it
behind her so she can continue to work him over.
Her other hand is on my chest, giving her stability.

I grip her thighs and begin pumping up into her, making sure her clit rubs my pelvis as she comes down. My breathing quickens.

"I need you to come for me, Beauty. I'm not going to last.", I tell her.

Kalan takes a hand from her breasts and moves it down to her clit. He starts rubbing circles. When I think I can't hold back anymore, he flicks her, and she comes apart. I join her, her tight channel milking every ounce of cum from my balls. Kalan moves away from her and her hand working his cock. He takes his cock in his hand and strokes it.

"Open up for me, Reegan, or I'll come on those pretty tits of yours," he says shakily.

She obliges and opens her mouth. With two more strokes, he comes on her tongue.

"I need to head home and grab some clothes. I'll meet you at school?" I ask.

"I'm going to drive her today. Professor Morley asked dad if I'd come in and talk a little about Politics among the fae.", Kalan says while he heads to the door.

I kiss Reegan one more time and leave. Last night seemed to do the trick of helping Reegan forget about the club. While she acted nonchalantly, I could see the fear in her eyes. It's all I think about on my way to the house. I try to determine who could want to hurt her. I know Calista is dangerous. She's already tried to hurt her twice. But the demon said it was on someone else's orders. The question is, who's? I muse over that question until I get home, coming up with no answers. Maybe they were trying to make us go easier on Calista. Make us question the attack like I have been all morning. When I entered the house, I searched for the guys. I find them all drinking coffee in the kitchen. I walk over to the pot and pour myself a cup. When I turn around, all the guys are looking at me.

"You reek of sex. Go take a fucking shower.", Asher says.

"Jealous?" I respond.

"As if." he laughs.

"Keep telling yourself that.", I tell him as I walk away.

I swear I hear Jaymeson say, "I am.", and I snicker.

I'm showered, dressed, and ready to go within ten minutes. Bentley and Jaymeson ride with me, and I tell them we have to meet after class to discuss what happened to Reegan. Kalan and I talked yesterday while Reegan was out. She thinks Kalan will be doing a sort of political show and tell for Professor Morley, but in reality, we set that up so we'd have one extra person on campus to look out for her.

We make it through the morning without running into Calista. I haven't seen Asher either. Elemental studies was fun. Since Prof. Morley didn't have a class first period, Kalan joined us in the arena. The dude has skills; I'll give him that. Watching some of the students try to take him on was a blast. He's royalty for a reason. The royal family is the strongest, most talented of the fae. When it's Reegan's turn to go up against him, they're pretty evenly matched, at least that's what it looks like. That is until Reegan releases whatever lock she has on her powers. She takes him down quickly when she stops playing. He doesn't look surprised. I'd say he seems proud. I think the same look is reflected in my eyes.

"Good job, baby.", he tells her as he kisses her on the forehead. "You did awesomely."

Reegan just blushes and pushes him away. Creator forbid she let anyone here see her emotions. Class ends, and we all change into regular clothes and head to the dining hall. I see Calista and Asher coming our way.

"Reegan, take Kalan and grab our table. I'll be there in a minute.", I tell her.

She overlooks Calista, but Kalan doesn't. He grabs her and steers her to the entrance. I divert to catch Calista and Asher before they can make their way inside. When I reach them, I put my hand around her throat and slam her into the wall.

"What the fuck, Trent?" she yells, choking a little.

Asher tries to remove my hand around her throat, but he stops when he realizes that all he's doing is causing me to tighten my hold. Calista is clawing at my hand to no avail. I won't release her until I have answers. Maybe I'll just go ahead and kill her.

"Dude, what the hell is going on?" Asher asks.

"What's going on is that your *fiancée* was behind the attack on Reegan Halloween night. I want answers. Who gave you the order to hire those demon thugs?" I direct toward Calista.

I lessen my grip so she can answer. "I don't know what you're talking about. If you don't believe me, ask Asher.", she says smugly.

"I wouldn't believe anything he tells me. He hasn't exactly been himself since he met you.", I tell her.

"You're letting Reegan ruin our friendship.", Asher accuses. "Calista is one of us."

"No, man, you are ruining it. You and this bitch you're fucking!" I yell in his face. To Calista, I say, "I will get to the bottom of this, Calista, and when I do, I'll make you pay. I don't know what you've done to Asher, but I will figure that out too. It's only a matter of time.",

"Oh, and Ash, She's never been one of us and never will be." I seethe.

With that, I release her and walk away. When I enter the dining hall, I see Reegan and the guys at our table. They're all laughing, and while Reegan is caught up in whatever Sam is saying, she doesn't notice Bentley looking at her with a soft smile. I grab my food and quickly make my way over to them. Asher and Calista enter a minute later but sit on the opposite end of the dining hall. They both keep staring daggers at me.

"What crawled up his ass?", Jaymeson asks.

"He just can't handle a little truth.", I say and continue eating. "Babe, the guys and I are going to town after class. Will you be ok without us for a bit?" I ask Reegan.

"Of course. Will you guys bring me tacos?"

"Yeah. I think we can handle that.", I tell her.

After lunch, Kalan walks with Reegan to Prof. Morley's room. I don't see her again until the end of the day. When we say our goodbyes, she hops in her car with Maddie in tow and heads off. The guys, Aldair, Kalan, and I, all congregate at the house I share with my boys. We all sit around the living room with beers in our hands.

"You called this little meeting, so start talking.", Bentley says grumpily.

"Ok, where do I even begin? Anything said here is to remain here. It cannot leave this room. We can't have this conversation without me revealing certain things about Reegan that she holds a secret, so I'm telling you now that if this gets out, I will kill you all with my bare hands.", I say.

"I already know her secret.", Bentley tells me. "I've always known, and I've never said a word. I wouldn't blab now. I may hate her, but her secret could get me killed, and I like being alive."

"What do you mean you already know? How?", Aldair asks.

At the same time, I say, "You don't hate her, man. You can try all you like to pretend, but I see how you watch her."

"Look, we don't have time to try and understand how Bent knows anything. We need to discuss more important things, like how Calista hired the demons from the attack."

"She did what now?" Bentley rages.

"Yeah, apparently, Calista hired the guys at someone else's orders. Now, I'm wondering if this person also ordered the jet ski incident.", I explain.

"Why would someone want to kill or take her?", Jaymeson asks.

"Because of what she is.", Bentley sighs.

"What is she," Jaymeson asks. No one answers him. "Really? You honestly think I would do anything to hurt my mate?"

"Mate?", Aldair asks, clearly confused.

"Dude, catch up. Everyone in this room except for you is Reegan's mate. The only one that doesn't seem to know they are is Asher.", Kalan says. "That's why he's not here for this little conversation. He can't be trusted right now."

"Yeah, can we discuss that real quick? What the hell is his deal?", Aldair asks.

"That's a long story. Asher has changed since he got with Calista. He used to be one of the guys. Now, it's like he's her puppet.", Jaymeson answers.

"That would explain the magic I sense in him.", Aldair muses. "It holds evil intent too."

"Can't you dispel it?" Kalan asks.

"Nah, man. I tried already, which means it's blood magic. I can't dispel that shit. Reegan might be able to, though.", he says. "Girl's got powers like we've never seen before."

"While this is true, what's to stop Calista from just performing the spell again? I'm pretty sure she's getting blood from drinking straight from the source.", Jaymeson claims.

"Isn't that illegal?" Kalan asks.

"Yeah, but Calista's dad won't do anything about it, and I'm sure Senior Hayworth is involved as well. I mean, they contracted for their marriage after all.", I reply.

"Could they be behind the orders?" Kalan asks me.

"I wouldn't put anything past Senior. If Marcus retires and Reegan disappears, that leaves an empty council seat he'd gladly step into. Calista's dad, however? He wouldn't do anything without Senior's approval. He's sneaky, but he's terrified to cross Senior. Most council members are. Marcus is the exception.", I tell him.

"But would they want her gone, or would they want to use her?", Aldair asks.

"That's a good question. Considering what she is, it could go either way.", I answer.

"Ok, again, what *is* she?", Jaymeson pushes.

"She's the weaver.", Bentley answers with frustration.

"That's just a legend, though. The Weaver lived centuries ago and then disappeared.", Jaymeson says.

"Most supes believe that yes, but there is a prophecy. My parents were the record keepers and historians for the council. They came across the prophecy a few years before they died. When Reegan started to show her powers, they went to Esme and Max with their theory, which was Reegan's parent's name. They swore never to tell anyone, and they helped make the plans that if anything happened, Reegan would be sent to Elfame to be protected by the fae. My parents died the same night hers did. They died protecting her. They left a son behind to help hide and protect a little girl with beautiful sapphire eyes and purple pigtails." Bentley tells the story.

"And that's why you hate her.", Jaymeson states. It's not a question. "You blame her for your parent's death. Man, she was only a little girl with no idea what she was."

"You think I don't know that! I hate myself for hating her. I loved her when we were little. I spent hours with her, pushing her on a swing or sleeping in a treehouse with her. She was so small. Even then, I was only a couple of years older than she, and I remember thinking how small she was. What hurts the most is that I didn't know we were mates until recently, but my parents used to tell me it was going to be my job to take care of her, to protect her always.", he says with tears in his eyes.

Listening to him, I realize. "Son of a bitch. We're all connected." They all look at me, waiting for an explanation. "Bentley was friends with her when they were little. His parents helped protect her. My mom and her mom were best friends at the academy. They moved away when Esme became pregnant. She shared dreams with Ash. And she was raised with the fae, with Kalan."

"Where's that leave me then?", Jaymeson asks, perplexed.

"I don't know. We'd have to talk to your parents.", I say.

"I could just call dad.", he states.

"No. It's too dangerous. We need to make sure Reegan makes it through the trials. It's teamed this year, and I've already signed us up. Once the trials are over, we'll deal with everything else. We can't tell Reegan about the connection. Not yet. Kalan, is there a way to get Marcus back here?" I say.

"Nah, he said he wouldn't be back until after the new year, something about rogue supes in Europe or some shit.", he says, shaking his head. "And the Asher situation. I don't think we should say anything about it either. I don't want to get Reegan's hopes up that the spell can be broken just in case we're wrong. I'll research it more."

"I need to make one thing clear. I will help protect Reegan, as my parents would have wanted, but I won't cement the bond. I can't.", Bentley interjects.

"Dude, that's on you. You know you'll never be able to mate anyone else, right? Like, the bond literally won't let you be with anyone else. You can fuck, but you won't be able to have a relationship.", Aldair tells him.

"I'm better off alone anyway.", is his only response.

Conversation over, each guy gets up to do whatever. Kalan and I take off to town to get our girl some tacos.

30

REEGAN

November goes by quicker than October. It's now Thanksgiving, and while it's not a supernatural holiday, and Fae holds a harvest festival, most supernatural on Earth celebrate it. Kalan is stuck in Elfame. As heir apparent, he has to be there for the festivities. Maddie has been invited to Kenneth's for the day, and I was told in no uncertain terms that I would be gracing the Strong's dinner table. I dress down for the occasion.

From, what I understand, today will be filled with food and football. I've never been much into sports, but I suppose I can suck it up for Trent. I drive to Meredith's house and find several familiar and unfamiliar cars in the drive. I walk up and knock on the door. I am engulfed in a warm embrace as soon as it's open. Meredith smells smokey and like pumpkin pie.

"I'm so glad you could make it!" she thrills at seeing me. "Come on in and make yourself at home."

I follow her through the house to the kitchen, where she has clearly been slaving away.

"It smells so delicious in here. Is there anything I can help with?" I ask.

"You wanna throw the salad together, and then you can check on the boys. Oh, where are my manners? Reegan, please let me introduce Sophia, Asher's mom."

"It's nice to meet you.", she says and then takes a drink of wine.

"Same here.", I say as I get busy putting together the salad.

When I'm done with that, I grab a bowl of pretzels and head toward the noise of jeers from the guys arguing over the football game.

"That call was bullshit.", I hear a voice say. I think it may be Jaymeson.

"Oh, come on. Don't be pissed 'cause the skins are losing again.", Bentley jokes. I hear a slap on the back.

I enter the room and see all the guys, including Asher. A man is sitting with Peter that I don't know, but by looks alone, I'd wager this is Senior Hayworth, also known as Asher's dad. Peter sees me and jumps us from his seat.

"My girl! When did you get here?" he asks, giving me a hug and a kiss on the cheek.

"Just a few minutes ago. Meredith sent me in to give you these and see if you men needed anything .", I tell him as I sit the pretzels down on the table.

"I could use another beer.", Bentley says. "You know, since you're playing waitress." I give him a look that says kiss my ass.

"The beer can wait. I want to introduce you to someone.", Peter says, pulling me over to the couch. Asher's dad stands. "Reegan, this is Senior Hayworth, Asher's father and one of the councilmen, right below your grandfather."

"Reegan, it's nice to meet the long-lost heir of the Winthrope house, and I understand you're all the rage at the academy.", Senior says, taking my hand.

That voice. That's the voice from my memories. My body wants to freeze up, but I fight through it. I give him a small smile. "I don't know about being all the rage, but I am most definitely excited to take my rightful place.", I tell him.

His eyes narrow slightly like he's trying to read me. He hasn't yet let go of my hand, and I feel a shiver of disgust rise up my spine. Trent comes over then and wraps his arms around me.

"Oh, did I tell you, Senior? Reegan is Trent's mate." Peter interjects as Trent pulls me from his grasp.

Senior's eyes widened in surprise. "Is that so? Well, we have more to celebrate tonight than I expected."

Trent pulls me over to his chair and into his lap. "Are you ok? You looked like you'd seen a ghost."

"I'm fine. Can we talk about this later?" I ask him. Then to the room, "Did anyone else need anything other than Bentley?"

Everyone yells out their orders, and I leave the room, trying not to let my emotions show on my face. I grab the drinks and take them back to the guys. I find out from Trent where the bathroom is, and I go there and lock myself in. I will not break down. I will not break down. If I keep repeating it to myself maybe it will be true. I splash cold water on my face and exit the room. Bentley is waiting for me.

"Come with me, Princess.", he commands. He grabs my hand and ushers me out to a little porch. "Tell me what happened back there. You were about to freak out."

"His voice. It's the same voice I heard the night my parents...." I trail off in sobs. Bentley holds me to his chest and lets me get the tears out.

"Are you sure?" he finally asks.

"I've never been more certain of anything in my life.", I tell him.

"Ok.", is all he says. He doesn't show anything on his face, so I don't know if he believes me or if he still thinks all of this is bullshit.

He leads me back in after drying my tears and ensuring I don't look horrible. When we return,

Meredith calls us to the table for dinner. I end up
seated on Peter's right with Trent beside me. Senior
takes up the other end of the table with Sophia
next to him on one side and Asher on the other.
Bentley ends up opposite Trent, and I see him surreptitiously nod to him. Jaymeson is across from
me. Meredith ends up in the seat next to Trent on
his other side. I find it hard to eat, so I mainly move
the food around my plate.

"Is everything ok, sweetheart?" Martha asks.

"Yeah, it's wonderful. I'm just not feeling too we
ll.", I tell her honestly.

"Well, let me wrap you up a plate. Trent can follow you home and make sure you're ok.", she states.

"Are you sure? I'd hate to take Trent away
tonight."

"Think nothing of it, sweetie. You just get home
and feel better, yeah."

I hug her and thank her again. She gets me a
fresh plate of food and pumpkin pie and gives it to
Trent with instructions to take care of me. Peter
hugs me as well. The other guys say goodbye, and
I get in my car and drive home; Trent's headlights
are the only thing I see behind me. When we get
home, he makes me eat. Now that I'm not in the
presence of Senior Hayworth, I find it much easier
to get my food down. I swear that man is pure evil.
Trent takes me into the den and plays a movie when

I'm done eating. We snuggle on the sofa together, and both end up falling asleep.

"Beauty, where'd you bring me this time?" I hear Trent ask from behind me.

Oh shit. Did I teleport us to Purgatory? "Um... Purgatory. Except we're not truly here. This is part of the dreamscape, I think." I say, looking around.

"It's not what I would expect. I always pictured a drab place where souls wandered.", he says, perplexed.

"Now, why would you think that Trenton Strong, Elemental with the strength and power of a drugon?" Neveah laughs, coming out of nowhere.

She comes over, and for the first time, she hugs me. "You got an answer tonight, didn't you? I could feel your distress earlier, so I had to pull you here.", she tells me.

"Senior Hayworth is responsible for what happened to my parents.", I whisper.

"Yes, he is. And he will get his due, but I need you to stay on track. The pieces are coming together. Aren't they Trent, mate of my Reegan." she says, turning her gaze to him.

"What are you talking about?" I ask.

"I realized the other night that we were all connected. I haven't figured out how Jaymeson comes into all this, but the rest of us? We're all connected in some way.", Trent tells Neveah.

"Yes!" she claps. "Jaymeson fits into this puzzle, but that's for you guys to solve. You'll figure it out.", she beams. "And how is training going?"

"Good. I plan to start concentrating on the spirit element now. That one has been the hardest to grasp, but I'll be ready for the trials.", I tell her seriously.

"Good. Stay close to your mates. Keep your eyes open. I fear that attack the other night won't be the last.", she says and disappears. How does she know about the attack?

"Ug. I hate it when she does that. Just gives a warning and disappears. And here I thought Marcus was the best person at disappearing at the most inconvenient times.", I gripe.

"Well, that was interesting. Who was she?" Trent asks with a tilt of his head.

"That was Nevaeh. The original Weaver and my great, great, something grandmother.", I tell him.

"Damn, she was hot for a centuries-old woman." he laughs, and I swear I can hear Nevaeh's laughter echoing through the meadow.

31

REEGAN

The following day I woke up on the sofa alone. I hear talking coming from the kitchen. I make my way there. The cook is plating up food for Trent. They are in a heated discussion over which is better, apple pie or pumpkin. I walk over and wrap my arms around Trent's neck from behind.

"Hands down, pumpkin pie is the best.", I say.

"You wound me, Beauty.", Trent jokes.

"Can I get you something to eat, Miss Reegan?" the cook asks me.

"No thanks. I'm good.", I tell her as I steal a piece of toast and bacon from Trent's plate. I go around the counter and make myself a cup of coffee.

"I'm going to go shower. I'll be back down in a few.", I say, taking my coffee with me.

When I come out of the bathroom, Trent is waiting for me.

"Hey. Can we chat for a second?" he asks.

"Yeah, what's up?"

"Were you serious about what you told Nevaeh last night?"

"What part?" I ask

"About Asher's dad."

"Yeah. There's no way I could forget that voice."

"That means that he likely was involved in not only your parent's disappearance but Bentley's parents' deaths?" he asks.

"Yeah, but I don't think his parents are dead. I think they're hiding away with mine.", I tell him. "

I don't know anything for sure, but it makes sense. I have to wait for Marcus to come home to get any real answers."

"This sucks. Did you tell Bentley about Senior?"

"Yeah. It just came out last night. You don't think he'll do anything stupid, do you?"

"I'll handle Bent. You just worry about getting through the next month. Trials are right after Christmas."

The next few weeks go by smoothly. Prof. Morley looks at my speech and deems it perfect for the debates. Two days before Christmas, we arrive at the council office. It's an ostentatious building. Prof. Morley meets us at the grand entrance to escort me and the others to the council chambers. The guys surround me as we walk down a long hallway. I look around at the marble floors and the pictures on the walls and wonder why all the fanfare.

"This is how it's going to work. There are two teams. Each team represents an issue that must be taken up with the council. You will debate for one minute after your team has given its presentation. At the end of the debate, the council will vote on one area where they will instill change. Reegan, as the future council seat holder, you will go first. This will be your introduction to all the council members and let them know where you stand on certain controversial topics. Are you guys ready?" Professor Morley asks us.

There's a chorus of affirmatives as we're led into the chamber. The first person I notice is Senior Hayworth. He's talking to a short man with reddish-brown eyes. I shiver automatically at the sight of him, and Bentley stiffens beside me. I grasp his hand and squeeze it in solidarity. We continue walking down the aisle.

The side door opens, and Dain, Alita, and Kalan walk in. I'm more than a little surprised. I knew Alita would be here as she holds the fae seat, but I didn't expect Dain and Kalan. The latter of the two makes his way over to me and pulls me into a hug. He then takes a seat behind the student area. Dain takes the principal chair at the council table. It looks more like what you would expect to see in a courtroom. The main seat sits above the rest. It's a seat fit for his station, but I suspect that the seat is typically meant for my grandfather.

"Shall we get started?" Dain asks.

"What's the meaning of this, King Dain? Why are you here?", Senior hisses.

"As you already know, Marcus is out of the country on council business. He has asked me to be here in his stead," Dain says lightly like he doesn't have a care in the world. "Our laws state that should a council member be indisposed, they may name someone to act on their behalf. I have been so named."

"Really, where exactly is Marcus? How do we know that you aren't trying to usurp his seat?", Senior accuses.

With a laugh, Dain responds, "Councilman Hayworth, I suggest you watch your tone. I do not answer to you or this council. My wife holds a seat to help keep the fae in line. We could leave now, return to Elfame and let the Unseelie among you wreak havoc."

With that, he dismisses Senior. Asher's dad is fuming. It's evident on his face. I stand and walk down to the table in front of the council. There on the table in front of me is a small microphone.

"Council members, allow me to introduce the heir to the Winthrope seat and future queen of Elfame, Reegan Esmerelda Winthrope.", Dain introduces.

I hear some gasps as it's made known to everyone that I will one day help lead the Kingdom of Fae. I look up at Dain. He nods for me to get started then

he winks. I can see the pride shining in his eyes.
It helps alleviate my nerves, and I jump right into
my presentation. It goes smoothly, and the council
members congratulate me on a job well done when
I'm finished.

I take my seat with my other team members. I
feel Kalan behind me squeeze my shoulder. I sit
there and watch the other students debate back and
forth. I can feel eyes on me, so I look up. Senior and
the shorter man are both staring at me. I lean back
and get Jaymeson's attention.

"Who's the short man there beside councilman
Hayworth?" I whisper to him, hoping I can't be
heard.

"That's Calista's dad. He holds the seat for the
witches. Her mother is a vampire and holds no
special place in the community though she likes
to think differently.", Jaymeson chuckles. "You did
amazing up there, by the way."

"Thanks. Who holds the shifter"s seat?" I inquire.

"Oh, that would be the guy on the end there,
Todd, my older brother and pack beta.", he says.
"He's kind of a placeholder like Bentley's uncle. Dad
retired several years ago, and since I wasn't old
enough to take my place, Todd took it for now.", he
explains.

"And everyone else?"

"Curious, are you? Well, I'll tell you about everyone else later. Alita, of course, you know, so I don't need to explain her role to you." he laughs again.

I turn back around and face the front. We're to the part where the council votes. I don't pay attention. Instead, I stare Senior down as a shiver slithers down my spine. *Yeah, asshole. I know exactly who you are.* Once everyone is done and the vote is taken, we are quickly ushered out while the council deals with other issues we aren't privy to. Honestly, I can't wait to get out of here. I need a damn shower. Of course, that isn't happening. Trent deems it necessary to have a training session for the trials, which take place in three days.

It's Christmas Eve, and I'm heading to town with Maddie and Sam to finish up last-minute Christmas shopping. While we don't celebrate the traditional Christian holiday, we celebrate the season. We do everything you would expect; decorate a tree, exchange gifts, those kinds of things. Humans like to start their celebrations right after Thanksgiving, but we wait to decorate until the day before. The guys are coming over later to decorate with me. I only have Alita and Jaymeson to shop for.

I find Alita a gorgeous cashmere sweater and a pair of emerald drop earrings. For Jaymeson, I buy him the latest video game he's been raving about. All the guys have matching pajamas they'll get tonight. I can't wait to see their faces. I buy Kalan an ugly Christmas sweater and then decide to get all the guys one. I don't know if Asher will show up, but I shopped for him too.

We get tacos and chai when hungry, sit at a window, and people-watch. The kids are adorable with their keen eyes and laughter. This is what I am meant to save. When we return to the house, Sam excuses herself to be with her grandma. I learned a while ago that her parents live in New Mexico, so she stays with her grandma while she attends the academy. Kenneth has already decided to go back with her once they graduate. Thinking of Sam and Kenneth makes me think of my future. It's hard to picture, but I hope it's a great future with all my guys.

I stand in the kitchen making homemade hot chocolate when the guys show up. Everyone is laden down with boxes and boxes of decorations. Bentley, being the big man he is, carries the tree. I direct them to the great room, where they begin getting everything ready.

"So, what's the plan for tomorrow?" I ask no one in particular.

"Dinner is always at the restaurant. We usually go to the shelter in the morning and feed the
homeless. Then we do whatever until dinner time.
Once we all get there, we exchange gifts.", Jaymeson
explains.

"That sounds awesome. I have brunch with Dain
and Alita, so if the shelter is early, I'd love to go.", I
say.

"Oh, that reminds me. Mom said to tell you all to
come for dinner tomorrow.", Trent says.

"Will the Hayworths be there?" I ask hesitantly.

"Not for the past two years. They spend their
holiday with Calista's family. We haven't talked to
Ash since shit went down on Halloween, so you
need to know that he won't be competing on our
team during trials.", Trent says cautiously.

"That doesn't exactly surprise me.", I huff. "Anyway, let's get this party started."

We spend the next several hours decorating the
tree, the mantle, and anywhere else we feel needs
to be festive. Dain and Alita join us, laughing at the
antics of the guys who have covered me in tinsel. At
some point, pizzas are ordered. We all sit around
on the floor of the great room, eating. Seeing the
king and queen lounging on the floor with us is
quite a sight. I excuse myself for a minute and grab
the bags holding the guys' pajamas and sweaters.
I hand them out. I was right. The looks I get are
hilarious. They all look at me in abject horror as

they take in their candy cane striped PJs with little dancing reindeer. They have the same looks when they see their sweaters, but they all promise to wear them tomorrow for dinner. After everyone is fed and everything is overly decorated, they leave. Well, everyone but Trent.

"Beauty, I wanted to give you one of your gifts before tomorrow.", Trent tells me when we're alone. He hands me a small velvet box. I open it, and my eyes get watery. Inside sits a beautiful necklace of my mark. It's the perfect infinity symbol made from a rainbow-colored feather. In the open oval parts are two beautiful sapphires. "I wanted you to have something that will always help you remember who and what you are. It's also a promise that I will always have your back no matter what, and we'll figure out everything together."

"It's perfect, Trent. It's perfect.", I whisper as I stand up on my tiptoes and kiss him. He doesn't deepen it; I know that's because he takes this moment seriously.

"Let me put it on you?" he asks.

I turn around and pull my hair out of the way. He clasps it behind my neck, and I can't help myself. I grab it and hold it in my hand.

"I love you, Trenton Strong. I know it's too soon to say it, and I don't expect a response, but I needed you to know."

He kisses me again but doesn't stop until we both need to come up for air. "Tell me again.", he implores.

"I love you," I say again and kiss him.

"I love you too, Reegan Esmerelda Winthrope.", he says reverently.

I go to bed that night wrapped up in my guys. Their bodies are sweaty and hot. It's perfect. After making love, I am exhausted. I wake to be poked in the side.

"Wake up, Beauty. It's Christmas.", Trent whispers. "Shhh. Don't wake Kalan. I want to show you something."

I stretch with a smile and get up to follow Trent over to the window. It snowed while we were sleeping. It's beautiful. We bundle up and sit under the rising sun, watching the sparkle of the snow where the light hits it.

We both shower and get dressed for the day before waking Kalan. I kiss him lightly and tell him where we'll be. We leave soon after and head to the shelter. I enjoy feeding the homeless immensely. Martha and Peter even bought the kids presents and stockings. My heart is whole as I see the looks on their faces. They are so thankful, making me wonder why the supernaturals aren't the same.

Just because we have powers and special abilities, it doesn't make us that different from each other. After the shelter, I head home for brunch, and Trent heads to his mom's restaurant to help get everything set for tonight. He takes all the wrapped presents with him to place under the tree there. Brunch is delicious. This is the first time I get to be with all of them simultaneously in months.

"Will you guys be here for the trials?" Maddie asks.

"Unfortunately not, sweetheart. The Unseelie are giving us some trouble, so we have to head back after dinner.", Dain says.

"Kalan is staying, though, right?" I ask, looking at him.

"I can't. I have to be there for the negotiations. I'm sorry, baby. Things will be easier after the new year.", he placates.

My spirits dropped a bit after his declaration, but I shut my mouth. I can't begrudge him for his duty. I know Aldair and Maddie will be there cheering me on, so I decide to let that be enough. After brunch, we all sit around watching cheesy Christmas movies until it's time to get ready for dinner. I wear a green sweater dress that hugs my curves and knee-high boots. Maddie is dressed similarly except for her deep red dress that goes perfectly with her hair. Kalan is wearing slacks and a white button-down under his sweater. His sweater has Christmas light strings all across it. I laugh when I see him. It's not so bad. Dain is dressed in just a pair of slacks and a red shirt, while Alita wears a stunning, deep blue dress with three-quarter lace sleeves. Aldair doesn't disappoint in his slacks with a black button-down shirt.

The restaurant is gorgeously decorated in shades of ice blue and silver. It looks like a winter wonderland. The tree has to be fifteen feet tall and is covered from top to bottom with giant ornaments. Meredith serves a meal of prime rib and ham with all the fixings. It is the most delicious meal I've ever tasted. After dinner, we have a scrumptious chocolate cake with cherries. It is decadent. We all move over to chairs Alita has set around the tree. Everyone is handed their gifts, and we all take turns opening them. Each guy gives me something small. Then there's one large gift with all their names on it. I open it to find a two-piece suit that looks like leather but feels as soft as velvet.

"It's for the trials. It will help protect you. It's covered in magic to dispel any nefarious magic thrown at you.", Bentley tells me.

"It's gorgeous and looks badass. Thank you, guys.", I tell them each sincerely.

The guys open their gifts next. They all seem thrilled at what they get. Everyone looks pleased. There's no more talk of the trials. We just bask in the glow of being together. After some time, everyone gets up to leave, and Kalan and I head home. I head to bed after saying goodbye to Dain and Alita.

Kalan joins me, not entirely done with our celebrations.

"Baby, you know I wouldn't leave you if it wasn't essential, right?

"I know. I just hate that you won't be here."

"If you need anything, call. If it's urgent, teleport to me."

"I will. I promise. How much time do we have." I ask him, hinting at what I want.

"Enough," he tells me and then wastes no time stripping us both out of our clothes.

Once he has me naked, he lifts me and lays me gently on the bed. He follows, kissing my throat and my breasts. He comes back up and takes my mouth. He enters me slowly, and instead of pumping quickly into me, he takes his time. He sets a leisurely pace. With each thrust, he twists his hips and grinds down on my clit. I come three times before he finally reaches his climax. I fall asleep in his arms, knowing that when I wake up, he'll be back in Elfame.

32

REEGAN

The trials are today. I wake up earlier than usual to get ready. It's cold outside, but the air will refresh my system, so I take off on my run to the lake and back. The run has my muscles burning, but I push through the pain. I wonder what to expect in the trials. Trent said they change the order yearly, but it will test us physically and mentally. The physical part you can train for, the mental aspect, well, that's all about your mental fortitude. When I get to the lake, there's a car and a man sitting on the bench. He looks deep in thought with his head buried in his hands. So as not to disturb him, I get ready to turn and head back. His head pops up, and I realize it's Asher. I don't need his drama today. I look at him once and then turn to run back the way I came.

"Reegan...Winnie, don't go.", He calls out to me. He sounds anguished.

"What do you want from me, Asher? You've ig-nored me for weeks; before that, you were nice to

me one minute and a complete douche the next. I
can't handle your back and forth."

"I don't know what's wrong with me, Reegan, but
I need help."

"I don't think I can help you."

"You may be the only one who can. Can a witch
spell you to do whatever they want?"

"You know they can, Ash.", I sigh. "All they'd need
is a little of your blood."

"Fuck!!!!" he screams. "That fucking bitch!"

"What are you talking about, Asher?"

"How would she get my blood? I get we heal faster,
but I'd know if she cut me, wouldn't I?"

"Who, Asher?"

"Calista.", is his response.

"She wouldn't need to cut you, Ash. She has
fangs. But you'd have to give her permission to bite
you, I would assume." when he hears those words,
his shame flashes across his eyes. "You deliberately
let that bitch bite you?"

"It made the sex amazing, Reegan. And this was
before I knew you were real."

"What makes you think you're spelled?"

"I honestly didn't figure it out until I heard a
conversation between my dad and Calista. Trent
said something to me a few weeks ago about how
I'd changed since Calista came into the picture. I've
spent the last week on my own away from the guys,
away from everyone, trying to figure this all out."

"Wait. You spent Christmas alone. Why didn't you come to Meredith's?"

"Because I'm ashamed of the way I've treated the guys. I'm ashamed of how I've treated you."

"I need more information. You should be telling the guys this. Can we meet up after the trials?" I ask.

"Dammit, the trials. I have to work with Calista."

"Yeah, just don't let her get you alone before they start. Find the guys and stick with them until then. She'll need your blood again if you've been away from her compulsion for this long. Promise me, Ash."

"I promise. Do you need a ride home?" he offers

"Creator, yes, please. I have to get ready."

Asher drives me home, and I rush to get ready while he calls Trent. It only takes me ten minutes, and when I come down, Trent is there.

"Good morning, Beauty. Wanna tell me what's going on?" he asks.

"I ran into Asher at the lake, and we talked. He's overheard a conversation between his dad and Calista, putting two and two together. He thinks Calista has spelled him.", I explain.

"Shit. Please don't get mad, but I already knew or suspected it."

"You what? Seriously Trent. Why the hell wouldn't you say something?"

"Because Aldair couldn't remove the magic attached to Asher, and we didn't want you to be involved with everything else."

"You should have told me. You should have told him. You can't keep shit like that from me. If Aldair tried and failed to remove the spell, then that means she's initiated a blood bond, right?."

"I'm sorry, ok. I didn't mean to keep it from you. We were going to tell you after the trials, and we couldn't tell him because he was under her control. What's changed now? Why did he talk to you?"

"I talked to her like I've wanted to for weeks because I have sequestered myself away from Calista for over a week. I spent Christmas alone after I heard the conversation between dad and her. I think Reegan can help.", Asher tells Trent.

"And I will do everything I can after the trials. In the meantime, Trent, I need you and the guys to stay close to Ash until the trials start. Do not leave him alone with that cunt under any circumstances." I order.

"We can't protect you both.", Trent argues. "Did you forget she's out to get you? Did you forget what Neveah said?"

"You don't have to protect me, but it doesn't matter. I won't be away from you guys, either. I don't need Calista to realize that things have changed. As you said, she's already gunning for me.", I tell him with a kiss.

"Ok. We need to go. The guys are on their way to the academy. They'll meet us in the quad.", Trent says as he ushers us out the door.

To keep up pretenses, Asher drives his car and follows us. The guys park side by side when we get to the parking lot. We get out and walk the distance it takes to get to the quad, where Bentley, Jaymeson, and Aldair are waiting. Maddie, Kenneth, Sam, and Mitchell stand close by. Bentley takes one look at Asher and lets out a sigh of relief.

"It's good to have you back, brother.", he says, and they fist bump.

"What? No inquisition.", Asher jokes.

"Nah, man. Not here and not now, but be prepared to have your ass kicked later.", Bentley says and laughs. It's the most genuine laugh I've heard from him.

"Hey, baby. What are you doing over here talking to the competition?" Calista says as she saunters over, clasping Asher's arm.

"I'll be right there, babe. I was talking to the guys for a few minutes telling them how bad they're going to get their asses beat today.", Asher says with disinterest in his eyes. That's his standard look when he's around the viper, so she should buy it.

"Oh, did Asher tell you? Daddy and Senior moved the wedding up. We don't have to wait until graduation to be married. Now we'll get married in May. Isn't that exciting.", She gushes.

"So very exciting.", Jaymeson says in a high-pitched feminine voice and an eye roll.

"Go back to the girls, baby. I'll be there in a minute." Asher tells her with a kiss. I think I just threw up in my mouth.

Everyone stands with their teammates while we wait for the signal to enter the arena. I'm talking to Maddie when I hear a voice behind me.

"Hey, Little Bit.", Marcus says.

I spin around, shock all over my face. He's not supposed to be here.

"I thought you wouldn't be back until after the new year.", I state.

"And miss my granddaughter's first trials? Not likely. Besides, I have to announce them and all.", he tells me.

"Nevaeh is pissed at you.", I whisper.

"Yeah, she usually is.", he laughs.

"You owe me answers, grandfather.", I state with authority.

"After.", he says, looking around. Is he worried that someone is listening?

"After so you can disappear again before you have a conversation with me?"

He slowly pulls me into a hug and whispers in my ear, "The only answer you'll get is to go West."

"Cryptic much, gramps?" I ask.

He cringes at the word gramps, and I can't help the smile that comes to my lips. I feel slightly vindicated.

"Enough of that, young lady. It's time to begin.", he says and walks over to a raised dais with a podium. "Students, welcome to the Trials. Most of you are aware of how this works, but for those of you that don't, let me take just a minute to explain them. As a task force member, you'll be thrown into situations that require both physical aptitude and mental fortitude. You won't always be able to rely on your supernatural abilities. These trials are meant to test your readiness. Some of you may be asking why first-year students are included. These trials will also help us to better prepare you for the future. With that, let us begin. First teams to your marks."

Asher leaves then and goes over to the magical door for his team, and we make our way to ours. We'll be going head-to-head with each other. It's like a race. While we can use our abilities to keep the other team from reaching their goal, we cannot maim or kill them. That's too bad.

"Rebecca sets these up every year. Instead of going in individually, we do this as a team. We watch each other's backs, and we make it across that finish line before they do.", Trent says. "Think of it like that escape room we completed a few weeks ago."

"We got this.", Jaymeson replies excitedly.

"Keep in mind that the supernatural creatures we may encounter here aren't real. They're magically crafted, and they're programmed. However, they will feel and sound very real. The only real beings in there are the other team.", Bentley tells me, squeezing my shoulder.

The buzzer sounds, and we enter the arena. It's been spelled to seem much larger than it is, and we're in a jungle. Lovely. There are thick trees everywhere. We come to our first obstacle; a pit filled with hundreds of nasty snakes. *They're not real.* I tell myself this, but their fangs will hurt even if they can't kill me.

"Come on. I can use my wind to carry you guys over, and then I'll cross.", I tell them.

The guys stand before me, and I blow up a large gust of wind. Jaymeson and Trent are carried across quickly, but Bentley, not so much.

"Well, shit. If I call up more wind, I'm afraid I'll knock you into a tree or something.", I tell him.

"Trent, can you call up vines and make a bridge?" Bentley calls.

Trent immediately comes over to the pit's edge and places his hands on the ground. Within seconds, vines have grown from one end to the other. We slowly make our way across. The snakes are so giant that they can reach the pit's edge and snap their fangs at us. When we're through, I destroy the vine bridge so the other team can't just cross it should they come this way. We walk for a while until we come to a wall that spans at least a mile in both directions and a mile straight up.

"Now what?", Jaymeson asks. "We can't climb it."

"Let me think.", Trent urges. He begins pacing. I take a minute to think as well. I walk about twenty feet in each direction, studying the massive wall in front of us. I run my hands along the stones. They're all smooth except for one tiny crevice."

"Guys check this out.", I tell them.

They come over one by one and look at what I found. The crevice is cut out to make a door, but how does it open?

"Look up there. There's a symbol or something.", Jaymeson says.

I look but can't see anything. "I don't see it."

"I do. It's the symbol for the water element." , Trent replies. "I think maybe we need to fill the crevice with water, which will cause the door to open."

He walks up to it, and water pools in his hand. He runs it along the crevice until it's full. Nothing happens. I stand there confused for a minute, and then it comes to me. I walk over and place my hand on the crevice sending my power into it. The water inside the gap begins to freeze. As the ice cracks from the constraints of the small space, the stones crumble. Behind the door, it is dark. I let a fireball form in my hand to try and see. On the side of the wall, there's a small sign that reads: Those who enter here will know what true nightmares are made of.

"That's not creepy at all.", I joke.

"This is the mental fortitude test. It's different every year. This year they must have decided to make us face our fears. It'll be spelled to work like a compulsion. When you go through it, you'll see what you fear most. The goal is to make it to the other side of the tunnel. Nothing you see in there is real. Keep that in your mind as you go through, and you'll be fine.", Bentley explains.

I enter first. I walk for a while, and nothing happens. Just when I think I'm immune, the darkness in front of me takes shape. A voice whispers, "I told your parents I would find you, little Weaver. I told them that before I killed them."

My worst fear is Senior Hayworth. I know this isn't real, but it doesn't feel fake. I can feel his hot breath on my back as he snatches me from behind.

"Get out of my head!" I scream. He vanishes.

I turn behind me to check on the guys and see Bentley crouched on the ground. He's mumbling something incoherent, and he's crying. I run to him and kneel on the floor. I call his name, but he doesn't respond. He just keeps mumbling and crying. I place my hands on both sides of his face. I don't try, but his nightmare comes to me anyway. He's standing in front of a beautiful woman. I realize it's his mom. She's screaming at him about how her death was his fault, how he didn't protect them. I insert myself into his nightmare and walk up to him, placing my hands on his face, mimicking what I'm doing in real life.

"Bentley, look at me." his eyes meet mine briefly but go back to his mother's face. "Bentley. Look. At. Me." I try again. This time he focuses on my face. "You did not kill your parents. You were just a child. There was nothing you could have done to change things."

It takes a minute, but he finally acknowledges what I said, and just like that, we're out of his nightmare. The other two guys are watching us. We get up off the ground and keep going. I don't ask what the others' nightmares were. I'm more concerned with Bentley. He blames himself for his parents. He also blames me, or is it just him projecting? As we make our way through, I have a few more fears show up. One of them was Asher telling me that he never loved me. That Calista was going to be his wife. I quickly shook them off and made it to the end.

"Is it just me, or have these trials been straight-forward so far?", Jaymeson asks.

"Don't speak too soon.", Trent tells him, pointing to the clearing ahead of us.

"Oh fuck.", Jaymeson grumbles.

In the clearing stand every kind of supernatural you could imagine, demons, shifters, witches, and others that boggle the mind. We don't get time to think as the ghouls rush us. We quickly dispatch them, and then we're faced with the shifters. I see a colossal tiger approaching me as they shift into their forms. I try to knock it back with the wind, but it dodges and keeps coming. It dodges my fireballs, and the water doesn't faze it either. I can't freeze it to the ground because it's constantly moving. It's backed me up to the tree line. When it gets ready to pounce, Jaymeson's wolf knocks into its side.

I'm concentrating so hard on Jaymeson that I don't notice someone coming up behind me. I'm grabbed, iron cuffs on my hands and some covering over my face. The man drags me off. I kick and scream until he punches me in the head. My vision blurs, and I feel like I might puke. I can't see any-thing. All I can feel are the cuffs on my wrists and the roughness of the man carrying me away. When we reach our destination, the cuffs aren't removed. Instead, the man attaches them to something and straps my legs, trapping me. The face-covering is removed. The man doesn't come out from behind me, so I can't see the bastard.

"I told you to watch your back.", Calista says as she rounds a tree. "You think you can come in and take what's mine? What was promised to me?" she hisses.

I tilt my head and look at her, "What did I take from you, Calista?" I ask her.

"You would take Asher from me after his father promised him to me. He's supposed to be mine.", she whines.

"He's not a fucking possession, Calista. What is wrong with you? I didn't come here to take any-thing. You know, though, don't you? You know he can never truly be yours because he's always been mine. He's my mate.", I yell.

"Lies. Why does everyone keep lying to me? Ash-er said he loved me and lied. Senior said Asher was mine and he'd make sure of it as long as I got rid of you and then changed his mind for some reason. Every one of you is a liar."

"The only person lying to you is you. You used blood magic and compulsion to keep Asher under your thumb and hold onto a man who never want-ed to be yours. You tell yourself you're that much better than everyone else when you are weak.", I goad.

I see something change in her eyes—some understanding. Then the man who held me captive comes out.

"Calista, sweetheart. You need to end her. She'll destroy us all. She'll ruin all our plans. If you don't stop her, she'll take Asher from you, and you'll be lonely." her dad says. "You'll never be queen."

Queen of what? Asher isn't royalty; he's just the heir to one of several seats on the council of supernaturals.

"You're right, daddy. She can't live. She's not like us. She's not worthy of taking the council seat. It should be mine.", she says.

She stalks closer to me and takes a small dagger out of her pocket. She slices my face over and over again. I do not scream. I won't give her the satisfaction. She then takes the knife and cuts through the front of my suit.

"Well, aren't we clever? A suit to dispel magic. It only works if it's on your skin, right?" she sneers.

Her father comes over and rips the fabric away from me. I'm now tied to a tree naked, but for my underwear.

"You know. Maybe when you're gone, I'll console your gorgeous prince. I'll make a wonderful queen, don't you think?" Calista asks with a huge smile. "Queen of two realms sounds so nice."

"You're delusional, Calista. Don't do this. You know this won't end well for you, right? Marcus will seek retribution.", I tell her.

"I doubt that. You see, Senior has a plan for him as well. This wasn't exactly part of it, but I can't have you around, even if Senior wants you for something. He'll have to deal with that now, won't he.", She says.

"Enough, Calista. It's time to get this over with.", her father says.

They both stand side by side and back up a few paces. They murmur something under their breaths, and I see magic balls build in their hands. They're black with a reddish outline. I don't know if they can kill me, but I'm certain it will hurt. Magic is all about intent. Calista throws hers first, and then her father throws his. They barrel toward me. At the last second, Asher jumps in front of me, taking Calista's magic into himself, while her father's is a direct hit to my chest.

"Asher!" I scream.

I hit the ground with a thud, the magic destroying the chains binding me. The last thing I see before everything goes black are the guys taking down Calista's dad as she looks on, frozen, with fear in her eyes. And I can hear my men calling my name.

33

THE END

The End for now...

Or maybe not. Want to know what happens next?
Book two is available now on Amazon.

Afterword

Thank you so much for taking the time to read my first book. I can't tell you how much I truly appreciate it. If you liked this book, would you consider leaving a review? Just a few words on Amazon mean so much to us little independent authors as they help keep our work relevant.

My Thanks

Where do I even begin. I have so many people to thank. First I'd like to thank you the reader for taking a chance on my work. I can't put into words how much it means to me that you picked up one of my books and I truly hope you enjoyed reading as much as I enjoyed writing it.

Thank you to my family for dealing with my crazy while I spent hours pouring over a keyboard to bring these characters to life.

To my bookish community; the authors, PAs, and everyone else that encouraged me through this process, I appreciate you.

About
Author

Angie lives in a small town in southern West Virginia with her husband, two children and six furbabies. She's surrounded by mountains and a true country girl. When she's not writing, she can be found reading or cooking; the two things that bring her so much joy. She loves interacting with her firends on social media and finding new ones to share her love of books with.

To find out more about the author and what she's working on next, check out her group. https://www.facebook.com/groups/angie swonderousweaversand follow her on her socials and Amazon https://linktr.ee/angie_cottingham_author

Also By Angie

Once Upon A New Year
https://books2read.com/Once-Upon-a-New-
Year
Lady of Nightmares (Book one in the
Lady of Nightmares and Heartache Duet)
https://books2read.com/Lady-of-Nightmares

Made in the USA
Columbia, SC
04 April 2024